QUARTER TO
MIDNIGHT

DARCY COATES

Poisoned Pen
PRESS

Published by Poisoned Pen Press, an imprint of Sourcebooks
P.O. Box 4410, Naperville, Illinois 60567–4410
(630) 961-3900
sourcebooks.com

Originally self-published in 2015 by Black Owl Books.

Library of Congress Cataloging-in-Publication Data

Names: Coates, Darcy, author.
Title: Quarter to midnight / Darcy Coates.
Description: Naperville, Illinois : Poisoned Pen Press, [2022]
Identifiers: LCCN 2022002255 | ISBN 9781728221816 (trade paperback)
Subjects: LCGFT: Novels.
Classification: LCC PR9619.4.C628 Q37 2022 | DDC 823/.92--dc23/eng/20220120
LC record available at https://lccn.loc.gov/2022002255

Printed and bound in Canada.
MBP 10 9 8 7 6 5 4 3 2 1

CRYPT

PART 1

MY SLEEPY LITTLE TOWN HAS A FEW NOTEWORTHY ATTRACTIONS. A novelty giant plastic banana sits just within the town limits, a sad attempt to lure families into stopping on their trips upstate. We host an annual carnival that boasts not one, but *two* hayrides. And now, according to Julie Haze, we have a vampire in our graveyard.

Julie used to be pleasantly plump, but age, a diet rich in sugar and fat, and a predisposition to spending her day in her stuffed recliner left her more bulgy than curvy. Still, she maneuvered through her tiny trailer with relative ease. Her three cats were attempting to outweigh her, and, although she gladly joked about her own size, she wouldn't hear a word of criticism against her pets.

When she'd been more mobile, she'd spent her life in the village, drifting from the restaurant to the park to the café, going anywhere she could find a soul to talk to. But with a bad hip and a hundred extra pounds weighing her down, she relied on visitors to her trailer to keep her company. And she made it very worthwhile to call in for an hour.

Julie seemed to know everything about everyone and had the town's entire history stored in her brain. Through her, I'd learned a bunker had been built under the church during the war but never actually used, that the mayor's family had enough skeletons in their closets to start their own graveyard, and that the music store's owner once had a whirlwind romance with a semifamous actress.

I visited her at least once a week. Making friends had been difficult when I first moved into the tight-knit community, but Julie had embraced my company with open arms. In turn, I loved listening to her stories.

She shuffled through the trailer, tipping packaged cookies onto a plate and filling a pitcher with iced tea while the cats wove around her legs. "I'm afraid, Sara," she said, placing the snacks on the folding table between the two overstuffed armchairs beside the window, "I've told you just about all of my best stories."

I took a cookie and nibbled on its corner while Julie settled into her chair. "Maybe you can retell some of the better tales? I wouldn't mind hearing the one about the priest's cat getting stuck in the drain again."

Julie waved away my suggestion. "Don't be ridiculous, honey.

I said I'm *nearly* out; the well hasn't run dry just yet. I spent all of this morning racking my brain for a good story to tell you, and I've remembered one I haven't thought about in decades."

I sat forward as Julie handed me a drink. "It's a classic, then?"

"Well, it's old, at least. And a lot of it is conjecture and guess-work, and I'm afraid you'll have to suspend your disbelief from the rafters to get through it. But I think you'll enjoy it."

Julie settled back in her chair as one of the cats leaped into her lap. Her eyes were focused on the window, where the off-white lacy curtains filtered the morning's sun and created a mosaic of shadowy patterns across her face. She was silent for a moment, seemingly to collect her thoughts, then she wet her lips and began speaking.

———

It started, well, it would have to be a little more than fifty years ago. The town was smaller then and not so well connected to the cities. Most people didn't have telephones, but we all had guns. A good number of wolves and bears would find their way into town, you see, and people needed a way to protect their families and livestock.

I was twelve at the time, just a few years older than Jack Suffle. The Suffles were one of the town's founding families, though there aren't any of them left anymore. Their father had died when I was a little girl, and the mother inherited his business. They were merchants—quite well off.

Jack and his younger brother, Charlie, played in the town

square most days. I don't remember much about Charlie, except that he was a roly-poly little thing who tagged along after his brother every chance he had. He cried at the slightest provocation. I used to think he was a baby, but then, he *was* very young.

Jack involved himself in some insane antics. He got himself stuck in the well one time, and he very likely would have drowned if Charlie hadn't run for their mother. Jack used to brag about going into the woods on his own, too, and say he'd shot wolves the size of horses. That was a load of bull, of course, but I suppose he liked to imagine himself as the man of the house, a real hero who'd protect his mother and brother, though he frequently caused more harm than good.

On this particular day—it was winter; I remember that because I'd gotten a new coat as a gift and was showing it off—Jack and Charlie came marching through the town. Jack had a shotgun over his shoulder, which wasn't so unusual back then as it is now, and Charlie looked on the verge of tears. I asked where they were going.

"To the cemetery," Jack said, sounding so proud of himself. "Charlie and me are going to hunt the ghouls there."

I laughed, mainly to pretend that I wasn't so impressed. Most of the town avoided the cemetery, except during funerals. The area was divided into two parts: the modern section—modern in that day, at least—and an older section full of cracked headstones and crypts. Our town was built over the ruins of a ghost town, you see. No one really knows who the original settlers were or where they came from, just that their homes had been long abandoned by the time the valley was claimed for our own town.

All of the original buildings were demolished, except for the old cemetery, which the founders left intact when creating the new graveyard beside it.

Charlie was sniffling and saying he didn't want to go, but Jack kept saying, "Go back to Mother if you're scared." Of course, the boy wouldn't. He loved Jack. Would have followed him to the ends of the earth, I imagine.

I followed with them past the town center and into the farming territory. The cemetery was a short walk into the woods, hidden from the town, so I left them there and went home. I assumed they would fool around among the gravestones for a few hours before coming back.

When I came down for breakfast the following morning, my mother told me little Charlie Suffle had gone missing. I was shocked. It felt…what's the word? *Surreal.* I remember digging my nails into the back of my hand until I drew blood because I was certain it had to be a dream. I asked what had happened, but my mother didn't know. I told her about running into Charlie and Jack before they went into the woods, and my mother said she supposed a wolf had gotten him.

You can imagine how I felt. Sad—mostly for his mother's sake—shocked, and very, very curious. Back in those days, an alley ran behind the pub, where we could wriggle into an alcove next to one of the air vents and listen to the men talking inside. All of the most important bits of news were aired in the pub. I went there as soon as I could after breakfast, but the alcove was already occupied—by Jack Suffle.

He'd been crying but was pretending he hadn't. "They don't believe me," he said before I could even open my mouth. "They think I'm making it up."

"Making what up?" I asked.

"The vampire."

I put two and two together. "Is that what got Charlie?"

Jack nodded, and though he wouldn't look at me, he beckoned for me to sit next to him. "It was in the crypt—the one in the old part, you know? I saw it first and fired my gun at it, but that just made it angry. I told Charlie to run. I thought he was behind me, but when I got to the crypt door, he wasn't there. They don't believe me. Not even mother."

He was doing an increasingly bad job of hiding his tears, and I'm afraid to say I wasn't much comfort. We sat for a while and caught snatches of conversation from inside. Men were arguing about what to do and whether they should arrange a second search of the forest. Apparently, a group had already looked for the lost boy shortly after Jack had returned home without his charge, but they had been forced to abandon the search when nightfall had made the woods too dangerous. Some of the men thought Jack had lost his brother during the walk and that there was a chance the boy was still alive in the forest. Others thought Jack may have accidentally killed him—maybe a slip of the gun or the child had fallen off a cliff—and was too ashamed to tell the truth. A third faction was in favor of believing at least part of Jack's story and searching the graveyard.

I left before the men reached a consensus, but from what I

gathered in the following days, the third faction eventually won. Half a dozen men armed with guns scoured the cemetery, paying special attention to the crypt where Jack said he'd lost Charlie. They didn't find so much as a hair from the boy's head.

Jack's mother was beside herself. She begged them to search the woods—and they did for the remaining daylight hours that day and for two days following. The woods were wild, remember. It was slow progress with just six men and Jack's mother.

On the third day, they found Charlie's body washed up on the shore of the river, quite a distance from town. He wasn't much recognizable, except for his shoes, which his mother remembered buying. They gave him a respectful burial—the carpenter had to make a special casket because the boy was so small—and agreed that it had most probably been an accidental drowning.

Jack, meanwhile, stuck to his story with the stubbornness of a mule. No, they'd gone nowhere near the river, he would say. No, Charlie didn't wander into the woods on his own. They'd gone to the graveyard, and a vampire had caught him.

Maybe things would have come out differently if people had believed—or at least pretended to believe—Jack. He was adamant and desperate for someone to take him seriously—and the town ridiculed him for it. Some of the other children found a cloak with a high collar and took turns jumping out from around corners wearing the cape and paper fangs. This went on for about a week before Jack lost it and attacked one of the children. Broke a nose and some ribs. My mother told me not to spend any time around him after that, so I really only saw him from a distance.

From what I understand, Jack's mother was patient and kind toward him, but she also believed her son had drowned in the stream. Over several months, Jack became less and less adamant about his story and started using phrases such as "I thought" and "it seemed like." He stopped exploring and became shy and withdrawn. I sometimes bumped into him at the grocer's, but he never spoke to me.

By the time I was nineteen, I had almost completely forgotten about the entire ordeal. I was engaged to my husband—rest his soul—and eagerly looking forward to my wedding the following month when Jack Suffle approached me.

Since Charlie's death, the family had withdrawn from town social life. The mother, Mrs. Suffle, still ran her late husband's merchant business, but mostly by correspondence. I sometimes saw Jack in town, but he didn't seem to have friends. I'd just finished selling some of our hens' eggs to the grocer when I felt a tap on the shoulder.

"Can we have a word?" Jack asked.

I saw him so infrequently that it took me a second to remember his name. "Of course," I said, then followed him out of the store and to a quiet alley.

Watching his feet, he wouldn't meet my eye. He kept opening and closing his mouth, and I was more than a little frustrated by the time he actually spoke.

"You remember the day Charlie died?" he asked.

"Yes," I said, scrambling to recall the details. He'd drowned, hadn't he?

"Do you remember talking with me behind the pub?" Jack chanced a glance at my face.

It was coming back to me quickly. "Oh, yes, you were upset because they wouldn't believe you."

"That's what I want to know. What did I tell them? What didn't they believe?"

I was becoming uncomfortable, but I answered him regardless. "You said a vampire took Charlie."

He let his breath out in a great whoosh, as though he'd been holding it for hours. "Good. Good. That's what I remember. I just... Good."

I was starting to regret agreeing to talk to him, but I was too fascinated to stop myself from asking, "Didn't you remember?"

He said, "Ha!" But it wasn't a proper laugh, more of an imitation of emotion. "I thought I did, but mother says...she thinks I made it up later... I just...wanted to make sure I wasn't crazy. This has been hanging over me for so long. I think I need to confront it before I can move on, you know?"

I didn't really know. Still, I nodded to keep him happy. Jack gave me a tight smile then abruptly walked away. That was the last time I saw him.

His mother says he came home, took the gun off the wall, and left again. She didn't think anything of it, as he sometimes went out hunting when he'd finished his chores. A few of the farmers say they saw him walking to the edge of the town by the road that led to the cemetery. He never came home.

Just as they had when Charlie went missing, the townspeople

searched the woods for several days. They didn't find his body, though. After a few weeks, they held a discreet funeral for him. I attended, but not many other people did.

The popular opinion is that Jack killed himself. Charlie, his baby brother, had died while under his care, and the grief and guilt had grown stronger and stronger until he was unable to escape it. His mother believed he'd taken his own life too. He'd brought up Charlie's death that morning, she said, during breakfast.

Everyone agreed it was a tragedy. Some thought the family was cursed with premature death. Mrs. Suffle didn't live more than a year after losing Jack. She died in her sleep. She'd had a hard life. Her husband and her two children had passed in their prime, and money can't replace family.

Well, I have a slightly different theory about what happened to Jack. I think Jack was telling the truth about the vampire. I agree that the grief of Charlie's death had been eating at him, but instead of choosing to end his life, he confronted his monster… and lost. They searched the woods, but no one thought to search the cemetery. I often wonder if they might have found his body in that big old crypt.

There's one particular reason I'm inclined to think that. No one else paid much heed to it, but that river they found Charlie in—well, it runs right past the north border of the cemetery. Yes, I think Charlie may have breathed his last in that crypt, then the monster dragged him to the river when it was done.

PART 2

THAT WAS A VERY, VERY DIFFERENT STORY FROM WHAT I'D BEEN expecting to hear from Julie. I frowned at her, trying to decide if she actually believed it. She was sitting back in her chair, sipping at her tea, watching me, clearly pleased with the effect of her tale.

"And no one searched the tomb after he went missing?" I asked.

"Nope. No one seemed to think of it. The search of the woods was mainly a token gesture for his mother, really. He wasn't a precocious child anymore; he was a depressed, sullen young adult who had gone into the forest with a gun. No one had much hope of finding him alive, so they had a quiet funeral and called it a day."

I thanked Julie, finished my tea, and left her trailer. It was past midday, so I stopped in at the smallest of our town's three cafés and chewed my way through a greasy burger. I'd seen the Suffle name on a few plaques around town and assumed their family either had moved away or hadn't had any children. Knowing the tragedy Mrs. Suffle had gone through, I thought I would be less likely to overlook their monuments in the future.

Every town has tales about mythical beasts lurking just out

of sight, for men to spread over a pint of beer or for children to whisper to each other during recess. I supposed the vampire was one of ours.

Still, the story niggled at me. Julie had made it sound as though Jack were approaching insanity on the day he disappeared, and the insanity had centered on the belief that a vampire had taken his brother. I didn't think it too far-fetched that he'd walked to the crypt, found it empty, then been overcome by depression and taken his life. It bothered me that no one had searched there.

I finished my lunch and began the drive home. It was a Saturday, and I didn't have anything to do except a bit of neglected house-cleaning. I toyed with the idea of going to see a movie or driving to the larger library in the next town. While I was chewing over my limited options, a third, more exciting possibility snuck into my mind: *Why don't I visit Jack Suffle's crypt?*

I almost laughed at myself then thought, *Why not?*

More than forty years had passed since the events in Julie's story had taken place. Even if there was a body to find there—and that was a very big *if*—it would be a skeleton. Best case, I would have an exciting afternoon, solve a long-standing town mystery, and give Julie a new tale to tell. Worst case, I would find an empty tomb.

I turned my car toward the cemetery.

The graveyard had grown from what must have been a few dozen plots during Julie's childhood to a few hundred. A stone wall and a dense band of trees divided the old section from the new. I navigated my car down the narrow lane to the cemetery,

admiring the dense pines that lined the road. Surrounded by mostly untouched natural woods, the graveyard was a few minutes' drive from the outskirts of town. It was shady under the huge trees, and the temperature felt several degrees cooler.

I parked off the road, beside the wall that surrounded the new section of the graveyard. Lichen and moss covered the wall, but it was still stable. The caretaker left the gate open during the day, so I let myself in.

A couple of the modern graves had wilting bouquets laid carefully under the headstone, and the caretaker kept them tidy and weed-free. I didn't have any family or friends buried there, so I made my way through the graves at a quick pace.

The tree divider grew unchecked at the back of the cemetery, hiding the old section of the graveyard. I pushed through the shrubs and found myself facing another wall. This one was very different from the sturdy, lightly aged wall facing the road; it was taller than my head and must have been centuries old. Sections had crumbled, showing slate-gray stone under the moss and vines. There was no gate.

I paced up and down its length then eventually settled on one of the crumbled areas. Using some of the dislodged rocks as footholds, I clambered up its side, gripping vines until I could pull myself onto the top. The moss was soft and slightly slimy under my hands and would probably stain my pants. I wasn't wearing my hiking shoes so took my time letting myself down the other side, aware that if I slipped and broke my ankle, it might take days or weeks to be found. That thought stuck in

my head as my feet touched the weedy ground. Could Jack have fallen and broken a leg? He'd probably gotten in the same way I had, and he would have been hampered by his gun. I walked up and down the inside of the wall, looking for clothes or bones that might tell the story of a man's last miserable days on earth, but I found nothing.

That was a relief, at least. It would be a horrible way to go.

The old half of the graveyard hadn't been touched in decades. Dry weeds grew up to my waist in sections, and almost all of the headstones were collapsed or overgrown. Gothic statues— some of angels, some of humans, and a few that seemed to depict monsters—sprouted from the underbrush.

Julie had said the graveyard had already been there when the town was settled. I hadn't thought much about it at the time, but as I wandered among the last records of passed souls, I became aware of how strange it was that a town with nearly a hundred graves could have been so thoroughly forgotten.

I pushed the weeds away from one of the unbroken headstones and tried to make out the worn-down inscription. *Elizabeth Claireborne: Beloved mother and wife. May her soul find rest.*

Insects scurried out of the weeds and began climbing up my arms. I flicked them off with a shudder and moved farther into the cemetery.

I found the crypt from Julie's story near the back. Made entirely out of black stone, it was almost as big as Julie's trailer, but much less welcoming. Heavily weathered and a haven for weeds and spiderwebs, the doorway loomed out of the gloom

like a tribute to Gothic masonry. The light penetrated no more than a few paces past the opening.

I pulled my car keys out of my pocket and pressed the button on the small LED light attached. The light was laughably weak, but it was better than being blind. I walked through the archway and took four steps before the floor disappeared.

I cried out and stumbled back, managing to catch my balance at the last moment. Shining my light at the floor showed the edge of a step, and I swallowed. What I'd assumed was the entire crypt was merely an entryway.

The steps were slimy and damp, so I took them slowly and kept my free hand pressed to the wall. My eyes slowly began to adjust as I moved deeper into the tomb and the darkness thickened, and the LED light became more useful. The walls were smooth stone, carved carefully and blemish free. Whoever had owned this crypt must have been either very wealthy or very important—or both.

I counted twenty steps before the floor leveled out. I had been expecting a single room, but the steps ended in a hallway that extended to the left and the right. Leaves, dirt, and even a few animal bones littered the foot of the steps, and the musty, stale air pushed against my eardrums as though the pressure had doubled. I peered as far as I could down both pathways, but the light was too weak to see more than a few meters. I chose left.

The path continued for twenty paces. Like the walls, the stairs were perfectly smooth. The leaves on the ground soon disappeared, leaving stone with a thin coating of dirt. The air was

heavy, almost as dense as soup, and it clogged my throat. Before long, the path ended in another intersection.

I thought I might have stumbled into a subterranean labyrinth, so I chose left again, so I could retrace my steps easily if the path kept splitting. The passageway ended, however, after a dozen steps, in a square room. The room was just a few meters wide. A raised dais took up most of the room; a carved stone coffin sat on top. Intricate runes were spaced around the lid, with words carved in the center. I approached it carefully and shined my light on the inscription:

Eleanor White
Loving mother, compassionate friend
Unlucky in marriage
May her sleep be eternal

The inscription felt unreasonably gloomy for someone's last resting place, but I supposed maybe her husband hadn't been liked. He would have been wealthy—possibly the wealthiest man in the town—to afford the below-ground temple. And, historically, the rich didn't always place well in popularity contests.

I left the room and followed the pathway straight, down what would have been the right-hand turn from the main passageway. It ended in another room that had a dais, but no coffin. I gave the room a quick search, but there was nothing to see: just smooth stone walls and floor and an empty waist-height dais.

The subterranean crypt was cold, and I pulled my jacket

around myself more snugly as I retraced my steps into the main passageway and past the stairs to the outside. The leaves crunched under my feet for a dozen paces before the floor returned to being empty. I was becoming disoriented and dizzy. The thick air and the identical empty walls and floors were clouding my head and making it hard to think. The farther I walked, the more aware I became of a stench. The heavy smell got down my throat and made me want to gag. It was musty, bitter, and dry, and it carried hints of organic decay.

For a moment, I thought it might be the smell of Jack's corpse, but he would have turned to bones a long time ago. It was more likely that an animal had gotten into the cemetery and died in a corner of the crypt.

Just as it had before, the path split. I chose left and soon found myself in a small room identical to the first, where a stone coffin rested atop a dais. I leaned over the coffin's lid, careful not to disturb the layer of dust, and read the inscription.

Christopher White
Taken in his infancy
His mother loved him

I turned, casting my light around the room in case I'd missed something, but it was completely empty except for the coffin and a dead beetle in one corner. The smell was only slightly better than it had been in the passageway, which meant its source had to be in the remaining unexplored room.

I returned to the passageway and continued on straight. In the final hallway, I found the first signs of imperfection in the walls. If everything else hadn't been so eerily smooth, I would have missed it, but the hollow caught my eye as soon as the LED's light fell over it. The small indent was the width of my finger, and something shiny and silver was inside…

A bullet. So, Jack was here after all… But which trip did this lodged round belong to? When Jack came with Charlie, had he accidentally shot his brother after all?

I could see the entrance to the final room ahead. The smell was nearly overpowering, but I sucked in a breath and stepped through the doorway. It was simultaneously very similar and very different from the previous rooms. It was the same size and made of the same stone, but the walls were pocked with nearly a dozen holes. *What was he firing at?*

The coffin on the dais was not intact. The stone lid lay on the floor, cracked in three places. Dust had gathered over the toppled lid; the coffin must have been opened for a long time. I couldn't see inside.

I'd come to the old graveyard with the specific goal of finding a skeleton, but faced with the possibility of actually seeing one, all I could think of was leaving the tomb and running to my car without looking back.

Don't be a coward. It's just bones.

I approached the lip of the stone box, my heart hammering and the hairs on my arms standing on end. Images flashed through my mind: a twisted corpse, its clothes in rags, scraps of

dried skin still stuck to the bleached-white bone. I squeezed my eyes half-closed as I peeked over the edge, then I let my breath out with a whoosh. The coffin was empty.

Grinning at my stupid anxiety, I gave my hands a quick shake to loosen my trembling fingers. I started to turn away from the coffin then stopped myself. It wasn't completely empty after all; as I'd turned, my light had caught something pale in the corner of the box. It looked like paper. I reached in and plucked it out with two fingers.

The sheet of yellowed, stiff, grainy parchment felt as though it could crumble in a strong breeze, so I unfolded it carefully. I squinted in the low light to read the black ink scrawled across the paper.

"By decree," I muttered to myself, trying to comprehend the challenging scrawl. "On this day, the fourteenth of March, 1879, the White family is to be interred living in their tomb, for crimes against God and against their fellow people. The council has concluded that Lord Fitzwilliam White has contrived to bargain with the dark powers to grant his flesh immortality and take on the form of the vampire. We pray his entombment will grant the town reprieve from its suffering and that the White family may eventually find forgiveness in the next life."

The paper was signed with five names, presumably the council that had written it. I shivered, feeling as though a cold wind had rushed through my clothes, and gently replaced the paper. The decree explained a few things, at least.

Julie Haze had said no one knew anything about the people

who had lived there before the current town was founded. It was only an hour's drive from the next city, but the original town would have been much more isolated in 1879. It had probably been a pioneering town, settled too far away from other cities to receive supplies reliably. If it had fallen on hard times—possibly failed crops or an exceptionally harsh winter—it wasn't difficult to imagine the desperate townspeople had looked for someone to blame. Jokes would become rumors, and rumors would become truth; drowning in stress, hunger, and grief, the suffering town could have easily turned into a Salem replica... except, instead of crying, "Witch! Witch!" they had screamed, "Vampire!" as they carried Fitzwilliam White, his wife, and his child into the crypt.

And they'd been buried alive. For a second, I imagined what it must have felt like to be pressed into the stone coffin then watch as the unmovably heavy lid dropped into place, blocking out light and sound. I shivered again, crossing my arms over my chest, and pushed the thought out of my head.

The human sacrifice hadn't done the town much good, anyway; it had still fallen, probably succumbing to disease, or starvation, or cold. The Whites' fate was horrible, but it might have actually been merciful compared to what their peers had endured as they struggled to survive in an unforgiving and hostile landscape.

Another thought occurred to me then. I imagined two boys, one set on adventure and the other begging to go home, entering the tomb. Of course Jack Suffle would have looked into the open coffin; that sort of morbid mystery held an allure he would have

found impossible to resist. He'd picked up the parchment and read it, and the word *vampire* had stuck in his mind.

Then something had happened to little Charlie on the way home. Maybe the gun had gone off accidentally or the child had slipped into the river and drowned. Either way, Charlie had died, and Jack had been unable to save him. Grief, fear, and guilt had crawled into Jack as he ran for home, and his mind had created a coping mechanism. He'd built an alternate reality based on the most memorable part of the note he'd read. *A vampire got Charlie. It wasn't my fault; I couldn't have saved him. It was a vampire.*

If he'd lived in modern times, Jack might have had a chance of being treated with therapy and counseling. Instead, he'd been ignored, ridiculed, and accused. The psychosis had taken hold, and as the years passed, it had deepened until he believed it too completely to be dissuaded.

Of course, he'd returned to the tomb to confront the vampire he was convinced existed. But instead of fighting a fictional monster, he'd found the note in the empty coffin. It might have been enough to bring up the suppressed memories of what had actually happened that day… and so he'd walked into the woods, gun in hand, unable to tolerate the truth. The depressing narrative was pure speculation, of course, but it answered the mystery of Jack's obsession and disappearance.

I turned toward the room's exit, thinking I might pay a second visit to Julie that afternoon so I could share my discovery. She would love to know the full story, though she would probably swear she'd never actually believed in the vampire either.

As I swung my light toward the exit, it caught on something bright and reflective above the doorway. I turned my mini flashlight toward the shape, squinting to try to make it out. Two circles a little smaller than my palm hovered near the roof, shining like the reflective posts spaced along the side of the main highway. I frowned and turned my head to the side, trying to figure out what they were.

They blinked.

My back hit the edge of the coffin as I leaped away from the creature, heart in my throat. *What is that? An owl?*

It dropped from its perch with a soft thud. I stared, fixated, unable to believe what I was seeing. The creature, only vaguely humanoid and nearly as large as me, crouched on all fours. Its skin was leathery gray, just barely a shade darker than the stone walls that had disguised it so well, and its huge, owlish eyes bulged out of a smooth head. Those eyes, flashing crimson in my flashlight's pitiful beam, were the only color on the creature. Its fingers were impossibly long, and its loose, wrinkled skin hung on what seemed to be little more than a skeleton. It quivered as it stared at me, and I swear I saw anticipation in its eyes.

Faster than I could have ever imagined, it sprang toward me. The frail appearance was a ruse: it gripped my shoulders in its long fingers and hauled me off-balance, slamming me to the ground. I struggled, revolted and terrified, as I tried to break out of its grip, and it bit my arm just below the shoulder.

I screamed as a dozen needle-sharp teeth cut through my shirt and punctured my skin. The key ring was still clasped in my hand, so I twisted it around and stabbed the keys at the monster's head.

Without the light, I couldn't see where I had hit it, but my attacker hissed in pain and released its hold, allowing me to squirm out from under it. I scrambled backward until I hit the dais.

Hot blood was running down my arm and dripping off my elbow. Fighting to keep my mind clear despite the searing pain, I fumbled to turn on the light.

The monster had retreated to the corner of the room, crouching, its huge eyes fixed on my face. It seemed wary to attack me again; the keys had cut through the skin on its head, and a flap of the gray flesh hung loose, exposing a white skull underneath.

I staggered to my feet. My breathing thin and panicky, I held the light ahead of my body like a priest warding off a demon with his cross. The beast watched intently as I stumbled in a semicircle around it, moving to get my back to the exit. Then I turned and ran.

Thankfully, the pain in my shoulder was numbing as my feet slapped on the stone floor, carrying me away from the monster. A thought hovered in my mind, terrifying me, blocking out all reasoning. *Vampire. That was the vampire.*

I glanced behind myself, shining the light over my shoulder, looking for the two reflective eyes, but the passageway was empty. My legs felt weak, so I slowed to a jog as I rounded the corner and saw the natural light coming from the stairway ahead.

The pain had almost completely subsided, and in its place, a gentle heat spread from my shoulder, radiating through my body. My thundering heart slowed, my hands stopped shaking, and I reduced my jog to a walk.

There's actually nothing to worry about, I realized as my feet crunched the leaves littering the hallway. *Yes, it was a vampire, but so what? Why did I let it scare me so badly?*

I felt tired and a little bit drunk as I reached the stairway and began to climb. My bleeding shoulder felt pleasantly warm, and my mind was going fuzzy. I thought I heard dragging footsteps from behind me, but they didn't matter anymore.

I need to rest for a bit, I decided as I lurched onto the fourth step. *I had a shock, and I'm tired, but a little rest would do me good. Just for a moment.*

The dragging sounds behind me grew louder. They were comforting, like the ocean lapping at a white-sand beach. My feet faltered on the steps, and I fell forward, hitting the stairs hard. I tasted blood in my mouth but, surprisingly, it didn't hurt.

This is nice. Maybe I'll rest here for a bit. Regain my strength before going home.

I rolled onto my back. My vision was blurry, but I thought I could see the creature crawling up the steps toward me. I smiled at it stupidly. *I wonder what its name is. Maybe it's actually Fitzwilliam White. Wouldn't that be something? I'll have to remember to tell Julie. She'll find it so funny.*

The creature's long fingers wrapped around my ankle and thigh, and it began dragging me away from the sunlight and down the stairs. Its lips were quivering with anticipation, and its lamp-like eyes bored into my face.

It pulled me off the last step, and something cool bumped my

cheek. I glanced at it; it was hard to see clearly, but I thought it was one of the animal bones that littered the entrance.

The creature was strong, and it pulled me quickly, dragging me back toward its room. I was vaguely aware of how cold the stone was under my back, but I didn't mind. All I wanted was to close my eyes and let sleep take me. I could worry about everything else when I woke up.

The motion stopped. We were back in Fitzwilliam's room. I still held the flashlight loosely in one hand, and it gave enough diffused light to let me see the broken coffin to my right. The creature circled me twice, inhaling deeply through the slits of his nose, then nestled his face into the crook of my neck. He bit me again—I was pleased it didn't hurt at all this time—and I turned my head to give him better access as he lapped at the blood that flowed freely.

I wonder if he'll let me float down the river when he's done? I thought sluggishly as the blood drained from my body and flowed into the creature's swelling, faintly translucent stomach. *Either way, I'll have to remember to tell Julie about this. She'll enjoy it so much.*

I smiled to myself as I let my head loll to the other side. There, in the corner of the room, only visible once my discarded light fell directly onto it, was a small pile of bones. Femurs, ribs, and a cracked skull lay in a haphazard pile, throwing twisted shadows over the wall behind them.

Oh good, I found Jack Suffle, I thought as I let my eyes drift closed.

THE MANNEQUIN

I FOLLOWED GEOFF DOWN THE STAIRS TO THE BASEMENT, KEEPING a few feet behind him as he wheezed and grunted his way to the landing. I suspected he didn't get down to the lowest level of his home very often. By the time he unlocked the heavy wooden door, his face was flushed and sweaty.

"This is it," he announced, ushering me into the concrete room. "It's a bit messy, but..."

I looked around. A single mattress, old and frayed, rested in the middle of the floor. It was surrounded by dozens of boxes of all shapes and sizes, as well as furniture shrouded in blankets. A barred, grimy window was positioned nearly at the top of the wall, letting in a narrow square of sunlight.

"Nah, it'll be fine," I said. "Fifty bucks a week, right?"

"That's right." Geoff hitched his pants as high as they would go under his bulging stomach. "You can use the bathroom and

kitchen upstairs too. Just clean up after yourself and replace any groceries you take."

I nodded and approached the mattress. There were more than a few disconcerting stains on it, but Geoff had been considerate enough to leave a stack of clean sheets, blankets, and a new pillow at the bed's foot. I dropped my backpack—which held the entirety of my worldly possessions—beside the bed.

"You can move the boxes and stuff around to give yourself more room," Geoff said, hitching his pants up again as he backed toward the door. "Most of it's junk, anyway. I never got around to cleaning it out. But there're some tables and a chair and stuff you can use. Just don't break anything, and we're good, okay?"

"Sure," I said. "Thanks, man."

"Later," Geoff grunted, closing the door behind himself. His huffing and groaning echoed through the room as he pulled his large frame up the stairwell.

I turned back to the basement and gave it a closer look. There was dust everywhere, and some of the boxes looked as though they hadn't been opened in decades.

When my girlfriend and I had broken up, we'd both said some pretty rash things. In retrospect, "No, don't bother. Keep the flat—I'm leaving," was one of my less-thought-out statements. I was between jobs and didn't have much in the way of savings, so it was pure good fortune that a friend at uni had told me how his uncle Geoff wanted to rent out his basement. It wasn't pretty, but it was cheap and didn't come with a contract, so I couldn't complain much.

I made the bed quickly, out of eagerness to cover up the yellowed stains more than anything, then started working on making my new home more livable. There was hardly any room to stand, so I began pulling boxes away from the bed and stacked them against the walls as high as I could reach. Moving them caused showers of dust and grime to rain down on me, sending me into sneezing fits. One of the boxes rustled suspiciously. Whether it held mice or a cockroach nest, I couldn't have been sure, but I shoved it out of the way as quickly as I could and then dusted my filthy hands on my pants.

I pulled the drapery off the furniture to see if any of it was useful. I found a spindly wooden rocking chair, which I set under the narrow window, and a small, round coffee table that could double as a bedside stand and a place to eat dinner. I was tempted to make use of the giant mahogany wardrobe that was missing one door, but my clothing storage needs were better met by the coatrack I found and placed beside the door.

Most of the other furniture—the broken washing machine, the unplugged mini-fridge, the bookcase, and the foldable camping chairs—weren't much use, so I replaced their cloths and left them where they were.

One final piece of furniture, tall and narrow, was nestled in the corner behind boxes and a few crates of what looked like children's toys. Hoping it might be useful, I struggled to it, but when I pulled away its cloth, I was disappointed and a little disturbed to find a mannequin.

The naked figure stood nearly a head taller than I did, and it

was made of a smooth, slate-gray ceramic. Its masculine face was tilted upward to gaze at a corner of the room.

It seemed shockingly lifelike, even though its features were only abstract imitations of the real things. The smooth surface below its eyebrows gave the impression of a steady gaze, even though the face had no eyes. The lips were set in a hard line below high cheekbones, and its arms were held out in some unfathomable gesture. Its long fingers were devoid of nails, creases, and fingerprints, but somehow, they seemed just as human as my own.

I threw the cloth back over its bald head and rearranged the fabric to ensure every part of the mannequin was covered, then I replaced the boxes and crates in front of it.

My back was aching, and I figured the room was about as organized as I could bother making it. Dust and whorls of grime still coated the floor, and my every step kicked up small puffs. I hadn't found a broom during my cleaning, but I supposed Geoff wouldn't mind if I asked to borrow his.

I jogged up the stairs and let myself through the door at the top. Geoff's house was large, and he'd only shown me the way from the front door to the basement. As I hesitated on the landing, wondering if it would be less rude to go looking for him or to call his name, my phone beeped. I pulled it out and saw two missed messages: one from Tony, asking if I wanted to meet him and the guys at the local pub to celebrate my breakup, and another from Clive, saying they were all waiting for me.

A grin slid across my face as I texted back, saying I would be there in ten minutes. Forgetting the broom, I raced back down

the stairs to get my wallet and jacket. I watched the signal on my phone as I descended, and the bars disappeared about halfway down the stairs. Clearly, the basement was a dead zone for Wi-Fi. It was annoying, but I was willing to put up with a lot in exchange for cheap rent.

I opened the door and froze as I felt eyes watching me. I looked to my left and saw the mannequin's head, barely visible above the stacked boxes, staring in my direction.

I dropped my phone into my pocket then circled the boxes to escape the gaze of the statue. I mustn't have put the cloth on properly, I realized. A breeze from the open door had probably caused it to slide off.

A minute of puffing and clambering got me next to the manne-quin. I gathered the fabric from where it was pooled around his feet then threw it back over him, being extra careful to make sure it would stay put before I extracted myself from the storage area.

———

The pub wasn't far from Geoff's house, and I got there in good time. My four friends were already halfway to drunk, so I made quick work of a pint of beer to catch up to them. When Clive asked me to share some of the ways my ex had wronged me, Tony had the bright idea to turn it into a drinking game.

We ordered a tray of shots and drank every time I told a story that made my friends hoot in disgust. They were predisposed to hate my ex and eager to drink, so it wasn't long before we were plastered.

We left—or we might have been kicked out; I really can't remember—shortly after midnight. I don't have any memory of finding my way home, but I did, which was a bit of a miracle, truthfully, as I'd only been there once before. I remember fumbling with my keys for what felt like an eternity before I realized I was trying to use the one from my old apartment. When I finally let myself into the house, I tried to creep toward my basement so I wouldn't wake Geoff, but I had forgotten where it was and ended up looping through the house twice before I found the right door. If Geoff heard me, he was generous enough not to disturb my drunken roving.

I woke up the next morning with a dry mouth and a splitting headache. I lay there, prone on my dust-covered mattress, for as long as I could before my bladder threatened mutiny. I pulled myself to my feet, ready to stagger upstairs, and nearly walked into the mannequin.

It stood at the foot of my bed, its arms splayed out as though to welcome an embrace, its head tilted down to angle its nonexistent gaze on me as I slept. I stumbled away from it, became tangled in my bed sheets, slipped, and caught myself on one of the boxes. My headache flared, and for a moment, I thought I would be sick on the floor. Then as I closed my eyes and breathed the dusty air through my nose, memories of the night before filtered through my mind. I remembered spinning around with the mannequin, laughing at how serious he looked and telling him he was almost stiff enough to be a replica of my ex.

For whatever reason, Drunk Me must have thought it would

be a brilliant idea to pull the mannequin out from the corner of the room and set him up to watch over me as I slept. I cursed, shambled around the statue, and stomped up the stairs.

I'd slept in my clothes and still had my wallet in my pocket, so after relieving myself and splashing water over my face, I decided it would be less painful to go outside than hide in the cramped, dusty basement. I went to one of my favorite local cafés. There was a corner with dim lighting, and the servers knew me well enough that they wouldn't pester me too often, so I hunkered down to drink coffee and wait out my hangover.

By the time I felt like a human being again, I was late for a uni lecture I couldn't miss and had to jog to get there on time. Afterward, Tony invited me to tag along for dinner at a barbecue one of his work friends was throwing. In the end, I didn't get back to Geoff's house until late that night. When I opened the basement door, I was surprised to see the mannequin standing beside the rocking chair under the window.

I paused in the doorway, confused and alarmed, until I realized Geoff must have moved it. When he hadn't seen me that morning, he'd probably come downstairs to check on me and found the mannequin poised above my bed. It must have confused him and likely disturbed him a little, so he'd moved it.

Great. Now he thinks I put the mannequin there on purpose. Talk about making a first impression.

I sighed and halfheartedly kicked my bed sheets back into an approximation of where they should have been then flopped on top of them. When I split from my ex, I'd left just about

everything I owned at our apartment—including my clothes, my laptop, and my uni books. I would need to ask for them back soon, but I dreaded having to carry them the twenty minutes from her apartment to my new basement. I supposed I could ask Tony for help—he was a solid friend and would brave my ex with me like a champ—but I was still holding out for slightly nicer, less-cramped accommodations, preferably without a mannequin.

I rolled over to look at the ceramic figure. He stood beside the rocking chair, his arms hung limp by his sides, and his face was turned to observe the door. His sightless gaze was disquieting, even when he wasn't looking at me.

Sighing, I got up, approached the mannequin, and gripped its arms. The fake skin was colder than I'd expected, almost as if he'd been sitting in a fridge. I shuddered, ground my teeth, tightened my grip on the muscular biceps, and began dragging the statue back toward the corner.

It was heavier than I'd expected, and I was winded by the time I reached the crates and boxes blocking me from his corner. It was incredible that Drunk Me had managed to pull him out the night before.

I looked at the boxes, judged them to be too numerous and heavy to struggle with, and decided it would be easier to leave the mannequin on my side of them. I pushed him into a gap between two boxes, turned him to face the corner, and borrowed the cloth from on top of the mahogany wardrobe to drape over him. When I was done, it was almost possible to pretend he wasn't there at all.

I went upstairs to brush my teeth, shower, and check for messages on my phone. When I got back into the basement, I barely spared a glance at my cloth-covered companion before sliding into bed. I rolled over to face the window and lay there for almost an hour before sleep finally claimed me.

My dreams were disjointed. I imagined I was in uni, taking an exam I hadn't studied for. Whenever I looked at the words, they squiggled across the page like worms and resettled in new places to form completely different questions. A tall, dark man with a smooth face stood beside me while I struggled to erase an incorrect answer, and as I watched the words writhe across the pages again, he bent down to whisper in my ear, "Close your eyes."

I sat up with a jolt. Pale light filtered through the window, telling me it was morning. I fumbled for my phone on the bedside table. The clock on my phone confirmed it was just after seven, so I got up and searched for fresh clothes on the coatrack.

I only had three shirts and two pairs of pants, and they were all grimy with settled dust. Grumbling, I shook one of the shirts and a pair of pants, sending plumes of tiny hairs and specks swirling in the early-morning light, then pulled on the clothes.

As I made for the door, I shot a glance at the mannequin. It was no longer where I'd left it, between the boxes. I froze then rotated slowly, my eyes skimming the room.

It wasn't hard to find him. He was posed directly behind the

head of the bed, staring down at where I'd been lying just a few minutes before.

A stifled laugh spilled out of me. I glanced about the room, searching for some explanation—and failing to find one. The mannequin stood, legs spread on his stand, his bald head tilted downward. His abs caught a hint of shine from the window's light.

I jumped through the doorway, slammed the door behind me, then jogged up the stairs. The house was quiet; Geoff probably wasn't awake yet. I let myself out through the front door, slung the backpack over my shoulders, and jogged down the near-empty street toward my favorite café.

I stayed there for several hours, stirring a cold mug of coffee and trying not to think about the statue in my new home. I needed someone to talk to who would listen patiently, wouldn't think I was crazy or stupid, and could give me solid advice.

Well, Tony can do two out of three.

Just before the lunch crowd started filtering in, I paid my bill then took the subway to Tony's neighborhood. It was a neglected part of town, but the occasional windowsill potted plant and a small park stopped it from being depressing. I let myself into Tony's apartment complex, climbed the three flights of stairs, and knocked on his door.

He was home, luckily, though he looked as though he hadn't been awake for long. His round, oily face split into a huge grin when he saw me, and he pulled me into his cluttered two-room apartment.

"How you doing, man?" He shoved a pile of clothes off his couch and waved me into the newly freed space. Then before I could answer, he asked, "Want a beer?"

I certainly did, and he fished two bottles out of his fridge. As I opened my beer, he sat next to me and fixed me with his brilliantly carefree smile. "What brings you here on such a lovely day?"

I took a gulp while I tried to think how to phrase my problem. Even Tony, who fervently believed in the Loch Ness Monster, had limits to what he would swallow. I settled on a vague answer: "Something weird is happening in my new apartment."

"What, like with the house owner?"

"No, no, he's fine." Things suddenly fell into place, and I felt acutely stupid for not seeing it sooner.

An explanation—the only possible explanation, really—for the moving mannequin was Geoff. He'd come down to the basement while I was asleep and put the statue behind my bed as a prank. It was a weird thing for him to do, and it definitely pushed the boundaries of personal space. Still, that was less disturbing than imagining the mannequin was sentient. I snorted and gulped down another bitter mouthful of beer. "You know what? It's nothing. Don't worry about it, man."

Tony shrugged and turned the TV on. He was quickly absorbed in a soccer match, and I let my mind wander.

Geoff had seemed like a jovial person when I'd met him. He was probably waiting for me to bound up the stairs, screaming about walking mannequins so he could slap my back and have a laugh at my expense.

Well, that wasn't going to happen. I loved a good prank, but the mannequin was just too creepy to tolerate. When I got back, I would have to confront Geoff and ask him not to move the statue again.

I didn't follow soccer, but Tony did, and it was an easy, distracting two hours. Tony kept fishing more beers from the fridge, and around midafternoon, he phoned for a pizza.

When I left Tony's house shortly after sundown, I was slightly drunk and much less anxious than I'd been that morning. The air was cool and smelled like rain was on the way. I took my time walking home, taking detours through the nicer parts of town to prolong my freedom before retreating to the basement.

When Geoff's house came in sight, I hesitated then quickened my steps. The two-story house stood out like a beacon. Every light in the place was turned on, and the front door stood open, spilling a rectangle of gold down the steps and onto the sidewalk.

I stopped in the doorway and listened to the heavy steps thundering through the back of the house. A moment later, Geoff rounded the corner, his large face beet-red from exertion, carrying a suitcase in each hand. He saw me and let his breath out in a rush.

"You're back! Good, good… I was going to write you a note…"

He dropped his suitcases beside the door, wiped the back of his hand across his damp forehead, and gazed about the room. His watery eyes scanned the stack of mail on the narrow hallway table and the phone on the wall.

"Did something happen?" I asked, eyeing Geoff's suitcases

warily. *If he's leaving, does that mean I need to find a new place to stay?*

Geoff caught my gaze and gave me a grim smile. "Don't worry. I'm not kicking you out. I've got to be out of state for a couple of days, lad. I'm sorry to do this so soon after you've moved in. It's my sister. She's had a fall, and I... I need to be there for her."

He pulled a handkerchief from his pocket and rubbed it over the rivulets of sweat slipping down his face, his eyes again scanning the room. "I don't think I've forgotten anything... You can use whatever's in the fridge, if you like, so it doesn't go off. The bills are all paid, so no worries there..."

"I'm sorry about your sister," I said, but Geoff didn't seem to hear me.

A taxi honked from the street, and he grabbed his travel cases.

"That's for me, lad. Got to go. I'll call if I'm going to be away for more than a few days. Take care, now."

He barreled past me, dragging his suitcases toward the waiting taxi. I closed the door behind him then watched through the curtained windows until the car disappeared.

Geoff had left the lights on in the house, so I went through each room, turning them off. He must have only just gotten the call. A mess of clothes littered the floor around his closet, and he'd left the bathroom cabinets open after collecting his toiletries.

The offer of free food was too tempting to pass up, so I grabbed some leftover chicken and a soda from the fridge for my dinner. I took a shower—much longer than I would have dared if Geoff had been in the house—changed into a pair of my clean

clothes, and set my phone to charge. Then I allowed myself the luxury of watching TV in the living room until tiredness started to gnaw at me.

It was getting close to midnight when I made my way down the stairs into the chilly basement. I didn't think Geoff would mind me using the rest of his house while he was gone, but it wouldn't feel right to sleep in his bed, no matter how inviting it was compared to my stiff mattress and dusty concrete room.

The mannequin stood where I'd left him, poised over the head of my bed. I closed the door behind myself, dropped my bag beside the coatrack, and picked the mannequin's discarded cloth off the floor. I threw it over his head, blocking his horrible blank profile from my sight, then dragged him back to his proper place, wedged between two boxes near the opposite side of the room.

"Looks like it's just you and me for a few days," I said grimly, patting the mannequin's covered head. "Lovely."

I turned the light off and stood by the door for a moment, letting my eyes adjust to the darkness. The rectangular window set high in the wall let in just enough moonlight to guide me back to my bed. I kicked off my shoes and crawled under the sheets, shuddering at how unexpectedly cold they were.

The rooms upstairs had felt so warm and comfortable that it had been easy to become drowsy, but back in my basement, the tiredness melted away. I lay on my back, frustrated and alert, my eyes seeking out patterns in the stained concrete ceiling while the weak moonlight gradually eroded shadows and built new ones in their place.

You've got to get some sleep, I thought after checking my phone and seeing it was creeping up on one in the morning. *You've got classes tomorrow, and you really need to pick up your laptop and study books... brave the fiery wrath of the dragon ex...*

I slipped into a thin, unsatisfying sleep, where dreams blended into reality. The light from the window was fading, like a flashlight whose battery was running down, while the mannequin strode past me, his ceramic joins bending unnaturally as his blank eyes bored into the back of my head.

The door gave a soft click, and I jolted into awareness, sitting up and rubbing at my face while I tried to center myself and shake off the dreams.

The noise had been too real—too close—to have been my imagination, so I fumbled for my phone. I swiped to turn on the flashlight and then pointed the thin glow toward the basement door.

A tall, dark man stood there, as still as stone, staring down at me. I stared back, horrified.

My heart was beating in my ear, like a bird trapped in a cage, thrashing its wings against its prison. Not daring to move, I sat in my bed, prepared to dive backward or defend myself the moment the man moved toward me. The stranger, barely visible in the thin light from my phone, had frozen as well. I could feel him watching me, waiting to see what I would do.

His stillness was unnerving, terrifying, and somehow much worse than motion. The seconds stretched out, each one lasting much longer than they had any right to, while we each waited for

the other to make the first move. Then a horrible, crazy thought flitted through my head. *What if it isn't an intruder? What if it's the mannequin?*

I glanced to the right, to where the mannequin should have been propped between the boxes. The phone's light was too weak to make out much more than a cloud of shadows, but I thought I caught sight of the cloth pooled on the floor.

Then darkness poured over us.

My phone had slipped into hibernation. A weak, terrified sound escaped my lips, and I swiped the phone again, calling the light back. I looked up.

The mannequin had moved a full two paces toward me in that second of darkness. He was frozen again, poised just shy of the foot of my bed as he loomed over me, his fingers spread by his sides, his blank face angled down at me.

I clambered out of bed, the adrenaline lending my shaking limbs strength, and darted backward, away from the mannequin. I kept my thumb rubbing over the phone's screen, refusing to let it slip back into darkness, as I pointed the screen toward the mannequin like a priest uses his cross to ward off a vampire.

I kept backing away, refusing to take my eyes off the statue's back, until I reached the door. I grabbed for the knob with my free hand and twisted it. It stuck. I pulled harder, pushed, then put my shoulder against the door and shoved it as hard as I could.

He locked you in, a nasty voice in my head whispered. *He's got you trapped.*

"No," I muttered. I stepped away from the door and searched

for the plastic box set in the wall. I found the switch and flicked it. Beautiful, sweet light filled the room.

I took a series of short gulps of air as I put my phone back into my pocket. I didn't dare take my eyes off the mannequin, but he hadn't moved since that second of darkness. I returned to the door again and jiggled the handle. It wouldn't budge.

The spare keys were in my jacket's pocket. I edged around the perimeter of the room until I reached the coatrack, where I fumbled for my corded jacket. The first pocket was empty. So was the second one. I kept going, turning out every pocket in it, until there was no room left for doubt. The keys were gone.

They'd been there when I'd let myself into the basement the night before. I remembered putting them back in my pocket before taking off the jacket and hanging it up. And if there was no one in the house except for me and…

I stared at the mannequin's muscular back. He wore no clothes and had no pockets. *If he took the keys, what did he do with them?*

The concrete floor was icy cold under my hands as I knelt before the door. There was a gap of nearly an inch between the wood slab and the ground. I spared a glance toward the mannequin to reassure myself he hadn't moved, then I turned my head and looked under the door.

The short hallway leading to the stairs was almost pitch-black, but a thin sliver of light stretched along the ground. I could just barely make out a glitter of silver at the foot of the first stair, offering tantalizing freedom that was impossible to reach.

A crash, a snap, and then the light was gone once again. I

scrambled away from the door, stumbled to my feet, and turned to get my back against a wall. The light from the window had faded as the night progressed, making it impossible to see anything except vague hints of shapes. I tugged my phone back out of my pocket, my eyes uselessly scanning the black room, and swiped it on.

The mannequin stood beside the light, barely a foot away from where I'd been kneeling. His body faced the wall, but his head had turned to follow me. He held something white in his hands. I stared for a moment, extending my phone forward to push the weak light toward him. He was holding a crumpled plastic rectangle with severed wires trailing from it. *The light switch.*

"You bastard," I whispered.

The mannequin didn't reply. He was frozen in the beam of my phone, the indents where his eyes belonged gazing at me. Once again, I felt the overwhelming sensation of being examined, as though his fleshless, lifeless eyes could see far more clearly than my mortal ones. I skittered sideways, toward the window, to get out of his gaze.

Panic was building like a knot of cords in my chest, binding my lungs so I couldn't breathe and restricting my limbs so I couldn't move. The waning burst of adrenaline was urging me to do something—flee, fight, just some sort of action!—but my exit was locked, and I would rather have died than touch the monster in the basement.

"That's what you are," I said, backing toward the window, my feet scraping across the dusty floor as I warded him off with the light from my phone. "A monster."

The back of my legs hit the rocking chair, and I let myself slump into it. The rickety legs creaked under my weight, but it didn't break.

My mind scrambled to find a way out, but every choice was a dead end. The window above me was too narrow for a person to fit through, even if I could break it open. My phone had no signal in the basement. The door was too thick and solid to break, and without the keys, I had no hope of unlocking it.

I glanced past the mannequin. If I could find something—a coat hanger, maybe—to slip through the gap under the door, I could probably hook the keys. But that would mean turning my back to the mannequin again. I instinctively knew that was a terrible mistake…while it was dark, at least.

I tilted my head back to gaze at the window above me. It was narrow and had bars like a jail cell's, but it let me see a strip of inky sky pinpricked with stars.

If I could hold him off until dawn, I might just have a chance to retrieve the keys and make a break for it. I looked back at the mannequin. He remained as motionless as a statue, posed by the defunct light bulb, looking the other way.

"Light's your weakness, huh?" I said. "You can't move as long as I can see you."

As usual, there was no reply. I kicked my heels against the ground, sending the rocking chair into a gentle swing. *How long until dawn?* I turned the phone toward myself for a moment. Three in the morning. I had at least two hours until sunrise.

I rotated the phone back to face the room. The mannequin had

moved. In the second I'd taken the light off him, he'd dropped the scrunched plastic from his hand and taken a step toward me.

My breath whistled through my lips in a shaky wheeze as we stared each other down. My first impulse was to move out of his line of vision, as I'd done before, but I stopped myself. I didn't want to show signs of weakness in front of my stalker.

"Maybe this is best," I told the mannequin while the light jittered over his slate-gray face, casting strange shadows about his eyes. "I can watch you, and you can watch me, but no one gets any closer than we are now."

Time dragged by. When my arm began to ache, I switched the phone to my left hand. I didn't dare break the mannequin's gaze, even as the shadows behind him jumped and leaped in my dim light, clamoring to surge forward and engulf me and my inhuman companion. As the air became colder, goose bumps rose on my arms, and mist began to plume in front of my face. A couple of times, I thought I saw tiny puffs of chilled air appear around the mannequin's set mouth and ceramic nose, but it might have been a trick played by the light.

It was easy to lose track of time in the basement. I kept my chair rocking, using the gentle motion to keep me alert. Each time I kicked against the floor, the worn wooden joints whined in protest. I had my eyes trained on the mannequin, watching the shadows around his eyes quiver as the light shifted from the motion, as I willed myself to stay alert.

Then my phone beeped.

I knew that noise, and a rush of frantic horror poured through

me. I stopped rocking the chair, letting it come to a halt as my feet hit the ground, and stared at the statue with fresh dread.

The beep was my phone's warning for low batteries.

How didn't I think of this before? It's been on for hours. Of course the battery's going to drain.

My mouth was dry when I swallowed, and I felt a small bead of sweat trickle down my neck. I imagined the light going out, dead beyond my power to summon it back, trapping me in the inky blackness with my inhuman companion. A strangled noise caught in my throat.

Calm down. Think. Where's the charger?

Upstairs, of course, where I'd left it after fueling the phone before bed.

"Damn it," I whispered. "Damn it, damn it, damn it."

My hand shook, and the unsteady light allowed the shadows to creep across the mannequin's shoulders and up his legs. The way the darkness danced made his face look as though it were moving.

How much battery do I have left? How much time?

I eyed the statue, calculating the risk of taking the light off him versus the agony of not knowing how long my battery would last. Then I turned the phone toward myself as quickly as I could.

He was in darkness for less than half a second, but when the light returned to him, he'd taken a long step forward.

"Damn you to hell," I snarled at him.

I had 15 percent of my battery left. I'd charged it just before bed, so having its light on was sucking its power quickly.

A headache set in to my right temple as I tried to calculate how long that would give me. It was just after five in the morning. *Surely dawn isn't far away.*

I remembered a quote, something I'd read in a novel years before, which suddenly felt much more personal. *The game of patience has changed into a game of endurance.*

There was nothing to do but wait and hope. I kicked against the ground again, setting my chair back to rocking.

I divided my attention. I still watched the mannequin, but I couldn't stop myself from flicking my eyes toward the window above my head. I kept expecting the fresh morning light to break through the black, but if anything, it seemed to be getting darker. I struggled against my desire to check the time. Taking the light off the mannequin for even a second would give him the freedom he craved, but the slow crawl of time was agony. When my limbs were trembling from exhaustion and cold and my eyes were bleary from staring into the dim light, I couldn't stand it any longer.

I flipped the phone around to face myself then immediately turned it back on the mannequin. He'd taken another long step forward, halving the distance between us. I recoiled in my chair, and the pained squeals of its dry wood filled the basement.

I'd seen two important things in the moment I'd been able to look at my phone.

First, it was five forty-two in the morning. I couldn't remember what time dawn broke, but I suspected it wasn't long after six. Second, and much more horrifying, my phone's battery was down to the last 2 percent.

47

As I held the shaking light toward the mannequin's face, I thought his thin, stern lips looked a little different. Maybe it was the exhaustion or the stress getting to me, but they seemed to have curled into a grim smile.

"No," I said, using both hands to hold the light, to stop my numb fingers from dropping it. "No, don't come any closer. Don't come any closer. Don't come any closer."

I kept the chant up, gasping thin breaths in between and stealing frequent, quick glances at the window, desperate to see any sort of abatement in the smothering darkness. The mannequin, ever still, ever patient, watched me with those intense, eager eyes. I met his gaze, shook my head…and then my light died.

———

"Here it is," Geoff said, huffing as he unlocked the basement door. "I haven't touched anything since I got back."

Tony followed the wheezing man into the basement, taking in the surroundings in a quick glance. He recognized his friend's jacket and shirts hanging on a coatrack as well as the backpack sitting by the door.

"He didn't take anything?" Tony asked, crossing the room and glancing at the unmade mattress on the floor.

"Not that I can tell," Geoff said, rubbing the back of his hand across his forehead. "Weirdest thing. He cleared out while I was visiting my sister. Didn't write a note or anything. He left the key at the foot of the stairs, though."

Tony stooped to pick up the phone that had been left on the

rocking chair. He pressed the power button, but the battery was dead. "Well, if you hear from him, tell him to get in touch with me. Tell him I'm worried, and his professors say he'll fail if he misses any more classes."

Geoff nodded grimly. "D'you want to take his stuff?"

"I guess I'd better."

Tony grabbed the clothes and phone, stuffed them into the backpack, then followed Geoff toward the stairs. At the threshold of the room, he glanced back, searching for any sign of where or why his friend had disappeared. He saw nothing except the unmade mattress on the floor, the stacks of boxes pushed against the walls, the dilapidated rocking chair sitting under the grimy window, and two slate-gray ceramic mannequins standing against the back wall.

MIRROR MAN

MY EARLIEST MEMORY OF THE MIRROR MAN IS FROM WHEN I was four. My mother was trying to coax me into brushing my teeth by myself, but I was more interested in the man standing behind the bathroom door.

"Who is he?" I asked.

"Who is who?" Mum had replied.

I'd pointed to the man in the mirror, but my mother couldn't see him. Frustrated, I'd turned around to ask him myself, but the room behind us was empty.

From then on, every time I looked into a mirror or highly reflective surface, I saw Mirror Man. Sometimes he was watching me. Sometimes, he was watching whoever was with me. Sometimes he wasn't looking at anything in particular, just swaying from side to side.

He always stood in the darkest corner of the room and seemed

to gather shadows about himself like a fog. I couldn't make out much about him except that he was tall. I tried talking to him a few times, but he either couldn't hear me or didn't care.

When I realized no one else could see the Mirror Man, he became my little secret, something to watch when I walked past high-gloss windows or to catch glimpses of when I turned the back of my spoon to exactly the right angle. On a few occasions, I snuck into the bathroom late at night to talk to him after my parents had gone to bed. He never replied, and I soon lost interest in him.

When I was twelve, I stayed at my best friend's house for a sleepover. I was brushing my teeth in their bathroom, which had a mirror larger than the one at my house, when Mirror Man caught my eye. I winked at him, as I often had when I was younger.

He was standing beside the towel rack, a place that was relatively bright compared to his usual corner haunts. The shadows still clung to him, but he was easier to see than normal. That was the first time I realized how impossibly thin he was. I'd always assumed he was an average weight, but I could see the bulk of his size came from his clothing—a long cloth wrapped around his body and limbs, crossing over itself and engulfing him. I thought I saw the fingers on his right hand twitch, but other than that, he was completely still.

"Damn, you're a weird one, aren't you?" I asked. I was answered with silence.

Mirror Man became bolder over the next few years. He left

his usual corner more and more and moved farther into the light. The closer he came to the mirror, the easier he was to see.

By the time I was fourteen, I could see his mouth: a thin gash with pale, cracked lips. Once or twice, I made silly faces at him, trying to get him to smile, but he never did. I was sixteen when I started being able to see his hands clearly. He had long, bony, grasping fingers that occasionally twitched. It was the only movement I ever saw him make, except for his sporadic swaying.

Not long after my nineteenth birthday, he began standing directly behind me, staring at my image in the mirror over my shoulder. This was close enough to let me see almost all of him. Only his eyes remained hidden in shadows. He had no hair, and his skin was dry, thin, and stretched tautly over his face. There were such sharp indents below his cheekbones that it looked as if someone had stitched a cloth over a skull.

I graduated high school and left for college. Neither I nor my roommate cared enough about our appearance to replace our broken dorm mirror, and to be honest, it was nice not to see Mirror Man hovering behind me every morning. I still caught glimpses of him in reflective glass doors and on the silverware, but he was easy to ignore. I graduated with good scores and a degree in IT.

The industry was booming at the time, and I received a job offer from a start-up a week after graduation. Even though the start-up failed after six months, I made connections through it and managed to get a job at Syneztic as their IT manager. I rented an apartment in a nice suburb just outside the city and,

eventually, found myself a boyfriend. He moved in after a year of dating, and that was when things went wrong.

Isaac liked to think of himself as a handyman and started renovating our apartment not long after moving in. One of the first things he added was a large wall mirror to the bathroom.

"We don't need a mirror that big," I said when I saw it.

"Uh, excuse you, but yes, we do." He pecked me on the nose as he strode by, and that was the end of the discussion. As close as I was to Isaac, I would never be close enough to tell him why I didn't like seeing my reflection.

I'd gone six years with nothing larger than a palm-sized mirror, and the sudden reappearance of Mirror Man was a shock. He no longer tried to hide himself in the shadows, but stood so close behind me that I should have been able to feel his cloth wrapping brushing against my arm.

His eyes were finally visible. He had no pupils, and the irises were a vivid red. They were the only parts of him besides his hands that moved. His head held still, but his eyes kept flickering, glancing around the room for a second before fixing on me once again.

Unlike the mirror at my mother's home, Isaac's installation was too large to allow me to avoid Mirror Man's stare. He was always watching. When Isaac brushed his teeth beside me at night, Mirror Man would stand between us, occasionally flicking his glance at my boyfriend before settling his eyes back on my face.

It began to wear me down. When I was a child, Mirror Man

had been a cool novelty, a private joke, something I'd winked at each night before bed. Now that I was an adult, his presence felt more and more like an invasion of my privacy and my home. I hated being watched while I showered. I hated seeing Mirror Man's dead red eyes and twitching hands when I washed my face at night, and I hated that he was there to greet me every morning. I hid my discomfort the best I could, though I'm sure Isaac noticed I sometimes skipped showers and brushed my teeth at the kitchen sink.

Over that year, I was promoted twice at work, and we got a shelter cat. I was shocked one morning when our cat, Smucks, jumped onto the bathroom sink and fixed its eyes on Mirror Man. That was the first time I'd seen another creature react to my companion's presence, and it was both validating and disquieting. I watched Smucks watch Mirror Man, and after a moment, Mirror Man's eyes flicked to the cat.

The reaction was immediate—Smucks hissed and arched his back, and the fur on his tail puffed up. He held that pose for a second then leaped to the floor and raced out of the room. Isaac found him hiding under our bed later that night, and I never saw him go into the bathroom again.

By that point, I could see every detail of Mirror Man perfectly: the bleached-gray wrappings, the blue veins that crawled across his bare head, and the flecks in his pupil-less red eyes. He was swaying more, and his fingers were twitching almost constantly. Sometimes, I thought I saw his bloodless, cracked lips tremble.

It ended on the morning of Saturday, the eighteenth of July.

When I stepped out of the shower and looked in the mirror, I saw only my own reflection.

That was the first time I could remember when Mirror Man hadn't been waiting for me. The glass was foggy from the hot shower, but there was no mistaking it—my stalker was gone.

I couldn't believe it. I blinked and stared at my reflection, repeatedly scanning the shadows of the bathroom, feeling an exhilarated relief grow inside of me.

Then I noticed a handprint left in the fog that had gathered on the glass. The mark had been made by someone with long fingers. I slowly turned to face the room.

There, behind me, stood Mirror Man.

WHOSE WOODS THESE ARE

Morrow Woods, an ancient tangle of conifers at the edge of a rural town, sprawled in front of Anna, and she slowed her car to get a better look. She hadn't seen the forest in over a decade, but amazingly, it was almost exactly how she remembered it.

A few things had changed, though. She'd tried to find the parking lot where her family had always left their car when they'd come there to camp, and she was surprised to discover it no longer existed. A gate blocked her access to a weedy field that had once been a dirt patch studded with markers.

Anna glanced from the cordoned-off parking lot to the mass of trees behind it and shrugged her seat belt a little higher on her shoulder. She turned her car back onto the gravel road that ran along the edge of the woods and followed it for a few minutes. When she found a shrubby stretch of grass, she eased her car off

the road and carefully parked it where it was hidden behind a thick clump of bushes.

The trees loomed above her as she stepped out of the car. She inhaled deeply, savoring the light scent of the pines and organic decay, and listened for familiar birdcalls. The air was a far cry from the lazy smog of the city, and it pulled her back to childhood memories of hiking through the trees and struggling to set up tents on uneven ground. Anna grinned at the forest, feeling as if she were greeting an old friend.

Something else was new about the woods: a chain-link fence, nearly two meters high, stood between her and the trees. It ran as far as she could see in both directions.

Anna couldn't remember seeing a fenced-off wood before, and it made her pause. She wondered why a small, quiet town like Gillespie—which she'd left just a few kilometers behind her, hidden by the rolling hills and scrappy patches of trees—would spend what must have been a small fortune on segregating itself from nature. Perhaps the forest had become a restricted area or they were trying to keep people, like her, from damaging it.

Or are they trying to stop something from getting out? The area was too far south for wolves, and there weren't any bears in that part of the country. *What else, then? Wild boars? Exceptionally annoying squirrels?*

Anna snorted with laughter and pulled her backpack out of the car's trunk. She couldn't imagine a single creature in the region that needed a fence to keep it contained, which meant the forest must have been turned into a protected area. She felt

slightly guilty about her plans to trespass, but a childhood full of camping had taught her how to respect nature. She knew she could leave the woods as clean and healthy as it was before she'd entered it.

Besides, she needed this. The hike was like a closure somehow—a final goodbye to her father, the nature lover, who had brought his family to the woods every year until Anna had turned fourteen. The catharsis was too important for her to turn back just because of a fence.

Scaling the chain-link barricade turned out to be harder than she'd expected, though. The fence was only a little taller than she was, but it took a good bit of heaving to throw her heavy bag over the top. It hit the ground on the other side with a hard thump, and Anna cringed, hoping none of the equipment had been broken.

She hooked her fingers through the holes in the chain-link and climbed it with less speed and much less grace than she'd hoped for. Still, she made it over the sharp wires at the top without cutting herself. She dropped to the ground on the other side, dusted the dirt off her cargo pants, heaved the backpack over her shoulders, and began walking.

As she moved deeper into the trees, the gentle downward slope gave way to a pine-needle-littered forest floor pocked with holes and exposed roots. Anna picked a dead branch off the ground and used it as a walking stick to prod at the piles of detritus to make sure she wasn't about to step in a concealed hole and break her ankle.

The air around her buzzed with life; the scent of plants and organic decay was rich and heady, and the ground felt pleasantly springy under her feet. *I should move somewhere like this,* she thought absently, running a hand over a tree's bark. *The city's killing me.*

She kept her pace slow, taking the chance to enjoy her surroundings and fill her lungs with fresh oxygen. The day was warmer than the forecast had predicted, and before long, she was too sweaty to keep her jacket on.

Just over an hour into the hike, her surroundings began to change. The lush green grasses and vines started to disappear; sickly, spindly plants took their places. The pine trees seemed to grow taller, but their trunks were darker and had fewer low branches. What needles she could see were discolored and looked unhealthy. A flicker of dark amber on one of the trees caught her attention. She stopped to look at it and found she was breathing heavily despite her slow pace.

She had to step right up to the tree before she recognized the amber color as sap. Dribbles of long-dried golden juice hung like stalactites from a six-inch gash in the bark. Anna ran her fingers over the cool, smooth substance. *What sort of jerk hacks into a live tree like this?*

She turned back to her path, but her steps faltered as she began to notice cuts in other trees. Some were only little nicks, but others were deep slashes that cut into the center of the trunk. A few of the trees had been damaged so badly that they had died. Held in place by lifeless roots, they stood waiting for rot or a strong storm to bring them down.

She'd never seen damage like that when she'd camped there before. *It must be why the city put the fence up. Makes sense.* She guessed clueless campers, bored teenagers, or possibly even someone with anger management problems had come in and cut up the trees, so they were protecting the forest until it could regenerate.

But as she moved farther through the forest, she had to wonder how much good the fence was doing. Some of the cuts looked fresh, as if they'd been made within the last month. *Why, though? What's the point of walking into the heart of a wood to spend hours cutting at trees?*

She stopped beside a tree with four deep slashes at her head height. They looked only a few days old. She stared at the honey-gold dribbles, suddenly feeling much less confident about spending the night alone in the woods. *What if whoever did this comes back?*

Anna turned to look at the path she'd come from. It wasn't too late to turn back, but that would mean wasting an entire day, not to mention the equipment she'd bought and the gas she'd burned driving there...

"Jeez," she muttered, and the heavy air around her seemed to swallow her voice. She'd come to the woods to remember her father on the anniversary of his death. She *could* leave, but she knew she would hate herself if she did.

The forest was vast, too, and her intended camping site was still a long way off. The chances of two strangers bumping into each other in the maze of trees had to be tiny. *Besides, I'm not completely defenseless. I brought a knife.*

Comforted, Anna turned back to her path. She picked up her pace, stepping briskly, only pausing every twenty minutes to check her compass.

She reached her destination, the river, late in the afternoon. The trees growing alongside it were healthier and less damaged, though they still grew taller than those at the entrance to the woods had. Anna sat on the rocky bank of the river for a few minutes, admiring how clear the liquid was as it rushed over the smooth pebbles. She caught flashes of motion in some of the more stagnant areas and was pleased to see that, no matter what had happened to the trees, the fish population was still thriving.

The air was filled with birdsong and animal calls. She closed her eyes and listened, trying to pick out sounds she recognized. She caught the high, light trills of treecreepers and thought she heard a hawk's screech in the distance. Other calls she couldn't identify, though: some cackling, some trilling, and one especially strange noise that sounded like broken laughter coming from a long way away.

Since she'd stopped moving, she was chilling quickly as her sweat dried. The sun was sinking lower, and she knew she needed to set her tent up before it became too dark to see. The ground around the stream was uneven and sloped, so she backtracked for a few minutes until she came across a relatively flat glade. She shrugged her camping backpack off then spent a few minutes clearing rocks, leaves, and sticks away from where she planned to put her tent.

The light was already dimming toward twilight, so she moved

quickly as she assembled the two-sleeper tent. Her father had sold his camping equipment many years previously, so Anna had bought a cheap model for this trip.

She had to admit, though, as she fitted the canvas over the tent poles, camping was more enjoyable with company. She'd broken up with her boyfriend only a month before her father had passed, and she was feeling the isolation.

"Still," she muttered, forcing a metal peg into the soft ground with her hands, "it's nice not to have to argue about what we eat."

Her parents had never agreed on what food to bring. Her father would have wanted sausages, steaks, onion, and eggs, all fried over the fire. Her mother, practical and cautious, had always insisted that meat was not safe to consume after spending the day in a warm backpack and suggested sandwiches and canned food instead.

As an adult, Anna tended to side more with her mother. The last place anyone wanted to get food poisoning was in the middle of the woods. Still, they'd eaten dubious sausages and steaks for ten years' worth of camping trips without any disasters, and because her visit was a testament to her father, she'd brought a pack of sausages wrapped in a small cooling pack.

Anna finished setting up the tent in good time. The ground wasn't firm enough for the pegs to anchor it properly, so she placed some largish, clean rocks inside each corner of the tarp base. She kicked and scraped the dead pine needles away from an area in front of her tent, creating a large circle of exposed dirt. A quick search turned up several more rocks, which she built into a ring to protect and contain her fire.

She needed to have water nearby before she lit it, so Anna pulled one of the larger pots out of her backpack and walked to the stream. The sun was halfway set, and the twilight played strange tricks on her eyes, blending trees with shadows. As she neared the stream, she once again heard the strange noise that sounded like wild laughter. She stopped short. The sound was much closer than it had been before and seemed too deep to belong to a bird. *An animal, maybe?*

The sound broke off, and Anna strained to hear it again. The atmosphere seemed different, somehow, and she realized that all other sounds—birds, animals, and even insects—had quieted following the strange call, leaving only the rustling of the trees.

The skin on her arms prickled into goose bumps. Suddenly wanting a fire more than anything else, she broke into a jog.

She was relieved to finally push through a patch of bushes and find herself at the bank of the river. A thinner canopy above her allowed more of the waning sunlight through, and Anna paused to soak it up for a moment before kneeling beside the running water and dunking the pot into it. The fish were gone, probably hidden somewhere to sleep for the night.

Anna stood slowly as the strangest sensation crept over her. She felt as though she were being scrutinized, as if her every movement were being followed. Anna lived in the city, where there were eyes everywhere. At any minute she could have half a dozen gazes on her, but she'd never before felt *watched* like she did at that moment.

You're in a forest. There's no one here.

She turned in a slow circle, pot clasped in both hands, as she scanned the woods around her. *It's so quiet. Even the trees seem to be holding their breath.*

Then the wind changed direction, and a strong, foul musk invaded her nose. Anna gagged, and water sloshed over the lip of her pot. It was unlike anything she'd smelled before; it reminded her of rotten eggs and decaying meat, with a bitter, metallic undertone.

She didn't wait any longer but began jogging up the incline toward her tent. Water spilled out of the pot and soaked her pants and hiking shoes, but she didn't slow down. By the time she reached her camp, she could no longer smell the odor, but it hung in her mind like a fly she couldn't swat away.

"No wonder they built a fence," she muttered, setting her half-full pot beside her tent and rubbing at her nose. "I would, too, if it kept me from smelling that."

Anna chuckled to herself then kicked off her wet shoes and crawled into the tent. She opened the backpack and rifled through it until she found her comfy sneakers. They were no good for hiking—she'd brought them to wear at night while she sat by the fire—but they would do well enough until her hiking shoes dried.

She climbed out of her tent and began gathering dry firewood. The sun was almost completely set, so she searched by feel more than sight. She'd badly underestimated how long setting up the tent and the firepit would take, probably because last time she'd been camping, she'd had two parents to help.

She put a small stack of fire starters in the center of the pit then stacked dry pine needles and small sticks on top. She lit them and sat to watch as the flames licked over and eventually caught on to the wood. Once the kindling had caught, she put a few larger pieces of wood on top and began pulling food and the frying pan out of her backpack.

The day's walk had drained her, and she almost settled on eating canned fruit for dinner, but she knew her father would have been disappointed. "If you're going camping, you'd better do it properly," he'd once said while he poked at the sizzling sausages and her mother dourly buttered bread.

"This is for you, Dad," Anna said, putting two of the sausages in the pan and setting it over the growing flames. She'd never felt so lonely.

The air chilled rapidly as night overtook the woods, and Anna pulled on her spare jackets. Twice, she thought she caught traces of the rotting smell on the wind, but it passed quickly. *Maybe something died down by the river.*

She kept the fire small, just hot enough to cook the sausages and warm her a little. She sat on the ground close to its heat as shadows danced around the edge of the clearing. The daytime birds had fallen silent shortly after sunset, and owls and night animals had taken over. Their hollow calls floated to her through the night air.

She pulled the sausages off the fire and ate them straight out of the pan, savoring the warmth as it pooled in her stomach and spread outward. They were overcooked—better over than under,

her mother would have said—but because she was famished, they tasted like a feast.

She'd also packed dessert: an apple with its core cut out and a chocolate bar pushed into the hole. She rolled the apple, which was wrapped in foil, into the coals to heat through. It was another of her father's favorites, and one dish her mother had approved of.

While she waited for it to cook, she went back into her tent to inflate her blow-up mattress and unroll her sleeping bag. The fire's light was strong enough to come through the tent's canvas and illuminate her. It threw jumping shadows on the wall opposite. They seemed to move independently of each other, some traveling left while others went right, and she paused her work to watch them.

Then she realized the light was growing dimmer. *The fire shouldn't need more wood yet.* She'd put two branches on it only a few minutes previously—but as she turned around to look at it, the campfire went out with a harsh sizzle, plunging the tent into darkness.

Anna's heart leaped into her throat as she stayed still, listening. The woods outside were perfectly silent. Then she smelled the stench again—thick, smothering, and nauseating. She had to suppress the urge to spit it out of her mouth.

Fear spiked through her, and she scrambled for the flashlight in her backpack. The pine trees were too thick to let any more than a few scraps of moonlight through, leaving her nearly blind, and she struggled to find the flashlight among the spare clothes, blankets, maps, and cutlery.

She finally found it in a side pocket and turned it on with shaking hands, holding it like a sword in front of her body as she advanced out of the tent. The air felt colder than it had before, as though the temperature had dropped five degrees in the two minutes she'd been inside. Her breath misted in front of her face, and her nose started to burn from drawing in the chilled air.

She stopped just outside the tent and moved her flashlight in a semicircle, searching for movement. Tree branches twitched and shook in the wind. Her flashlight's beam was too narrow to light much; all it could do was tease her with small snapshots of her surroundings.

She moved toward the fire. It was completely dead; there weren't even any coals left. Anna pressed a shaking finger to one of the logs. It was still warm, but not hot, and felt slightly damp. Unnerved, she pulled away from the dead fire and swung her light across the border of the glade again. *What could make the coals wet?*

The answer came to her quickly. *The pot of water, of course. Did someone find me and tip it over the fire?*

She turned to where she'd left the pot beside the tent. Chills crawled up her spine as she dipped a finger over the rim and found it was still filled with water. *Then what...?*

The sickly, thick smell still permeated the air, though it seemed to be lessening. Anna rotated slowly, trying to hold the light steady as she searched the trees. She knew she had only two options: pack up and hike out of the woods as quickly as possible or stay the night.

It wasn't much of a choice. The hike alone was five hours, never mind the time it would take to pack her equipment, and she would be much, much slower in the pitch black. By the time she left the woods, it would be dawn—or close to it—and she wasn't sure she had the energy to stay alert and conscious of her surroundings until then.

Looks like we'll be spending the night here.

Anna shivered and retreated into her tent, zipping it closed behind herself. She pulled her knife out of her bag and sat for a long time, too scared to sleep, gripping the flashlight in one hand and the knife in the other. Eventually, exhaustion dampened the anxiety enough to let her crawl into the sleeping bag and close her eyes, but she kept a firm grip on the knife just in case.

Her last thoughts were about the smell, which was almost gone, and the calls of an owl perched somewhere above her tent.

────────

She dreamed about the last time her father had brought them camping to Morrow Woods, when she'd been fourteen years old. They'd stopped at the town that bordered the forest to pick up a few last-minute supplies. Her father had gone to see if he could find a more up-to-date map of the woods, while she and her mother bought fresh bread, a small square of butter, and a tub of live bait for fishing in the river.

Her father was gone for a long time, and when he came back, he looked older, somehow. He'd pulled Anna's mother off to one side and talked to her in a hurried, hushed tone. When he

turned back to Anna, he put on one of the most forced smiles she'd ever seen.

"Your mother and I were thinking, Annie," he said, "there's another forest an hour's drive away that we've been wanting to visit. We thought we'd give it a try."

"What? Now?" Anna glanced out the shop's window. She could see the edge of the woods not even fifteen minutes' walk away. "But we always camp here!"

Her father just laughed and ushered her back into the car then drove them to the smaller, tamer pine forest he'd mentioned. It had been nowhere near as pretty as Morrow Woods was, and Anna hadn't been able to understand why he'd wanted to visit it so badly all of a sudden.

———

Anna woke up with a start. It was still dark. The flashlight illuminated the inside of the tent, turning it into a small, golden cave. The smell was back, saturating the air. She held still, wrapped in her sleeping bag, knife clasped in one hand and flashlight in the other, listening hard. She thought she could hear breathing, but it was so well disguised by the rustling trees that she couldn't be sure.

Then the sound from the day before split the silence. A twisted, broken, wailing laugh came from just outside the tent's entrance.

Anna bit the inside of her cheek to keep herself from crying out as the laugh cut off abruptly and silence rushed in to fill the void.

Don't move, she thought as she tried to control her heavy breathing. *Don't let it hear you.*

The silence stretched out. An itch crawled across Anna's back, but she didn't dare move to scratch it. Sweat was drenching her clothes and beading on her forehead despite the cold, and she struggled to slow her thundering heart.

Szzzzzzzzrch…

Anna jumped at the new noise but couldn't immediately tell where it was coming from. The source became horribly clear when she saw the zip at the tent's entrance was moving along its track, pulled by a force outside the tent, creating a gaping hole in her meager fort.

The time for silence was over. Anna scrambled out of her sleeping bag, kicking at the thick, fluffy fabric when it got stuck over her feet, then scrambled backward until she was pressed against the rear of the tent.

Her sudden movement didn't disturb the zipper's progress. It glided in a smooth arc, and as the released part of the door began to flop out of the way, she caught a glimpse of the outside.

She focused her flashlight on it, hoping to blind the intruder or at least see it, but whatever was unzipping her tent stayed out of view. She could see the trees, twitching and shivering, and even parts of her ruined fire, where the foil-wrapped, half-baked apple still sat in the blackened patch, winking at her like silver treasure.

Szzzzzzzzzzrch…tch!

The zipper hit the end of its runner, leaving the door wide open. Anna's hands were shaking too badly to hold the flashlight steady; it jittered over the opening but failed to show her the opener.

"Who's there?" Anna called. She had never heard a silence as complete as what followed her voice.

The trees had fallen still. The animals of the night seemed to hold their breaths. She heard no sound at all, not even the gentle tap of falling pine needles.

The smell invaded her nose with each breath, turning her stomach and making her dizzy. She pressed herself against the back of the tent as she waited, her shaking hands pointing the flashlight and knife toward the tent's opening.

Then claws, large and viciously sharp, plunged through the canvas at her back. One snagged her jacket, and she lurched free with a shriek.

Carrying only the flashlight and the knife, Anna threw herself through the doorway and into the dark embrace of the night. At once, noise returned to the woods, swelling and growing in pitch as though the trees were exhausted from holding their breath. Birds—both those that belonged to the day and those that lived in the night—began to cry. Animals screamed. The wind, after holding still for so long, burst through the trees and brought down a shower of pine needles. The sound surrounded her, deafening her. She could barely hear her own gasping as she ran for the cover of the trees.

Something large, dark, and fast was racing around the edge of the tent. It was moving too quickly for her eyes to fix on it, and she only got a vague impression of ragged clothing and brightly white teeth. As it ran it called to her, adding its hideous laughter to the noise of the woods.

It—whatever it was, human, animal, or something else entirely—darted across her path. Anna was running too quickly to change direction or stop, so she raised the point of her knife and let her momentum force it into the creature's chest.

Blood sprayed from where the blade pierced its flesh. The creature wailed, and its scream was a terrible cacophony that filled Anna's head and made her ears feel as if they were about to explode. She closed her eyes, let go of the knife, and continued running, her blood-dampened right hand held in front of her face to shield her from branches, her left hand doing a poor job of focusing the flashlight on her path. Her breath sticky and thick in her lungs, she ran until the woods quieted and the stench left her nose. She ran until her legs ached and her arms throbbed from scratches. She ran until she thought her heart was about to burst and her lungs burned.

Then she let herself fall to the ground. She was too exhausted, physically and emotionally, to cry, so she lay on the floor of pine needles and roots, doing her best to draw breath quickly enough to replenish her oxygen-depleted muscles. She could hear the gentle rustle of the trees and the occasional animal noise, but she didn't think she had been chased. The smell was gone too.

Anna pulled herself to a sitting position and found she was dizzy. Her head throbbed, her arms stung, and her legs ached. The moon wasn't strong enough to penetrate the unnaturally tall trees, so she picked up the flashlight from where she'd dropped it and gingerly inspected her stinging forearms. They bore dozens of tiny cuts from the branches and vines she'd raced through.

She could feel some tender patches on her cheeks too. Her right hand—the one she had held the knife in—had a pale-pink, jelly-like liquid sprayed over the fingers and wrist. She tried to shake it off, but it clung to her skin. Disgusted, she picked up a handful of pine needles and used them to rub off most of the liquid. Then she brushed the hand over her sweater and jeans to clean it further.

She had no idea which direction she'd run in or how far she was from the fence. She knew she could find her direction reasonably well once the sun came up, but until then, she couldn't risk moving farther into the woods, so she huddled at the base of the tree.

Anna didn't let herself fall asleep as she waited. Every ten minutes, she got up and paced in circles to ward off the exhaustion that threatened to lower her guard. She focused on searching for the smell, assuming that, as long as the air was sweet, danger wasn't too close.

The night air was freezing, and before long, she was shivering. Her jacket did a reasonable job of protecting her top half, but the jeans she'd slept in did nothing to warm her.

She was immeasurably relieved when dawn arrived. Anna felt exhausted and fragile, as if she were held together with fine threads that might break at any moment. The trees were too thick for her to see the sun directly, but she clambered to her feet and guessed which direction the light was coming from. She then turned herself in a quarter circle, so that she would be walking south. She knew the park was north of the town, so if she walked far enough, she would eventually arrive at the fence.

With the light at her back and the flashlight batteries starting to fail, she began walking as briskly as her sore legs would let her. After about an hour, she stumbled on the river that wound through the woods. She was parched, so she stopped for a drink and to wash the scratches on her arms. Then she followed the river for another kilometer before she recognized the section she'd visited the night before.

She was tempted to bypass her camp entirely, but curiosity and necessity won out. Her camping equipment had been expensive. Besides, she didn't fancy the idea of walking for five hours without water or food. Anna traced the path from the river to the clearing where she'd set up camp, and stopped at the edge of the trees.

Her campsite was wrecked. The tent was shredded. Its torn tarp, still tethered to the ground with pegs and rocks, flapped limply in the breeze. Her gear had been ripped from the bag and lay about the clearing like shrapnel. Even the stones she'd used to make the fireplace had been hurled away from the cold charcoal and half-burnt branches. The trees surrounding the clearing had suffered too. Deep gashes marred their trunks, and many of the lower branches had been torn off.

Anna stumbled through the remains, stunned, hardly absorbing the sights. She paused to pick up one of her saucepans—one side had been crushed in, and it was pocked with holes. She dropped it to the ground.

What did this? What's strong enough to cause this much damage?

She didn't stay long; it felt too unsafe to linger, and she saw

almost nothing worth salvaging. Her backpack had been torn in half, but she managed to tie one of the pieces up well enough to act as a bag. Into it, she loaded the only undamaged saucepan, a spare jacket, tent pegs, and an empty water bottle. She also found her shoes—thankfully intact, though a little dirty—and switched them with the comfy sneakers she'd been wearing. Everything else had been destroyed.

Anna paused to look about the scene one final time before turning back toward the river. She had a long hike from her campsite to the edge of the woods, and she knew she would be grateful for a full water bottle.

She'd been drained by the fear, the running, and the night without sleep, and Anna found herself stumbling over the exposed roots and rocks as she made her way down the incline. She kept her eyes focused on her feet and didn't look up until she was nearly at the water's edge.

A girl was standing in her way. Anna stopped short, nearly crying out from shock. The girl faced away from her, watching the water swirl over the smooth river stones. She was wearing a tattered dark dress, and her thick black hair was matted with twigs and small leaves.

Anna gaped at her, trying to understand what she was seeing. *What's a child doing in these woods? Does she live here?*

As the girl swayed gently from side to side, a new thought entered Anna's mind. *Does she know what attacked me last night?*

At that moment the wind changed, and Anna gagged on the sudden thick stench that blew over her. It was much stronger

than it had been the night before. An automatic fear response made Anna stumble backward, her shoes slipping on the forest floor, until her back hit a tree.

The girl turned languidly, and Anna clamped a hand over her mouth to stop herself from screaming. The child's eyes were entirely black: no iris, no whites, just black gashes sitting in the impossibly pale face.

No...they're not eyes... They're holes.

Where her hands should have been were claws. Thick and curved, they were as long as Anna's forearm. They draped down the side of the child's dress and nearly touched the ground. Something was also protruding from her chest. Something metallic and familiar. *My knife.*

The girl opened her mouth and laughed. Her eyes—or where her eyes should have been—crinkled, and her red lips spread wide. The harsh, cruel sound that came out of her throat was far louder than any human could have made.

Anna dropped the water bottle and started running. The smell was making her dizzy, so she held her breath as long as she could. Her aching legs screamed under this new strain, but she didn't let herself stop as the laughter followed her up the incline.

She ran through the demolished camp, not even sparing a glance at the slashed trees or shredded tent. She thought the creature was right on her heels, just waiting for her to slow down before it dug its claws into her back.

She was exhausted. As the smell and the laughter gradually faded, Anna let her sprint slow to a brisk walk. Her limbs were

shaking badly, but she didn't stop moving. She knew which direction she needed to go to get out of the infernal forest, and she focused on walking as quickly as her burning muscles would move.

She hadn't collected any water, and by midday, she was parched, but the reappearance of healthier trees and vines encouraged her to keep walking. The cuts in the trunks soon disappeared, and she thought the atmosphere felt lighter.

Then she unexpectedly broke through the trees and found herself facing the fence. Its new significance hit her as she gazed up at it with mingled relief and revulsion. *What's the chance it has nothing to do with protecting the woods, and everything to do with protecting the town?*

She didn't want to linger inside the forest for even a moment more than she had to, so she threw her makeshift bag over the fence then wrapped her fingers through the metal wires and began to climb. The effort drained her remaining energy, and when her feet touched down on the other side she sank to the grass and closed her eyes. The sun, something she hadn't felt since she'd entered the woods, played over her skin. She smiled, then her smile turned into tears. She covered her face with her sweaty, dirty hands as the enormity of the events finally caught up to her.

She didn't have long to rest, though. As she took a deep breath to clear her pounding head, she caught traces of the bitter, rotten scent she'd come to associate with danger.

She sat up, her fear returning and feeding energy into her aching joints and weary bones. She scanned the edge of the woods

but couldn't see anything. Still, she stood, feeling the blisters in her feet burn, and began walking again. She made a guess about which direction she'd left her car, and after forty minutes, she found it, still hidden behind the bushes. She slid into the driver's seat with a sigh of immense gratitude.

———

Anna was famished and thirsty, so she stopped by the town's small eatery. She must have looked ghastly—the patrons all stared at her with either curiosity or pity as she pulled herself onto the stool in front of the counter.

The server, young and plump, with a short crop of black hair, eyed her cautiously. "You okay?"

"Yeah," Anna said, rubbing at her raw eyes. She'd decided on a white lie during the drive into town. "Been backpacking. Couldn't find a hotel for last night. Can I get the biggest breakfast you sell and a jug of water?"

"Oh, yeah." The girl's demeanor changed instantly as she motioned at the line cook. "Backpacking can sure do a number on you, eh? I went through England last year, and I stayed in a place with roaches everywhere and cold showers. I thought I was going to die."

Anna laughed weakly, but her attention was focused on the progress of her breakfast on the grill.

An aged, grizzled man sitting next to her chuckled. "If I didn't know better, I would've thought you'd come out of the woods."

"Lay off it, Bern," the server said, scorn and affection mingling

in her voice. "She don't want to listen to your horror stories, I'm sure."

Anna waited until the server had gone to clear off one of the tables, then she turned to Bern. "What about the woods?"

The man's cracked lips split into a grin, and she saw that he was missing at least half of his teeth. "Oh, you haven't heard of the monster, huh? It's our local legend. I'm the resident expert on it, you know."

Anna leaned on the counter, indicating that she was giving him her full attention, and he continued gladly.

"Twenty years ago, those woods used to be very popular for camping. Lovely place, it was, with lots of wildlife and a big stream weaving through it. Then, all of a sudden, campers started disappearing. At first, the police thought it was particularly bad luck that three couples had gotten lost on the same weekend, but then they found the bodies. It was a real horror show. They were torn apart—hardly recognizable—with their organs scattered about them like a halo.

"Then the search parties—the ones who had been looking for the missing people—started coming forward with strange stories. Talking about seeing a little girl, and saying there was a really bad smell too. I never went into the woods, but one gent who stopped by my shop told me it gave him such bad heebie-jeebies, he'd had nightmares for a week.

"Well, the police assumed it was some sort of serial killer and called in reinforcements from nearby towns. There was a big investigation about it. Just about everyone within a ten-kilometer

radius got questioned. Then some of the officers who'd been searching the woods started going missing too. Those that got out repeated the same story—they'd been attacked by a girl with dead eyes and claws instead of hands. The cost and body count escalated. The deaths only ever happened in the woods, so eventually, the town decided the smartest thing to do was make the whole forest off-limits and put up a fence. It's been eight years since then, and whatever lives in those woods never comes out, but no one who goes in there to stay overnight is ever heard from again.

"There are a lot of stories about what the monster is and where it came from, but it usually involves witchcraft. People reckon it's either a girl who's been cursed or a witch whose spell backfired. They say it appears as a child wearing a black dress during the day, but after midnight, it transforms into an unspeakable monster and tears apart anyone it finds in its woods."

Bern finished his story and slurped at his coffee with a satisfied smile. Anna's plate of food had been placed in front of her, but she hadn't even noticed. After a moment of silence, she picked up the fork and began eating mechanically, hardly tasting the greasy food.

———

Anna returned to her car, unlocked the driver's door, and slid into the seat. She set it into gear and began cruising out of town, her slow speed disguising how badly she wanted to escape from its grip and never see it again.

Bern's story sounded fantastical—impossible even—except that she had seen both the girl and the beast with her own eyes. She'd heard the laughter, smelled the overpowering odor, and looked into its ghost-white face. Bern had said no one escaped from the monster's clutches if they stayed overnight. *I got lucky. I had a weapon and used it at the right time.*

As she turned out of the town and onto the freeway, a strange smell filled the car. Anna froze, taking her foot off the accelerator and letting the car slow to a crawl before she dared raise her eyes to the rearview mirror.

The girl sat in the middle of the back seat, clawed hands draped in her lap, her wild hair framing her ghost-white face and empty eyeholes. Her mouth spread into a brilliant smile at the cleverness of her trap. Anna's eyes met the place where the girl's should have been, and the girl broke into her terrible, consuming laughter as she lunged forward.

CUTTY STREET LAMP

GROWING UP IN A RURAL FARMING TOWN, I HEARD A LOT OF advice that was supposed to keep me safe. *Don't wander into the woods, don't get into strangers' cars, and don't go near the lamp halfway up Cutty Street.*

The Cutty Street Lamp was half superstition, half urban legend. Just like some people tried not to walk on cracks in the sidewalk or didn't like it when black cats crossed their path, people avoided going through the light cast by that street lamp.

During the day, the light was off, and no one paid it any more attention than the other four lamps on that street. But after dark, anyone sitting on the low brick fence that bordered the cemetery opposite the lamp would see something very interesting.

Cutty Street was the most direct route from the east side of the town to the shops in the center, so it wasn't a quiet road.

When I was a child, I liked to sit opposite the light on nights

when I didn't have homework. It made ten-year-old me feel like a hero to have my back to the cemetery and my face to the light no one wanted to walk through as the blood-red sunset faded into darkness. I would sit on the brick wall and weave braids out of the long grass that grew there or pick up a handful of gravel and try to throw it through the third slat in the storm water drain half a dozen feet away while I counted how many people avoided the light.

Pedestrians looped around the light. Some gave it a wide berth, even crossing the street to be clear of it, while others walked in a tight semicircle, just barely skirting the circle of light the lamp created on the sidewalk. For most people, it was almost a subconscious action.

To be fair, it was a strange sort of light. The other four lamps lining the sidewalk cast a normal, warm-white glow, but that particular lamp's light was tinged blue. It wasn't so strong that it looked clearly wrong, but compared with the lamp twenty feet down the road, it was slightly off.

My mother was a very superstitious woman, and among her other advice—don't break any mirrors, don't go to sleep in the middle of a fight, and don't play with Ouija boards—she occasionally reminded me to keep away from the light on Cutty Street. When one of her friends saw me there and passed on the news that I'd been watching the lamp at night, she panicked and, through tears and threats, made me promise not to go near it again.

She was a good woman, and I loved her dearly, so I stopped my nightly habit. For the next few years, I saw very little of the

light. I still traveled down Cutty Street, usually during the day, and I couldn't stop myself from glancing at the lamp every time I passed it.

When I was twelve, my cousin came to stay with us for a few weeks. His parents were going through a nasty divorce, and his mother had wanted to give him a break from it. Todd was a year older than me and impressed me as being the height of cool.

Todd wasn't an unpleasant person, per se, but he was surly and not entirely happy about being turned out of his home. I was overly eager to please and let him have whatever he wanted. After he complained about how uncomfortable the spare mattress on my room's floor was, I swapped with him so he could sleep in my bed. When we watched movies at night, I always let him pick. I tried to introduce him to my friends, too, but they didn't like hanging out with him.

"They're babies," he told me one night, lying in my bed, arms folded behind his head as he stared at the ceiling. "I don't blame them, though. There's nothing exciting in this town. If they were in the city, they'd harden up real quick."

I hated hearing Todd complain about my town, so I cast around for something that would impress him. "We had a murder here a few years back," I said. "A guy killed his wife and buried her in his backyard."

Todd snorted. "Just one murder? No serial killers? We've got plenty of those in the city."

I was deflated but not deterred. "There's also lots of bears in the woods. We've got to bring a gun whenever we go in there."

"I've seen bears in the zoo," Todd retorted. "They're not that scary."

Then my brain lighted on the relatively insignificant six feet of Cutty Street that had always fascinated me. "We have a haunted streetlight."

Todd glanced at me out of the corner of his eye, and I knew I'd gotten his attention. "What?"

"There's a lamppost that kills anyone who walks under it." That was, I admit, a pretty big exaggeration. I'd seen a few people walk through the light before, and they'd always shivered and picked up their speed as soon as they realized they'd stepped into the unnatural light. I was twelve, though, and trying to impress one of the least impressible people I'd ever met.

My cousin had rolled over to fix me with a scrutinizing stare. "You're making this up, aren't you?"

"No!" I felt offended. "It's real. I can show it to you."

"Right now?"

"Yeah, sure, whatever."

And just like that, we rolled out of our beds, pulled clothes on over our pajamas, and snuck out the back door. My mother watched TV in the front room of the house in the evenings, so it was easy to climb over the backyard fence and into the lane that ran between the houses without her knowing. From there, we could follow Roger Street toward the city center.

I knew my mother would check on us before she went to sleep, but that wouldn't be for another hour at least, and I hoped I could show Todd the light, prove that our sleepy little town

could be just as impressive as his stupid city, and get us back into our beds without my mother being any wiser.

Todd was showing more interest in me than he had since he'd arrived. He asked about the lamp, and I told him about its blue sheen, the cemetery it sat opposite, and the way no one walked through its light.

I led Todd to my familiar seat on the cemetery fence and was pleased to see it had hardly changed in the years I'd been away from it. I sat, waited for Todd to grudgingly sit next to me, then pointed to the lamp on the other side of the road.

"That's it?" he said, skepticism lacing his voice. "It doesn't look that scary."

I was miffed but tried not to let it show. "Can you see the blue light? It's darker than the lamp down that way."

Todd squinted between the two lights, not looking impressed. "Maybe a little."

"Well, just wait," I snapped.

We did. It was a quiet night, and Todd was becoming fidgety by the time a woman entered the street from a side lane and began walking toward the light. I poked my cousin to get his attention then nodded to the lady. She had her hands in her jacket pockets and was watching the road in front of her, apparently absorbed in her own thoughts. Just as she approached the edge of the light, though, she changed course and stepped onto the road. We watched as she walked in a neat semicircle, leaving at least a foot between herself and the glowing circle cast on the concrete, before returning to the pathway and continuing on her journey.

Todd didn't say anything, but he didn't take his eyes off the woman until he'd seen her walk straight through the light cast by the normal lamp down the road. Then he turned to me. "Okay, that was cool."

I kept my face serious as I nodded, but I was rejoicing inside. "Okay, we can go back now. There's still fifteen minutes until Mum's program ends, so if we hurry—"

"Not yet." Todd slipped off the brick wall. "I want to check this out."

Nervousness fluttered in my stomach as I followed Todd across the road. "Hey," I said, trying to keep my voice casual, "we can't hang around. If Mum finds us missing—"

"Shut up. This will only take a minute."

Todd paused just outside the circle of bluish light, staring up at the lamp. I hovered ten feet away. I'd loved watching people circumnavigate the light, but I'd never considered passing through it myself.

Todd spent half a minute staring at the lamp then stepped directly into the light. The blue glow cast strange shadows on his face, giving him a sickly gray pallor. His eyebrows pulled into a scowl as he turned to look at me. He opened his mouth but closed it again, apparently deciding against whatever he'd been going to say. He looked a lot less comfortable than he had a minute before.

"Okay," I said, anxiety seeping into my voice, "you've seen the lamp. Let's go."

Todd looked upward. His eyes widened as he gazed directly at

the light, then his face contorted. A horrible high whine filled my ears, and I realized it was coming from Todd's open mouth. He seemed to be trying to scream but couldn't get the noise to form properly. His eyes bugled, and sweat beaded over his forehead. Every muscle in his face strained, and veins stood out over his forehead like purple worms. Tears started to leak from the corners of his eyes, mingling with the perspiration on his cheeks, as he stared directly into the light.

I screamed his name, but he either couldn't hear me or couldn't react. His jaw stretched wider, and the whine became higher then cut off abruptly as Todd went completely limp and crumpled to the ground.

My heart beat painfully in my throat as I stood frozen on the sidewalk. Todd wasn't moving, and he was still inside the circle of light. The entirety of my being screamed against the idea of getting any closer, but I couldn't leave Todd. I squinted my eyes nearly closed, lunged forward, and plunged both hands into the blue-tinted glow. In that terrible second that my hands were inside the light, I felt it—the air was charged with a faint electric current. My skin prickled, and the hairs on my arms stood on end. It felt like what I'd imagined radiation would feel like, but at the same time, it had an otherworldly sensation, like that column of air belonged to a different plane.

My fingers seized the back of my cousin's jacket, and I hauled him out of the light as quickly as I could. I dragged Todd at least ten feet away from the lamp before rolling him over to look at him. His face was frozen in that horrible grimace, eyes open,

a small smear of blood marking where his temple had hit the sidewalk. He was as pale as a ghost and completely still.

My memories from the rest of that night are disjointed and strange. I don't know if I ran for help or if someone found us, though I suspect it was the latter. I have a clear image of riding in the passenger seat of our car as my mum drove in the wake of the wailing ambulance. As tears ran down her face, I realized I'd done something unforgivable when I'd told Todd about our lamp.

I remember sitting in the waiting room, listening to the doctor explain to my mother that my cousin had suffered a massive cardiac arrest and died at the scene. Todd had only been thirteen. He'd been healthy and active and had no history of heart problems. My mother turned to look at me, her eyes swimming with grief and terrible knowledge. Neither of us dared say it, but we both knew the light had taken Todd's life.

I never went near the street lamp again. If I needed to get to the town center, I took a longer route to skirt around Cutty Street completely. I never spoke about it, didn't let myself think about it, and tried to ignore the persistent nightmares. It was a relief when we moved to a different town some years later, though it looks like I'll never completely escape the light.

I'm twenty-six now and was recently diagnosed with cancerous growths in both of my hands. The doctors say a combination of surgery and chemo has a good chance of being successful, but I don't think the light will let me go that easily. I've had an idea lately—a crazy, crazy idea—about making a pilgrimage back to my hometown. My mother passed away a few years back, so

there's no voice of reason to dissuade me. If I'm going to die, it'll be on my own terms. I want to go back and see the lamp again. I want to stand in its light. I want to know, once and for all, what it is.

I want to see what Todd saw.

DEAD CALL

5:08 p.m., Friday the 28th

Hey, guys, can I get some advice? I've been receiving a lot of dead calls lately. You know the type—you answer the phone, and there's complete silence on the other end. No matter how many times I say, "Hello? Hello?" they won't speak. Eventually, I hang up in frustration.

At first, I thought they were prank calls, but this is the third day, and they won't. Stop. Calling. It's happening fifteen, maybe sixteen, times a day. Sometimes, I'll get a clump of them together—five or six within an hour—then they'll space out to one every couple of hours. To be frank, I'm going crazy. Anyone had this happen before?

11:35 p.m., Friday the 28th

Thanks for all the messages. To answer the most common questions: yes, it's a private number, and no, I can't hear any giggling or breathing on the other end. It's just complete silence. From what you guys are saying, it's probably a machine dialing me from a call center, but I don't know why I never get a human on the other end. I actually yelled at them last time they called, so hopefully that will shut them up.

9:42 a.m., Saturday the 29th

Quick update: they called nine times last night. *Nine. F-ing. Times.* I set my cell phone to silent before I went to bed, but it recorded the messages. They never hung up, just let the voice mail run until it was out of memory, so now I've got an hour and a half of messages filled with complete silence.

Fun way to start the weekend, huh??

10:11 a.m., Saturday the 29th

No, unfortunately, I can't just ditch my phone. I don't

have a landline, so this is the only way my friends and family can contact me.

Thanks for the suggestion to do a redial. I'll try that now.

10:18 a.m., Saturday the 29th

K, tried redialing. Honestly, I don't know what I expected, but I just got a lot more of the same. They answered after one ring, but I couldn't hear anything. I've tried calling a few times, even hung on the phone for a couple of minutes at one point. Nada.

Any other suggestions?

1:55 p.m., Saturday the 29th

So. They're still calling. I'm ignoring them for now and letting the phone ring out. That's not what I'm updating about, though.

I played through a couple of the voice mails from last night while I ate my lunch. I figured I'd better, just to make sure there was nothing in them.

Now, I'm not superstitious or easily scared. I've gone on ghost tours and can watch horror movies

without a problem. But, honestly, those recordings freaked me out. I can't explain it well enough, but I really started to feel like someone was on the other end. It's the strangest, most inexplicably skin-chilling thing I've ever experienced.

I'm going to take a walk to clear my head.

3:31 p.m., Saturday the 29th

Thanks for the many kind messages calling me a pansy. You're such sweethearts.

I downloaded the first couple of messages onto my computer so I could get a better audio quality. Just in case, y'know? Well, when I adjust some of the levels, there IS something there. It's not much, and it fluctuates in and out, but it sounds sort of...echo-y. Like the message came from a really big, really empty room. I'm going to keep looking.

3:38 p.m., Saturday the 29th

I downloaded the rest of the messages. Most are empty except for that echo, but one had a patch of actual noise. It lasts for about fifteen seconds and

sounds like someone scratching their fingernails over fabric. That's the best I can describe it.

The phone's still ringing, by the way. I've had twelve calls since I got up. I'm not answering them.

4:03 p.m., Saturday the 29th

I uploaded the audio clip like you guys asked. You can hear the sound start at around 00:08 and last until 00:21. It's the only one of its type I got out of the messages last night. I let the clip run for another minute so you can hear the echo-y noise too.

Honestly, I don't care who's doing it or why. I just want it to stop. You don't know what it's like hearing that blasted ringtone every hour. I've turned my phone to silent a few times, but I don't want to keep it off for too long in case my family or work needs to contact me.

Help?

7:55 p.m., Saturday the 29th

Ryan—because it's a private number, my phone company won't give me any details on who owns it.

Tory135—I tried following your instructions on blocking the number, but it didn't work. They called again barely ten minutes after I'd finished. Maybe it only works on certain phone models?

HJVerve—any help you can give would be greatly appreciated. Yes, my phone contract is with [REDACTED].

9:15 a.m., Sunday the 30th

Great news, guys. One of the members here (not going to say names so he doesn't get in trouble) has a brother who works at my phone provider. He bent a few rules and was able to get me the number that's been calling me. I'm off to do some research now. If I can figure out who they are, I should be able to contact them and make them stop.

4:41 p.m., Sunday the 30th

I'm leaving this here in case you guys can make any more sense of it than I could.

Once I matched the phone number to an address, it was easy to find information about them

online. Really easy, actually. It's been all over the news.

Here's a link to one of the articles. The day it occurred is the same day I started getting the calls. I don't know what to think...except that it's time to get a new phone.

Copied from the *Harob Weekly*:

SUBURBAN HORROR by Natalie Mur

At 2:00 a.m. on Wednesday, March 26, a sinkhole appeared in Jacaranda Street in North Harob. The sinkhole, approximately thirty-two meters across, occurred directly under the home of publicist Georgina Gray.

In a statement issued by the Harob police, Inspector Patterson said: "The entirety of the Gray home, plus part of the adjacent property, collapsed into the sinkhole. It is believed that Mrs. Gray and her two children were inside the home at the time of the event. Attempts to retrieve them have so far not yielded results."

Police searches have been hindered by the depth of the sinkhole, which is estimated to extend at least ninety meters. According to Inspector Patterson, the chances of any of the Gray household having survived are "slim to none," though police are continuing their efforts.

LUCY

THIS HAPPENED A COUPLE OF YEARS BACK, BUT IT'S NOT THE SORT of thing I could forget easily. I was driving to visit my hospitalized mother, who'd suffered complications following a hip surgery. She lived across the country, so it was virtually a full day spent in the car. The weather was foul. A strong wind forced the rain nearly horizontally across the road. Though it was only midafternoon, the street lamps had come on in the absence of sunlight, but the weak circles of illumination did little to clarify the road.

Normally, I'd have taken a lunch break at Dorchester, but the traffic had slowed to nearly half its speed due to the bad visibility, and I figured it would be smart to stop early and hope the clouds broke up before the second stretch of my trip.

I took a turnoff marked West Harob. The road narrowed quickly, and scrubby trees crowded up to the edge of the asphalt.

I leaned forward in my seat, squinting to make out the white stripes indicating the center of the road. Fog was rising out of the ditches on either side of my car, spilling onto the street and clinging to the tree trunks. For a moment, I worried I might have taken a road to nowhere. Then the trees thinned, and I began to see a handful of houses—many made out of wood, though a few were brick—sitting on the hills that overlooked the road.

I didn't see a single car for the entire drive. In fact, I didn't see any signs of life at all until I reached what had to be the city center, where a bundle of buildings were arranged haphazardly into a strip mall.

The pub's parking lot was full. I supposed, if this were a farming town, the men wouldn't have much to do during such a severe rainstorm. I passed a real estate office with boarded-up windows and spray-paint tags on its door. A group of squat houses broke up the shops, then a little farther on, I found a café.

A few cars were parked out in front, and I drew my worn-out Chevy in as close to the door as I could get. Thunder rolled in the distance as I turned off the engine. I plucked my jacket off the passenger seat and opened my door.

I moved as quickly as I could, but I was still drenched by the time I opened the diner's door. It was a small place and was dirtier than I'd expected. One of the fluorescent lights flickered every few seconds, but it didn't seem to bother the other occupants, who were mostly huddled at the back of the café and talking in low voices. I slipped into one of the tables close to the front window. The plastic tartan tablecloth crinkled as I rested my forearms on

it, and the saltshaker was empty except for a few grains of rice. I picked up the menu and cringed at how tacky it felt.

"What can I get you?"

I turned to see a sallow-faced server hovering behind me. She forced a smile when I looked at her, but it didn't reach her eyes.

I scanned the menu for something that had a low chance of giving me food poisoning and settled on the burger. In a burst of genius, I added, "Can I get that to go?"

The server didn't reply, and I think I caught her scowling as she went through the double doors to the kitchen, but I didn't care as long as I could get out of the diner and back into the familiar comfort of my car. Maybe it was the rain, or maybe it was because of how anxious I was about my mother, but the town gave me the creeps. I gazed out the window at the rain pounding on the hood of my Chevy. Like the real estate office, the squat two-story building on the other side of the road looked abandoned.

The only person on the street was a girl running through the rain, going from door to door on some mysterious errand. Only a handful of buildings had lights on. I caught hints of the discussion at the table at the back of the room, but it sounded flat and vapid.

The server dropped a Styrofoam clamshell box onto my table. "That's eight fifty."

I wasn't very reassured by how quickly the burger had been made, but I handed her a ten dollar note, took the box, and left

the diner. I unlocked my car door, put the box on my dashboard, and was about to sink into the driver's seat when I heard a voice calling.

The wind and rain were ferociously loud, making it nearly impossible to catch the words, but the voice's tone was urgent. I cautiously closed my car door and searched through the rain, shivering and cringing as the drops hit my face.

Then I saw her—the little girl who'd been going door to door was dashing down the center of the street, fighting to be heard over the drumming rain and thunder. I watched as she banged on a house door then set off running again when no one answered.

I was getting drenched, but I couldn't leave while the girl was obviously struggling to find help. I stepped forward and raised my hand to hail her. She saw and ran toward me.

That's when I finally got a good look at her. She couldn't have been older than ten or eleven, and her simple white dress was discolored with mud and oil. Shoulder-length brown curls hung wet and limp about her cheeks, and her eyes were bulging out of her pale face.

"Help!" she called, her bare feet slapping the muddy asphalt as she ran. "Our car went off the road. My mum's hurt. She's hurt really bad. I can't get her out."

I felt my heart stutter. The girl was close enough for me to see a trickle of red coming from her temple. The blood mixed with rain, which diluted it to paint a pale-pink streak down her cheek.

"Okay," I said, looking about the street. It was empty. I turned back toward the diner and felt a flush of shock: the sallow-faced

server stood at the door. She gazed at the girl for a moment then looked at me and raised her hand to the doorknob. I expected her to come out to see what the commotion was, but instead she turned the door's lock then pulled a discolored cloth curtain over the glass part of the door.

Shocked, I blinked at the locked door, unable to understand why the server would so pointedly refuse to help us. I turned back to the girl. Her eyes were fixed on mine, terrified and desperate, and I felt overwhelmingly underqualified to help.

"Okay." I gazed at my car, the café, then down the deserted street. "It's going to be all right. Can you show me the way?"

She grasped my hand. Her fingers were cold from running through the freezing rain as she led me off the main road and down a lane. She ran flat-out while I jogged beside her.

The rain had gotten through my jacket and soaked my shirt. I'd hoped the storm would ease during my stop, but if anything, the rain was getting heavier. I couldn't see more than a dozen paces ahead, though the girl seemed to know where she was going. We came to the end of the street, and she led me down a narrow dirt path that ran between two brick houses. Behind the houses, an incline led into a wooded area. She let go of my hand then so that she could scramble up the slope with all four limbs. I glanced at my shoes—they were leather and only a few weeks old—and cringed. A run through the woods would ruin them. I glanced up and saw the girl waiting for me at the edge of the woods. I took a gulp of air and clambered up the incline after her.

She led me through the trees. The high branches caught the

rain and poured it down on us in dribbles and splashes rather than drops. The wild, dark area had no clear paths and very little light. I nearly tripped over a root and cursed.

"Please hurry," the girl begged, barely pausing to look back at me. "She's hurt bad. There's so much blood."

Nausea grew in my stomach. If the mother was still alive—and I didn't want to think about what would happen if she wasn't—would I be able to carry her through the forest and back to the town? I wasn't sure I would even be able to get her out of the car. I'd had some basic first-aid training at one of my previous jobs, but I didn't have any medical supplies. I pulled my cell phone out of my pocket and cursed when it showed no reception.

The girl was able to weave through the woods faster than I could, and she quickly drew ahead of me. I tried to keep up, but the trees were close together, and I kept getting tangled in vines and bushes. "Slow down!" I called. "I don't want to lose you!"

"Please hurry!"

I gritted my teeth and pressed forward, ignoring the bruises forming on my shins and my stinging toes from where I'd stubbed them. I focused on keeping up with the pale girl weaving through the trunks ahead of me.

I suddenly broke through a patch of bush and skidded to a halt, just inches from a steep ravine. I teetered, caught my balance, and took a step back. The cliff dropped down more than twenty feet before ending in a stream that shimmered dully in the rain. I looked across the ravine and saw a road chiseled into the side of the opposite mountain.

"Down there," the girl whispered, pointing into the ravine. I crouched and squinted, looking for the car among the boulders and bushes around the creek. I couldn't make out the crash through the rain no matter how many times I passed my eyes over the gully.

"Where is it?" I asked, glancing up. "I can't see—"

She was gone. I stumbled to my feet and turned in a complete circle, searching for the girl among the trees.

"Hello?" I called. All I could hear was the wail of the wind and the persistent drum of rain on the woods about me.

I stood there for far too long, waiting for the girl to come back or call for me. I kept looking down into the gully, searching for the car, but I still couldn't see anything. When I finally looked up at the road on the opposite side of the ravine, I realized the railing was intact for as far as I could see it.

I felt stupid and confused. With no other options, I turned and began walking back toward the town.

It was a long, cold hike through the woods. I found it was easy to become disoriented in the pathless, dark maze, but I tried to walk straight as much as possible and eventually broke through the trees into a field. Another twenty minutes of walking brought me back to the city center.

Drenched, shivering, and bruised from the trip through the woods, I sloshed through the puddles, passing the rows of deserted buildings and empty houses, until I reached the café and found my car waiting for me. I hesitated with one hand on the door as I tried to think of what the most reasonable action

was. Should I tell someone about the girl? Should I just get into my car, drive out of the town as quickly as possible, and pretend none of the last two hours had happened?

"Hey," someone called.

I turned to find a police officer standing in the entrance to the café, leaning against the doorframe with his arms folded over his protruding stomach. He nodded toward my car. "Is that yours?"

"Yeah," I said.

"You'd better come in for a minute, son."

I hesitated, wondering if I was in trouble. The officer had already turned and disappeared into the café, though, and I felt too cold and miserable to refuse him.

Inside, the diners from earlier were gone, leaving the room empty except for me and the officer, who had sat at a table near the window. I sloshed over to him, leaving a wet trail on the wooden floor, and sat down.

"Let me tell you, I'm glad you came back." The officer scratched at the stubble on his chin as he regarded me with amused gray eyes. "Annette told me you'd followed Lucy, so I was going to organize a search party if you didn't turn up soon. Not pretty weather for it, though."

I blinked at him, trying to understand what he was getting at. Something bumped my arm, and I jumped as the sallow-faced server placed a mug of coffee on the table in front of me. "On the house," she said flatly then pressed a bundle of dish towels into my hands.

"Annette, you're a doll," the officer said as the server left. He

turned back to me and grinned. "Did you make it all the way to the drop-off?"

"Uhh…" I dragged the towels through my damp hair as my brain scrambled to catch up. "There was a girl. She, uh—"

"Yeah, that's Lucy McKenzie." The officer took a sip of his coffee. "I wish I could say she's the strangest thing about this town, but then, this is West Harob."

My frustration built as I rubbed my neck dry. "What do you mean? She said her car had crashed—"

"It sure did, son. Decades ago. It was a night not too different from this one—horrible rain. You could barely see the road in front of you. Yeah, their car went off the ravine on the Woodsons Trail. The mother died at the scene, but Lucy managed to climb out of the creek and made it through the woods. Got all the way into town before she died from a…whatcha call it? A brain hemorrhage. Passed away in the middle of the road before anyone could help her. It was a real tragedy."

I had frozen, wet towels still clasped in my hands, as I processed what he was implying.

The officer nodded at my stunned expression. "She comes back any time there's a big storm and runs through the town, asking for help. We usually just shut our doors and block our ears 'til the rain passes, but I guess you didn't know about her, being from outside town and all. I'm glad you found your own way back, though. Not everyone does, and let me tell you, it's not fun looking for Lucy's helpers on nights like tonight."

He put his empty coffee cup on the table and stood. "I'd better

be going, son. The radio says the storm will clear up in a couple of hours, so you might like to wait it out. If you do leave, though, make sure to be careful on the roads."

The officer inclined his head toward the server and left the café with a bright jingle of its doorbell. My brain was reeling. I wanted to believe it was a big practical joke—but I'd seen the girl myself, watched the blood run down her face, heard her beg for help…only to have her disappear and leave me with an intact stretch of railing and a gully that no longer held her car.

I only stayed in the café for a few minutes. I nodded a mute thanks to Annette before leaving, and the smile I got in return was marginally more genuine than the one I'd received on arrival. Back in the car, I stripped off as many layers of soaked clothing as I dared, put them in a spare bag to stop them from leaking, turned the heater up, and drove straight out of West Harob. The officer had said Lucy wasn't the strangest thing about the town… and I had no intention of staying long enough to see what else there was.

LIGHTS OUT

JODIE SWORE UNDER HER BREATH AS SHE BALLED HER FROZEN hands into fists and pushed them under her arms, trying to warm them. Her fingers felt like ice that could snap off at any moment. Beside her, Earl lit a cigarette and puffed on it until the smolder took hold. His eyes were bloodshot under swollen lids, and deep crevices around the corners of his mouth told Jodie he was working off a hangover.

On her other side, Miho huddled against the loading dock's brickwork, bundled up in layers of coats and scarves. Her nose was red, barely visible above the fur lining of the jacket she'd pulled up around her ears, and she kept sniffing and rubbing at it with the back of her knitted glove.

Jodie pulled one hand out and checked her watch. It was ten past. She swore again.

"I say we go back inside and let them bring 'em in themselves," Earl said.

"Your dad would have our necks," Jodie retorted. The words came out more harshly than she'd meant them to, but Earl didn't seem to notice.

"I've already told him I'm not working here anymore." He exhaled a cloud of smoke in a slow stream. "I'm a damn laughing-stock, working in a girls' clothing store."

Jodie bit her tongue. The cold was making her want to bicker, but she knew better than to upset the boss's son. Besides, he wasn't going anywhere. He hadn't been able to hold down any other job, and though he said he hated the supposed degradation of being surrounded by fashion, he enjoyed partying too much to give up his only source of income.

"It's here," Miho said with evident relief. She pushed off the wall and started hopping from foot to foot, trying to get some warmth into her legs as she watched the truck backing into the loading dock. Its flashing lights and an intermittent beep warned of its arrival. Earl squinted his eyes closed as though that could block out the sound.

Jodie waited until the truck came to a stop, its rear roller doors facing them, then shuffled toward the cabin. A wave of heat swept over her face as the driver rolled down the window and gave her a toothy grin. "Enjoying the weather?" he asked, passing the clipboard out for her to sign.

"Yeah, it's a gorgeous spring day, huh?" Jodie said, forcing a smile. Outside, the loading dock's doors were obscured by sheets of heavy rain that blurred the outlines of the trees just beyond the parking lot.

"You got it from here?" The driver took the clipboard back. Jodie noticed a well-worn novel on the passenger seat and a refillable mug filled with some steaming substance in the cup holder.

"Yeah, we'll be all right." She, Earl, and Miho were already freezing and miserable; there was no point dragging the driver out to help them when he so clearly wanted to enjoy his break in the truck's warm cabin.

Jodie shuffled to the back of the truck again, where Earl had already pulled up the roller doors. Miho stood by with the trolley as Jodie climbed into the back of the truck.

She found eight wooden crates strapped to the truck's floor. As she started to unbuckle them, a chilled sensation that had nothing to do with the cold crawled down Jodie's back. She sometimes got the feeling late at night, when her apartment suddenly seemed wildly too big and too empty for her, and she would pause the TV to listen, convinced she'd heard a door open, and imagine she heard footsteps, foreign and heavy, creeping across the scratched wooden floors.

The sensation was so strong that she stopped, one hand holding the strap's buckle. Her other hand rested on the lid of the crate, which was long, narrow, and large enough for a person to fit inside. *Like a crude coffin.* Jodie dropped the buckle and stepped back, the sensation growing stronger, digging its claws into her chest and gnawing at her stomach. She imagined opening one of the wooden boxes, pushing aside the packing material to find a face, blanched white from death, eyes stitched closed, hands clasped over its suited chest, waiting for her.

"What's'er matter?" Earl slurred around his cigarette. His small eyes were scowling at her as he stood over his own crate. The sound of his voice snapped Jodie back to reality. She took a deep breath and shook her head.

"Nothing. Nothing at all. Let's hurry and get out of this damned cold."

———

They managed to squeeze four crates onto the trolley, stacking them on top of each other. Earl and Miho stood on either side, bracing the wooden boxes, while Jodie pulled the handle, guiding their cargo through the concrete back passageways of the shopping center.

Their store was in the eastern end of the Inglebrook Center. The complex was nearly two decades old, but scrupulous cleaning and frequent renovations kept it looking brand new. The public enjoyed polished tile floors, natural lighting via the glass ceiling, and frequent clusters of potted palm trees and shrubs that were so shiny they looked fake upon first glance.

Jodie got to see a very different part of the center, though: the back passageways used by the cleaners and store staff to carry equipment through the building without disturbing the carefully cultivated atmosphere of the public section. There were no polished tile floors in the back passageways, no potted plants, and no air conditioning. The back held only concrete, which showed its age with discolored patches and stains, and weak fluorescent lights that cast a sickly glow over the tunnels.

Jodie felt like a maid in a historical novel, condemned to use the servants' passageways to travel through her wealthy lord's manor.

"Can you go any faster?" Earl barked. "I'm freezing back here."

"They're ceramic," Jodie retorted, "and I'm not about to explain to the boss that we dropped and broke them."

Earl muttered something under his breath, but Jodie ignored him. They were almost at the door that opened into their shop's cramped storage room. It would be warmer there—and brighter.

"Careful!" Miho shrieked, and Earl shouted a series of expletives. Jodie turned to see that the top crate had shifted, slipping off its pile, and Earl was struggling to get it back on.

"What did I just say?" Jodie snapped, hurrying to help him. For the second time that morning, her words came out harsher than she'd intended, and Earl noticed. He gave the crate a final, hard shove to get it back into place then turned on Jodie, his bloodshot eyes furious.

"It wasn't my fault. Miho pushed it!"

"I didn't!" the girl squeaked from behind the crates. "I was just holding it, and it started falling toward you!"

"Liar!" he yelled back, his voice cracking. "You shoved it really damn hard. You were trying to get me into trouble."

"Enough!" Jodie pressed her numb fingers to the bridge of her nose, where a headache had started. "I don't care what happened. It didn't fall, it didn't break, and Mr. Heinlein has nothing to yell at us about. That's the main thing."

Earl didn't look happy, but he wisely kept his mouth shut. Jodie wrenched their storage room door open and carefully

guided the trolley inside. The small area was stuffed with far too much stock; shelves on one wall held bags full of layaways, and racks were crowded with shirts and dresses that hadn't fit into the front store or were damaged and waiting to be returned. They'd carved a space in one corner by stacking boxes full of clothes and bags up to the ceiling to make room for their delivery. They carefully unstacked the crates, laying them upright in the narrow space.

The door at the opposite end of the room opened, and a small, mousy woman with large teeth poked her head in. "You're back?" She sounded breathless, as if she'd just run a marathon. "Thank goodness. There are at least eight people waiting to be rung up, and the crazy lady's back."

That's the last thing we need today, Jodie thought, smothering a groan.

"I'm going to get the rest of the boxes off the truck." Earl's voice sounded uncharacteristically bright. "Better not keep the driver waiting."

"I'll help you!" Miho took hold of the trolley's handle and pushed it toward the door, which Earl held open, their fight forgotten in their mutual desire to escape the storefront.

Allie, her eyes huge and pleading, hovered in the doorway. Jodie shrugged at her. "Guess it's just you and me. I'll take the crazy lady."

"Thank you," Allie breathed, and darted back into the store. Before following her coworker, Jodie glanced at the crates, which stood just over head height once they were upright. Tall and

imposing, the boxes looked even more like coffins than they had on the truck. Their bare, cheap wood took on a strangely gloomy tone in the harsh lights of the storeroom.

Movement caught Jodie's eyes, and she started as one of the crates near the back rocked slightly then stilled. *Probably something in it was settling.*

Jodie hesitated for another moment, her hand on the doorknob, worried that the rocking crate was a sign that they might topple. They held firm, though, stacked like impractically tall dominoes, sending thick shadows running up the walls behind them. Allie called her name, the girl's voice tense with stress under her thin veneer of polite friendliness, and Jodie let herself through the door.

"I'm afraid not," she said for what felt like the hundredth time. She leaned on the store's counter, holding a bag of clothing in front of her. To her right, Allie swiped clothes across the barcode scanner, checking out customers as quickly as she could. Her spiel was the same every time: "Found everything all right? Do you have a rewards account? Cash or card? Would you like a bag for that?"

Mrs. Danvers, their crazy lady, stood in front of Jodie. Her small eyes were watery, their irises so dark that they looked like little pits of coal in her face. She kept licking her lips as though it were a compulsion, while she repeatedly nudged the bag toward Jodie.

"I want to return them," she said, speaking slowly, as though Jodie were too stupid to understand her. "I have the receipt."

Here we go again. Getting Mrs. Danvers out of the shop in under ten minutes was a miracle. They'd been going at it for nearly twelve by that point, and Jodie's patience was wearing thin.

The first time she'd met Mrs. Danvers, she'd assumed the older, overweight woman had a mental disorder. With each visit, though, she'd become more and more convinced that Mrs. Danvers was completely sane but had developed a habit of repeating the same phrases over and over again, like a dog that refused to release its bone, knowing that, eventually, she would win simply by wearing her opponent down.

Not with me. Not today.

"These clothes are outside the month return policy," Jodie repeated, forcing herself to speak calmly, echoing the phrase as though it had become her life motto. "And they show significant signs of wear and tear."

"I haven't worn them," Mrs. Danvers objected, licking her lips again.

"This one has lipstick stains on it." Jodie pulled the clothes out of the bag one by one. "This shirt has a tear down one side. This singlet has stains under the arms. And this skirt isn't even from our store."

Mrs. Danvers turned her head to one side, her shrewd eyes narrowed. "I want to speak with your manager."

"I am the manager." Jodie gripped the bag in both hands to stop herself from giving in to the temptation to shake the older woman.

"I have the receipt." Again, the thick tongue, moist and flabby, slipped out to wet the cracked lips. "I want to return these clothes."

Allie shot Jodie a sympathetic glance as she bagged a customer's purchases. No one liked dealing with Mrs. Danvers. Jodie was the best at it, but she usually had to take a break afterward. She would go into the storage room and punch the bags of clothing or glare at the stain on the ceiling and pretend it was Mrs. Danvers's face while rehearsing the things she would say if there was no risk of being fired. "You're banned from the store for life. Never return!" was always at the top of her list. She was sure Mrs. Danvers had already been blacklisted from most of the other clothing stores in the center. But Mr. Heinlein, their boss, had a strict—and, in Jodie's opinion, idiotic—policy of never turning away customers.

"No," she said, speaking so loudly and firmly that the customers waiting in the checkout line stared at her. "You may not return these clothes. You bought them more than eight months ago, and you've clearly worn them multiple times. You *cannot* return them."

The tongue darted out again. Mrs. Danvers turned her head to the other side, her beady black eyes never leaving Jodie's face. After a moment of thought, she said, "I want to speak to the manager. I need to return these clothes. They don't fit right. I have the receipt."

"No," Jodie said, biting down on the frustration and lowering her voice. "No, no, no, no. You're not returning these clothes."

She waited for the almost inevitable repeat of *I want to return*

these clothes, but Mrs. Danvers only stared at her for a moment, looking her up and down, sizing her up to see if she was worth it. Then she reached her fat hands forward and snatched the bag from Jodie. "I'll come back when the manager's in," she said, clutching the bag to her chest, then turned abruptly to the store's exit.

Jodie sagged, feeling exhausted. Allie gave her shoulder a brief squeeze as she hurried past to throw a stack of unbought clothes onto the pile of items waiting to be returned to their racks.

"Fourteen minutes," she said on the way back, her smile bright and fake. "Could have been worse."

"Hmm." Jodie straightened her back, remembering that the store was full. She wanted to slip out the back and take her ten-minute break to mentally argue with the stain on the ceiling. However, Miho and Earl hadn't returned from picking up the final four crates, and Allie couldn't cope with the rush on her own.

"Can I help you?" she asked the next customer in line, forcing the retail-fake smile onto her face.

Her expression wary, a teenager approached, arms full of skirts that wouldn't flatter her short figure. She'd heard Jodie raise her voice at Mrs. Danvers and clearly didn't want to create a similar scene. Feeling guilty, Jodie widened her smile and put some effort into making it more sincere. "Find everything you were looking for?"

"Thanks so much, guys," Jodie said, pushing through the door to the storeroom. "You were terrific out there, helping Allie and me."

Miho jerked upright, turning red from embarrassment, but Earl remained lounging against one of the few empty patches of wall. He raised his eyebrows. "Crazy lady gone yet?"

"Yes." Jodie sighed and ruffled a hand through her hair. "And the store's quieter now. Allie and Miho are only on shift for another forty minutes, though, so we'd better unpack these suckers quickly before we lose half our manpower."

Miho, looking guilty for hiding in the storage room, hurried to fetch the crowbar Earl had brought into the store that morning. Jodie took the cold steel in her hands and approached the first coffin.

No, not coffin. Crate. Get your head together, girl.

There was no room to lay them on the ground; they would have to be opened while they were upright. It was dangerous, but Miho stood to one side, bracing the crate and ready to catch the contents if they fell out. After pressing the narrow wedge of the crowbar into the gap between the lid and the sides of the crate, Jodie began pulling and pushing, slowly working the nails free. The wood groaned, and one by one, the nails popped free. The gap widened, and Jodie passed the crowbar to Miho so she could use her hands instead. The lid came free after a hard tug, and Jodie pushed it against the wall so she could get at the crate's contents.

The crinkled white tissue paper stuffed inside looked, she thought, like fake flowers purchased at a premium from the

funeral home and poured across the coffin's corpse. Then the papers shifted, puffing outward and tumbling toward her as the crate's contents moved. For a second, Jodie thought there might actually be a body inside, buried before it was truly dead, waking up and stretching out of its prison. She smothered a shriek.

As the tissue paper fell away, she caught a glimpse of a mannequin's face, immaculately white, beautifully smooth, and shaped to give the barest impression of human features. The figure, packaged with such care, had overbalanced and fallen forward. She reached out to stop its fall, but it slipped through her hands, landing against her chest instead. The motion swung its arms forward, and they snapped around her, catching her in a lover's embrace. Corpse-cold and chillingly unforgiving, the dummy's hard cheek rested against the nape of her neck.

Jodie staggered backward, shocked by its weight, repulsed by its intimate presence, but terrified of dropping it. She thought the statue tightened its grip on her a fraction, then Miho pulled it off her, babbling apologies while Earl laughed.

"It's fine. It's fine," Jodie said, stepping away from the mannequin. Shaking, she raised her hands to brush over where the statue had pressed against her. *Nothing to be frightened of. You caught it. It's not broken.*

And yet, as she looked at the figure Miho had propped upright, she half wished it *had* broken. There was something unnatural about its face. It was bald, and its features had been shaped to represent a woman; the smooth brow sloped gently until it met the indents where the eyes belonged. The nose was straight

and long, a wedge set above stern lips and a smooth jawline. Its head was pointed away, facing the opposite wall, but Jodie felt as though she were being watched. The unusually dark shadows hanging around the indents of its eyes seemed to hide a sidelong glance. She shuddered, even though the storage room was nearly as warm as the main parts of the store.

"Ugly things, aren't they?" Earl sucked on a cigarette with a smug grin, fully aware that the room was supposed to be smoke free. "Dad's such an incredible cheapskate. Apparently, he got them from a store that was closing down in the seedy part of town. He said they were practically giving them away."

"They seem awfully clean if they're secondhand," Miho said. There was something strange about her voice, and Jodie glanced at her. The younger girl had backed away from the mannequin almost as soon as she'd set it upright. Hands crossed over her chest, she chewed on the ends of her hair.

She only does that when she's anxious. Does she feel it too?

Jodie sucked in her breath. She wanted to take a break, go outside, and sit for a while where it was quiet and less claustrophobic, but they had another seven cartons to open before the end of Miho's and Allie's shifts. "Let's get a move on. Earl, take that box out to the bins. Miho, where'd you put the crowbar?"

Jodie opened the rest of the boxes quickly, almost recklessly; her desire to escape the storage room outweighed her anxiety about breaking one of the ceramic statues. The team unceremoniously shoved the mannequins into the corner one by one, and Earl carried each box out after it had been emptied, gradually

freeing up room. By the time she was done, Jodie was panting, and her torso was covered in sweat. She threw the crowbar onto an open box of clothes and faced the store's newest acquisitions.

The eight mannequins—two male, six female—faced her with identical, inscrutable expressions. Their long white arms were outstretched, their stiff fingers angled into strange gestures. The light shined off their perfectly smooth skin, and Jodie thought back to what Miho had said about them being unusually clean for secondhand. They were more than clean; they were flawless. Jodie would have expected them to have sustained at least *some* damage at their old store, but she couldn't see a single scratch, chip, or crack. She didn't like the way it made her feel.

She checked her watch; Allie and Miho would be off shift in five minutes. "Better get them into the store and throw some clothes on them before you go."

Jodie approached the nearest one, a woman, and hooked her arms around the mannequin's chest. It was much heavier than she would have expected, and she strained to lift it and carry it toward the door. She eased her way into the front of the store then dragged the mannequin to a corner of the room to stand it next to one of their old dummies.

The replacement mannequins were long overdue. The old figures, which had been thirdhand when Mr. Heinlein bought them, dated back to the '60s and showed their age. They were scratched, chipped, and grimy around their joints. Two of them had limbs stuck on with duct tape. Jodie had, after months of gentle nagging, convinced the boss to invest in new ones.

She glanced between the two figures. One was horribly dirty, missing two fingers and nearly a third of the white paint on its face. Its torso was a little too large to hold the clothes well. The other looked brand-new, immaculate, and perfectly formed. Still, Jodie suddenly wished they could keep the old ones.

She stripped the clothes off the old mannequin and pulled them onto the new figure. She hated the feel of its ceramic skin, and moved as quickly as she could. When she was done, she dragged the old dummy into the storage room, where Miho and Earl had already finished two.

Jodie picked up another of the new mannequins and pulled it back into the storefront, aiming for the display windows. A middle-aged woman with short hair—one of their regulars—was riffling through a rack of discounted clothes. She smiled at Jodie as she passed. "Finally got some new models, eh?"

"Yeah," Jodie panted, trying to smile despite the crawling feeling covering her arms and back. "About time, huh?"

"They'll certainly brighten the store a bit." The woman moved away from the rack of clothes to watch Jodie set up the manne-quin, and the expression on her face changed as she got a good look at the statue. Jodie was halfway through pulling the old mannequin's sweater off when she glanced at the woman. Her face had changed from bright warmth to confusion, and as Jodie watched, it morphed into concern.

"Everything okay?" Jodie asked, pulling the sweater free. The woman had turned her head to the side to watch the mannequin out of the corner of her eyes and, at Jodie's voice, started.

"Oh, yes, thanks. I just… I'm supposed to meet my husband in the food court. I'd better go. Don't want to be late."

"Sure." Jodie, nonplussed, watched the woman leave the store with long, fast strides, disappearing among the milling shoppers in seconds. She turned to look at the mannequin, again feeling the unnerving sensation of being watched. She frowned and threw the sweater over the flawless white head.

———

"Seriously?"

Earl jolted and moved to hide the bottle, but Jodie stalked around the desk to where he was crouched and snatched it from him.

"Tubbi Wine, huh? What? Doesn't this job pay enough for a decent brand?"

"Give that back," Earl snarled, getting to his feet, his face twisted in frustration. "It's nearly the end of shift anyway—"

"So you thought you'd get a head start on tonight's plaster session?" Furious, Jodie shoved the bottle back into his hand. "Nuh-uh. Not on my watch. I'm not working with a drunk."

She was aware her voice had that hypercritical edge again, but she couldn't stop. The afternoon shift, despite being unusually quiet, had exhausted her more than the weekends did. It was the mannequins; she kept turning, sure that someone was in the store, watching her, only to find herself facing one of the statues. *You're just not used to them,* she kept telling herself. *In a week, they'll be so familiar that they won't bother you anymore.*

"Have you even swept the floor?"

"Sure I did." Earl had adopted the sulking, saggy expression she'd come to loathe. He raised the bottle to his lips and took a drink, glaring at her with his small, dark eyes.

Jodie breathed deeply through her nose, trying to quash the anger that threatened to spill out. "You could've fooled me. The floor's filthy."

Earl shrugged and screwed the bottle's cap back on.

It was just past their five thirty closing time. Jodie glanced about the store, taking a quick assessment of what still needed to be done. The floor needed sweeping; that was Earl's job. The trash behind the desk was overflowing with unwanted customer receipts and price tags, also Earl's job. Stock needed to come out of the back room to fill up the empty slots on the racks, two layaways needed filing in the back room, and the security system had to be set on the way out. *Earl, Earl, Earl.* The only completed tasks were hers.

Jodie, aware that she was seconds away from slapping her coworker, pulled her gloves on with harsh tugs. "Okay, I'm going home. You can close up on your own tonight. Ass."

Earl called her a very unflattering name in response, but Jodie pretended not to hear him as she stalked to the shutter on the front entrance and raised it just enough to slip underneath. A dozen stragglers were still meandering through the center, either on their way to their cars or waiting for a movie. She could hear shutters closing a little way off as another employee locked the doors to a nearby store. Turning left, toward the nearest exit,

Jodie walked as quickly as she could, glad to be out of the store for the day. And not just because of Earl.

———

Miho was waiting for Jodie outside the shop the following day, yawning and huddled in her jacket. Jodie's morning had been filled with disaster, from lost car keys to catching every red light between her house and the shops, and her shift should have started ten minutes before. "Sorry I'm late," she said, hurrying to find the store's key in her overfull key ring.

"'s fine," Miho mumbled, shifting from foot to foot, either to keep warm or stay awake. "I forgot my keys at home."

Jodie pushed the key into the shutters' lock and frowned. The lock didn't turn like it normally did. She pulled on the shutters and swore as they rose without resistance.

"What's wrong?"

"Earl didn't lock the doors last night." Jodie pushed them up, locked them into the slot in the roof, then swore again when she saw the inside of the store.

Earl's now-empty bottle still sat on the counter. The broom was propped against the jewelry stand, though the floor hadn't been swept, and bundles of clothes had been draped across the store's racks. Worse, the mannequins had been stripped of their clothes, which lay in clumps on the floor.

"Unbelievable," Jodie hissed, stalking into the store. "He's going to get an earful this afternoon."

She started snatching the clothes off the dirty floor and pulling

them back onto the mannequins. Miho picked up the empty bottle and frowned at the label, chewing the ends of her hair again. "Do you think he has a problem?"

"Oh, he's got a problem, all right. And its name is Jodie."

Miho laughed, and Jodie felt herself relax. She liked working with Miho; the girl was quiet and unpresumptuous, and she worked hard. *Unlike some people I know.*

"Quick, throw that bottle away so the customers don't see."

Jodie continued re-dressing the mannequins Earl had stripped while Miho tossed the bottle into the storage room and gave the dirtiest parts of the floor a quick sweep. The shopping center was filling up as the stores opened, and their first customer came in just as Jodie shoved a cap onto one of the male mannequin's heads in a failed effort to make it look less sinister. The woman flicked through a rack near the door for a few seconds before drifting out without buying anything. Three more customers quickly replaced her then left again in under a minute. As Jodie hurried through her morning tasks, she noticed more and more customers were entering the store then leaving almost immediately. Casual browsers weren't uncommon, but at least a few would always stay for a while and try on some of the clothes.

It was so unusual that Jodie found herself counting how many seconds each of the shoppers lingered. A regular customer stopped at one of the discount racks. The woman flipped through the shirts then started as though something had alarmed her. She swung to face the mannequin behind her and stared at it for a

moment before hurriedly pushing the shirt she'd been holding back onto the rack. Her aim was off, and the hanger and shirt clattered to the floor, but she didn't stop to pick it up as she pulled her jacket about herself and strode out the door.

"Did you see that?" Jodie asked, but Miho, who had been arranging the shoes on the shelf beside the desk, only looked at her questioningly.

Feeling uneasy, Jodie approached the discount rack. She faced the mannequin and searched its blank, soulless face, trying to find what had disturbed the customer. The statue only gazed back, expressionless, inscrutable. Jodie turned and picked the dropped shirt off the floor. *Of course, it's in the one place Miho didn't sweep.* She grimaced, trying to brush the dust and bits of fluff off the fabric, then froze.

The strangest sensation came over her—the same one she'd felt in the truck, when she'd hesitated over the coffins—*the crates.* It also came over her very late at night or in the early hours of the morning, when she was walking home and couldn't shake the feeling that she was being followed through the empty streets; she would put her hands in her pockets and quicken her step. Jodie was never brave enough to glance into the dark alleys that ran between the buildings like empty veins, though she would swear she heard a second step masked by the echo of her own hurrying feet.

She turned slowly, not wanting to see what was behind her but too frightened to do otherwise. The mannequin stood where she'd left it, its face wearing the same empty expression, its hands

still raised in odd gestures. It seemed different, somehow. More aware. *Awake.*

Stop it. Stop it, stop it, stop it.

"Jodie?" Miho called from behind the desk. "Something wrong?"

The customers felt it, too, Jodie realized, staring at the mannequin and feeling, with overwhelming certainty, that it was staring back.

Then laughter, raucous and mocking, shocked her, and she was finally able to break the gaze. A gaggle of teenagers had gathered in the male wear corner of the store, where they were yelling and pushing each other.

"No, really, dude," a scrawny and pale one said, his loud voice easily carrying across the store. He was shifting in agitation, hopping from foot to foot and shaking his arms to make his jacket flap. "It *blinked.*"

"*Dude,*" his companion said, stretching out the syllable and leaning on the nearest rack for support as he struggled to stop laughing. "It doesn't even have *eyes.* Just how high are you?"

Jodie approached them without being aware that her feet were moving. Her mouth was dry and had an odd taste, and tension spread across her shoulders. "Can I help you?"

The teenagers looked at her and laughed. "Nah," the tallest one said, slapping his pale companion on the back. "We're going."

Jodie felt frozen to the ground as she watched the teens leave with the peculiar loping gait that their social circle always seemed to favor. The pale one started laughing along with his

companions as they mocked him. Slowly, Jodie turned to look at the mannequin they'd been standing beside. It was the one she'd thrown a cap on. The cap had only succeeded in darkening the shadows under its eyes, once again giving her the sensation that it was watching her through the shrouded depths.

"I'm taking a break," Jodie said, crossing the store so quickly that she knocked several clothing racks askew. "Be back soon."

Without giving Miho a chance to answer, she jogged into the storeroom and closed the door behind herself. Her hands were shaking, and the tightness over her shoulders had spread down her chest and knotted in her stomach like a cold, thick snake coiled in her abdomen.

The storage room felt comforting, though. Its haphazard stacks of boxes overflowing with clothes, the shelves crammed full of layaways, and even the garbage bag left by the door were mundane, safe, and familiar. Jodie sank to the floor and pulled her knees up under her chin, closing her eyes and breathing deeply. Her heart rate slowed, and strength gradually eased back into her limbs.

What's gotten into me? She listened to the muted noises coming from behind the door that led to the main part of the store. *They're only mannequins. Yeah, they're creepy, but they're not actually* doing *anything. Except for maybe bankrupting the store.*

Calm washed over her as the tension left her shoulders and the sweat dried. She thought of Earl, who would be coming in for his shift that afternoon. She hoped he wouldn't give Allie any trouble. If he tried to drink during work again, she would have to tell the boss—and she wasn't looking forward to it. Earl's father

was surly, and although he wasn't fond of his son in any sense of the word, he hated criticism.

Maybe I could move on. I might need to, anyway, if the manne-quins are scaring the customers away. I could start putting out resumes again. Maybe actually make it into the journalism field and get some use out of my degree. Wouldn't that be amazing? I could get out of this awful store and away from Earl and Earl's father and the new mannequins—

The door creaked open, and Miho's round face peered through. "Jodie? You okay?"

"Yeah, fine." Jodie found her words were almost true. "Need help out front?"

"The crazy lady came in," Miho said.

Jodie sighed and got to her feet. "Sure, I'll take her—"

"But she left again."

"What?" Jodie went to the door and looked out. The store was completely empty.

Miho shrugged, chewing on her hair. "She stood by the discount rack for a minute then left. Didn't even *try* to talk to me."

"Huh." Jodie looked toward the rack and the tall mannequin fitted out in slacks and a hoodie that stood beside it. She could guess why Mrs. Danvers hadn't lingered. *Maybe those mannequins have some perks, after all.*

————

Jodie sat behind the desk, tapping a pen on the scratched wooden surface as she surveyed the empty store. Calling it a slow day

would have been an understatement. She'd kept herself busy dusting shelves and rearranging clothing racks, but without any customers, there was nothing else to do. Miho had gone home, and Allie, whose shift had started ten minutes previously, was drifting among the racks, looking lost.

"And it's been like this all day?" she asked on her third lap around the store.

"Pretty much. One woman came in to exchange her shirt for a different size. Otherwise, nothing."

"Maybe it's the weather."

The rain from the previous day had continued through the morning as a drizzle, but Jodie doubted that was to blame for their deserted store. "Maybe."

She checked her watch. It was ten minutes past the end of her shift, but Jodie was waiting for Earl. She'd spent the morning rehearsing what she wanted to say to him—in a calm, moderate voice, she'd promised herself—but he was, predictably, late.

He must know I'm angry about the state he left the store in last night. He's probably hoping he can wait long enough for me to leave and avoid the lecture.

"This is ridiculous," Jodie grumbled. She picked up the desk phone and dialed the number written on a Post-it Note hidden just out of the customers' sight. It rang four times before going to voice mail. She hung up without leaving a message. "He's not answering."

"Maybe he's driving here right now," Allie said, shaking out the top shirt on its stack and refolding it.

"Maybe," Jodie said. Earl couldn't afford a car, and his father refused to lend him the family vehicle, so he took public transport on days he couldn't get a lift.

A customer drifted in through the doors then floated out like a leaf caught in a swirl of wind. Her large teeth worrying at her lower lip, Allie watched the woman go. "Well, you might as well head home. Even if Earl doesn't come in, it's not like I'm going to be overwhelmed."

Jodie pursed her lips. She hated the idea of letting Earl win, but his stalling tactics were gradually eating away at her afternoon off. She'd already made plans that involved the three latest episodes of her favorite show, an extra-large duvet, and Chinese takeaway. "Thanks, Al, I might do that. Look, Earl was acting up last night. I caught him drinking behind the desk, and he left the store unlocked. If he gives you any sort of trouble today, give me a call, all right?"

"Will do."

———

Just before nine in the morning, the clouds from the previous two days had parted to offer a little weak spring sun. The weather forecast had said another storm was coming that evening, though, but Jodie had been thinking there might be just enough time to dry the laundry before her shift that afternoon. She was nearly done when a bright jingle disturbed the silence and sent Jodie searching her pockets for the phone.

She glanced at the number and recognized the work landline.

Who's scheduled this morning? It's Miho and Earl, isn't it? Or maybe someone else is calling...

The sensation of something being not quite right was so strong and so sudden that it knocked the breath out of her lungs. The morning didn't seem bright anymore, but cold and alien. In her mind's eye, she saw a hand reach for the clothing store's phone on the worn wooden counter, pick up the receiver, and dial her number. But the hand wasn't flesh and blood. The perfectly white porcelain fingers that should have been frozen moved dexterously as they danced over the number pad—

Then the phone rang again, and Jodie shook herself out of the stupor. The work number still flashed on the screen, and she pressed the answer button. "Hello?"

"Jodie, thank goodness!" The notes of fear and anxiety in Miho's voice doused Jodie's momentary relief.

"What's wrong?" She dropped a wet shirt into the washing basket.

Miho hiccuped then took a steadying breath. "I think we've been robbed."

"What?" Jodie was already jogging into her house to find her car keys. "Are you sure?"

"Pretty sure." Jodie pictured Miho standing behind the counter, holding the phone's old-fashioned receiver in both hands as she surveyed the store. "The doors weren't locked again. And there's stuff everywhere—pulled off shelves, off racks. It's a disaster."

"Hang tight. I'm on my way." Jodie hung up as she slid into

the driver's seat of her car and turned the key in the ignition. Her mind was racing, trying to make sense of it.

The doors were unlocked... Only five people had keys to the store: Jodie, Allie, Miho, Earl, and Mr. Heinlein. Allie and Earl had been on closing shift the night before. Her first thought was that Earl had gotten drunk again and left the doors open, but she'd warned Allie about it the previous afternoon. Allie was too much of a worrier to let Earl close up shop alone, anyway.

"Jeez," she hissed, weaving through traffic a little too quickly to be safe. She tried to think about how much might have been lost; it was a low-price store, and their most expensive pieces cost sixty dollars, so a thief couldn't have made off with a fortune. Mr. Heinlein would be furious, though, no matter how small the loss was.

Jodie parked haphazardly and jogged through the near-empty center. Miho was waiting just inside the store, and one look at the girl's face told Jodie the last ten minutes had been hell.

"Hey, it's okay." She put an arm around Miho's shoulders and gave them a squeeze. "You're not hurt, are you?"

Miho shook her head, but her face was still scrunched up. "The store—look at it—Mr. Heinlein–"

"It's not your fault. He won't get angry with you." Jodie gave the girl's shoulders another squeeze then stepped forward to survey the damage.

Miho hadn't been exaggerating—it was a disaster. Virtually every shelf was empty. The shirts, the jeans, the dresses, the jewelry, the skirts, and the shoes all lay in piles about the floor.

A few items hung from the top of the shelves, and one scarf dangled from a ceiling light. Most of the clothing racks had been overturned, and the T-shirt table had been jammed into the corner. Most of the mannequins had been knocked over. It hadn't been casual riffling; it had been pillaging.

"I didn't touch anything," Miho said, watching Jodie, who was turning in a slow circle to examine the room. Despite the gravity of the situation—or perhaps *because* of it—Jodie had to bite down on a laugh. She could imagine Miho saying exactly the same thing to a pair of police officers at the scene of a violent murder.

"Okay." Jodie pressed her fingers to the bridge of her nose as she thought through their options. "Close the doors, Miho. We can't let customers into the store like this. I'll call Allie."

She gingerly stepped over the sea of discarded clothes to get to the checkout table while Miho pulled down and locked the shutters. Customers would still be able to see through the windows—and, in fact, a couple of curious faces were already peering through the empty display at the other end of the store—but at least they wouldn't be interrupted while they assessed the damage.

Jodie dialed Allie's number from the Post-it Note then shifted from foot to foot as she waited. The phone rang four times before going to voice mail. Jodie pressed on the switch hook and tried again, with the same result. She sighed and waited for the beep. "Allie, call work, please. It's urgent."

Next, she tried Earl's number. Again, her call went to voice

mail. She didn't bother leaving a message. It was a quarter past nine, which meant he was probably skipping work...*again.*

Finally, she called Mr. Heinlein's number and scowled when his phone, too, rang out. No answering machine took the call.

Miho was hovering beside the desk, chewing at the ends of her hair. Jodie gave her a helpless shrug. "Well, we did inventory last week, at least. That'll help us figure out what we're missing. Better get started."

The cleanup consumed the entire morning. Jodie stood at the desk, comparing sales receipts with their inventory to come to an approximate tally of what they were supposed to have, while Miho picked up the clothes off the floor, checked them for damage, and rehung them. Once Jodie's list was complete, she joined Miho. Her back ached by the time they stopped for lunch.

"We're getting there, at least," Miho said from her perch on the corner of the desk, eating the kebab Jodie had treated her to. They'd rehung almost all of the scattered clothes but hadn't counted them yet.

Jodie checked her watch. "It's nearly the end of your shift. D'you want to go home? I doubt we'll be able to open today, anyway."

Miho shook her head quickly, and strands of her sleek black hair stuck to the grease around her mouth. She rubbed them away with a grimace. "Nah, I'll stay and help out here, at least until Allie comes in."

Jodie was anxious for Allie's shift to start too. The five calls

she'd placed throughout the morning had all ended up in voice mail, and they still hadn't been returned.

If she could just speak to Allie, she would at least know who was responsible for the damage. Allie or Earl might have dropped their key somewhere, giving a thief easy access to the store, or Earl had possibly gotten plastered and invited some of his buddies in to help him pull apart the shop he hated.

Jodie tossed her own kebab wrapper into the trash and hopped off the corner of the counter. The mannequins still needed righting; she's been putting it off, but with the rest of the store mostly sorted, she couldn't ignore them for long. They'd been stripped, just like the night before, and Jodie picked up the first one gingerly.

The white face stared down at her as she righted it. Even after being thrown to the ground, the porcelain was blemish free. Jodie found herself staring at it, searching the skin for imperfections—a hairline crack, a smudge, anything to abolish the niggling idea that the statues couldn't be damaged—but as her eyes darted over the face, she felt as though she were being scrutinized in return. In that moment, she became convinced that the lips weren't set in a neutral expression but that they were *smirking*. The face wasn't blank; it was arrogant and intense.

She swiveled the mannequin away so it faced the opposite direction and dressed it as quickly as she could manage with shaking fingers.

Jodie knelt on the cold tiles, shaking out the tangled necklaces and bracelets that had been knocked off the jewelry stand. Every thirty seconds, she paused to check her watch then glanced at the shutter doors before frowning and returning to the jewelry. Two minutes past the start of Allie's shift, she still hadn't arrived.

Allie was notoriously punctual. Everyone—including Jodie—occasionally missed the start of a shift, except for Allie. She sometimes arrived as much as half an hour early if she'd heard traffic was likely to be bad.

A tight ball of anxiety began to build inside Jodie's chest. What-if scenarios fluttered through her head, and they became increasingly difficult to push aside. *What if*, instead of being busy, she'd been unable to answer her phone? *What if* the break-in had happened while Allie was still in the store? *What if* she was in trouble, hurt, or worse? Jodie's fingers faltered as she tried to pry apart a necklace and a watch, then she threw them onto the floor in frustration.

Since Mr. Heinlein hadn't answered her first call that morning, she'd been reluctant to call again, partly because he tended to shoot the messenger and partly because she'd been hoping to finish the inventory and have exact details for him before delivering the bad news. But Mr. Heinlein held the contact details for Allie's family, and he was Jodie's only other link to Earl, who might be able to shed light on what had happened the night before.

One hand on the receiver, she hovered behind the desk, breathing deeply and wishing Allie would just *turn up* so she

could delay the call for another few hours. The eyes were on her again; it seemed like every mannequin in the store had a direct line of sight to her. Their attention was fixed on her movements, the way the lump in her throat made her grimace when she swallowed, and how her eyes couldn't stay still. They were anonymous spectators, faintly amused, and she was their entertainment for the afternoon, a dull little distraction for them to judge at their leisure.

Jodie squeezed her eyes closed, trying to block out the faces and struggling to clear her head. She took a sharp breath then bent over the counter to obscure the mannequins' view. Jodie dialed Mr. Heinlein's number.

He answered after two rings with his characteristic, "What?" Based on the way he slurred the word, Jodie thought he must have had a cigarette in his mouth. *Either that or he's drunk.* She braced herself and described the situation as briefly and factually as she could.

She tuned out a lot of what he said after that. He uttered copious swear words, most of them directed at her, and vague threats of suing for negligence. He also asked a series of questions she had no way of answering: "How much is this going to cost me? Huh?" and "Who's responsible? Who the hell did it?"

Jodie stared at her watch through the ordeal, letting her attention focus on the beautifully predictable second hand twitching its way around the dial. It was eight and a half minutes past by the time Mr. Heinlein's anger had ebbed enough for her to move the conversation along.

"Allie's shift was meant to start ten minutes ago, but she's not here. Has Earl said anything about—"

"Haven't talked to Earl," Mr. Heinlein spat, sounding disgusted. "Not for a couple days. We had...*an altercation*, so he's gone to sulk at one of his idiot friends' house."

That would explain why he hadn't been to work. It might also have been his motive for destroying the store, if he really was responsible.

"Well, I can't contact Allie. I'm worried something's happened to her."

"Maybe she's run off with my son," Mr. Heinlein said, and Jodie cringed as his cold laughter broke into a hacking cough.

"The police should be contacted." Jodie grimaced, knowing Mr. Heinlein had a deep-seated hatred for their local police.

"What the hell for? You want to cause trouble for the store? Is that what you're doing?"

She could feel the mannequins' amusement. They were gloating, mocking her for turning to such an unstable ally. Jodie turned her back to them, facing the wall behind the counter, where a giant poster of a woman wearing fashions nearly five years old was stuck. Every time Mr. Heinlein tried to divert the argument, Jodie repeated, "Allie's missing. Someone should be contacted." It became a mantra, which she interjected any time her boss paused to take breath.

I've turned into Mrs. Danvers. Hysterical laughter rose inside her, forcing her to bite her cheek to keep it contained.

"Fine," he snarled after she'd said the phrase for the fifth time.

"I'll call her family, and if they haven't seen her, I'll tell the police, and they'll probably shut the entire store down for a month while they figure out she skipped town with a drug-addict boyfriend. Happy? Now get my store fixed."

He slammed his receiver down, and the crack echoed in Jodie's ears long after she'd replaced her own receiver on the cradle. She turned back to face the store, and the mannequins, and forced a ghastly smile onto her face for Miho's benefit as she returned to the jewelry rack.

———

At nearly four in the afternoon, they finally finished the inventory. Jodie ran through the numbers one last time, incredulous. The stock left in the store perfectly matched the list of what they were supposed to have. If there'd been a break-in, the thief must have spent upward of an hour tearing the place apart then left without taking so much as a bangle.

"That's good, isn't it?" Miho leaned on the desk, looking drained. There were dark circles under her eyes, and the ends of her hair were split from her chewing on them.

Jodie gave her a sympathetic smile. "I guess it is. Head on home. I'll call Mr. Heinlein then close the shop early. We can reopen properly in the morning." She hesitated. "I know tomorrow was meant to be your day off, but…"

"Yeah, of course I'll come in." Miho sounded bright, despite her exhaustion. "None of my classes this week are really important, anyway."

"Thanks." Keeping the store open with both Allie and Earl gone would mean a lot of extra work, and Jodie hated the idea of having to spend time alone with the mannequins. Even just having half a day of company would be a huge relief.

Jodie ushered Miho out under the shutter doors then pulled them back into place. She glanced about the store, feeling the solitude acutely, and tugged her jacket around her body as she made for the phone beside the desk.

Mr. Heinlein answered almost immediately. Not only had he calmed down since the first call, but the news that his stock was intact actually made him cheerful. "Good thing too," he grunted. "Can't afford to buy in anything else until the start of the new season. They cost us a day of business, but we'll recover from that."

Jodie licked her lips. The mannequins were watching her again, their empty eyes fixed on her as she paced behind the desk. "Did you get in touch with Allie's family?"

"Yeah, a dead end. Her contact was her father, who died last year."

"And then you called the police, right?"

Mr. Heinlein's guilty silence stretched out, and Jodie snapped, "She's not answering her phone, and she missed her shift. She could be in serious trouble—"

"Fine," he snarled then ended the call before Jodie could say another word.

Jodie threw the receiver onto the desk, disgusted and furious, and looked up at her audience of mannequins. "What?" she snapped at the rows of faces then turned and half walked, half

ran to the supply room and pulled the door closed so sharply that the thin wall shook.

Frustration and fear for Allie collected inside of her, knotting into a painfully hot ball inside her chest. She pressed herself into an empty space between the shelves and an open box of defective sequined shirts and pressed her hands over her face.

She hadn't needed to work a full day in the store for a long time, and the constant bending and stretching had set a dull ache in her lower back. The storage room was comforting and safe. She was warm, and the sequined shirts under her cheek were unexpectedly comfortable. The store waited for her beyond the storeroom door, filled with the impersonal mannequins, and instead of mustering her strength and returning to them, she let her eyes close. *Just a moment's rest. Then we can go home.*

———

Jodie started awake, heart racing, palms clammy. After a second, she realized she was still huddled in the corner of the storage room. Grimacing, she rubbed at the side of her face where the sequins had bitten into her skin. The store was completely silent. Something had disturbed her, though, and she struggled to remember what it was. Some sort of beep…

She found the source after a moment. A cell phone had been left on one of the shelves, propped against a box of bags bearing the store's logo, and the message icon was flashing. Its owner might have set it down for a moment while putting a coat on or retying a shoe and forgotten it.

Jodie guessed whose phone it was and swiped it on to make sure. Sure enough, the background was a photo of Allie's cats. There were eight messages. Five would have been from her; the rest must have come from friends or relatives.

That explained why the calls hadn't been returned, at least. And if Allie used her phone's calendar to keep track of when she was working, she might have easily forgotten that she'd been scheduled for the afternoon shift. The anxiety in Jodie's chest eased slightly, and she replaced the phone and rubbed at her sore eyes.

It was just after seven thirty, which meant the only shops left open would be the grocery store at the end of the center and the movie theater in the food court. Jodie pushed through the storeroom door and back into the main part of the shop.

It was pitch dark. The only light came through the windows, from the shopping center's large ceiling lights, and they were at the wrong angle to reach far into the store. Jodie hesitated. *I left the store lights on, didn't I?*

After her call to Mr. Heinlein, she'd been too angry to do anything except storm into the storage room. Perhaps one of the security guards had passed by, thought the store was empty, and turned the lights off for her. *Impossible. They wouldn't have a key to get inside.*

Except...she hadn't locked the door after letting Miho out. Jodie hurried through the store, weaving past the racks and tables that were only barely visible, to reach the shutters. She gave them a tug, but they held fast.

Whoever had turned off the lights must have had a key, then, to lock the door. *Did Miho come back? Allie, possibly, or even Earl?*

Jodie turned to squint at the room. The ten mannequins, barely visible shadowy figures, were spaced around like sentinels, some half-hidden behind their racks, others posed on their stands by the windows.

Wait...ten?

Jodie recounted them quickly, and her heart rate shot up. There were definitely ten figures in the store. And yet, they'd only received eight crates.

Her mouth was suddenly dry. She moved quickly and quietly, not daring to take her eyes off the room, which suddenly felt claustrophobic, as she sidestepped toward the light switch by the door. Her foot landed on something soft, and she hopped back, horrified. It was a T-shirt, casually discarded.

Did we miss one of the shirts when we cleaned the place? No, we couldn't have. We were too thorough.

Jodie reached out a hand and fumbled for the switch beside the doors. It turned on with a quiet click, and light filled the room. Any thought of two of the shadowy figures being intruders disappeared with the darkness. They were all mannequins, their flawlessly smooth faces turned in her direction. Shaking and struggling to breathe, Jodie counted them again. *Ten.* Two more than had arrived in the back of the truck. Two more than the coffins she'd wrenched open. *Ten. How is that possible?*

It's a prank. Her eyes danced about the store, skimming over the figures. *It's Earl's doing, I'll bet. He knew I was scared of them; he*

saw my face when we were unpacking them and the first mannequin fell on me. He was angry because I made him close up himself and because I complained about the alcohol. And he said the mannequins were cheap; he must have been able to buy two more of them and bring them in... When? Tonight? No, I would have heard. It must have been last night. And he destroyed the store while he was here to add atmosphere.

And then he came back tonight to lock me in...

The mannequins were naked again, Jodie realized. Their clothes lay scattered across the floor. That accounted for the shirt she'd stepped on. The one thing she couldn't understand, though, was why someone would bother undressing all ten dummies... and how she hadn't heard it.

"Very funny, Earl," she called, trying to sound braver than she felt. "Your dad's mad at you, by the way."

Silence. Chills crawled up Jodie's arms, setting the hairs to stand on end. Earl had both the motive and the ability to set up the prank, but the more she thought about it, the less certain she was that he was responsible. It wasn't Earl's style at all. It was too subtle and nuanced—too clever. Earl would have been just as happy to throw a dozen eggs at her car.

He's got to be working with someone, then. A friend? Are they building up to something? Should I get out before I get a metaphorical bucket of pig blood dropped on me?

The store keys were in her bag under the front desk. Jodie skirted the racks to get to it, not daring to take her eyes off the store. There were a dozen places a man could hide in that room

without any effort, and being alone in the store while shoppers milled around just outside the windows was very different from the isolation once the shops were deserted.

Jodie ducked under the desk to pull her bag out from its shelf. She tugged open the front pouch where she kept her keys and licked at her dry lips as she found it empty.

It's fine. I must have put it in a different pocket; that's all. Everything's okay.

Straightening up, Jodie surveyed the store again. It was still and quiet. And yet, something seemed wrong. *The mannequins.* She could have sworn they'd been facing the shutter doors a moment ago, but now they were looking toward the desk. Toward her.

Jodie swallowed thickly as she unzipped her bag and began digging through it. She'd been meaning to clean it out for months—the crumpled receipts, empty tissue packs, mouth fresheners, spare makeup, and hairbrushes hindered her search.

It was hard to focus while she felt so scrutinized. Desperate, Jodie turned the bag upside down, scattering its contents across the desk, and searched for the metallic glint of her key ring. It wasn't there. Jodie swore under her breath. Frustrated, she knelt behind the desk again, running her hand along the shelf in case the keys had fallen out. Nada.

"Damn it, Earl!" Jodie choked as she looked up into the dark glare of one of the mannequins.

It had moved, impossibly, across the store to place itself on the other side of the desk, its hands spread and fingers resting lightly on the wooden surface. The head had turned to the side to regard

her, and as Jodie looked up at it, she found there was something terribly, horribly familiar about it.

Earl's heavy brow, his small eyes, his slightly crooked nose, and his thin lips had been warped, changed, and reinterpreted into smooth ceramic and white gloss. The features were simultaneously familiar and hideously alien.

Speechless, Jodie backed away from him, trying and failing to understand what she was seeing. She turned to her left, where another of the mannequins stood beside the shelves of jeans. This one, too, was familiar. Allie's lips. Allie's jawline. Allie's high cheekbones.

"No," Jodie whispered. "No, no, impossible."

There was a crack, and the lights died with a whine. Jodie skidded away from the sound, and her back hit a rack of coats, sending them rocking as the store succumbed to darkness. She turned toward the windows that looked out into the shopping center. Those lights there were gone too.

What is this? A power outage?

Lightning cracked across the sky. The harsh flash burst through the center's skylights and into the store. In that split second, she saw the mannequins had stepped off their stands and come out of their corners to inch closer to her. Earl's mannequin had reached out, its fingers extended toward her face. Then the light faded, and darkness rushed back in to take its place.

Terror made her legs give out, and Jodie tumbled to the ground, panting and shivering, feeling as though she were about to be sick. She could hear them, she realized. Stiff joints

creaked as they moved. The faint, sharp taps of ceramic feet on tile accompanied shifting noises as they brushed past the racks, disturbing the clothes.

Think! Think! The store has a generator, doesn't it? Why hasn't it come on yet?

Something cool and hard brushed across Jodie's exposed neck, and she shrank back from it with a gasp. Her skin chilled where it had been touched, as though the ceramic had been frozen. The entire store felt colder than it should have, and her muscles were cramping in the chill.

She couldn't see them, but she could picture them, moving languidly, confidently, knowing she was blind and trapped. The infernal tapping noise was coming closer—so close that they must be on top of her. Jodie shrank down close to the ground and balled her hands into fists, even though she knew her flesh would be useless against rigid ceramic.

A whirring noise shocked her, and she opened her eyes. While the lights in her own shop stayed cold, the main center lights flickered back to life. They couldn't illuminate her store completely, but it was enough, and Jodie risked raising her head.

She was surrounded. Hands extended toward her, faces leaned close, and bodies barred her path. But they'd frozen. *It's the light. They can't move in the light.*

Cold radiated off their ceramic. Jodie shrank as far from the grasping hands as she could, her mind scrambling for an escape. If she could just get outside the store and find a place with lights and other people...

The shutter doors were locked, though, and the keys had been stolen. The store windows were reinforced to prevent breaking, and there was no other exit. Except…

Jodie's eyes landed on the door to the storeroom. If she could get through the back room and down the concrete hallways, she would be able to make it to the center court, where the movie theater would still be open. And that meant light and company and safety.

They're slow. She glanced back at the empty faces leering down at her. *Surely I can outrun them.*

The light only penetrated into the first few feet of the store, though. From there to the back room was a mess of shadows.

Go, Jodie urged herself as desperation battled with fear that had frozen her to the ground. *Go, before the lights go out again. Go, go!*

There was no way to push past the mannequins without touching them, so Jodie pulled herself to her feet and threw herself over the top of the service desk, tumbling to the floor on the other side. Her weak legs held her, and she began running between the racks, dodging the clothes on the ground that the mannequins had shed. Her hand latched onto the handle of the stockroom door, and she twisted it, pausing just long enough to glance over her shoulder. The mannequins had turned their heads to watch her progress. Jodie swore as she slipped through the door and pulled it shut behind her.

Apparently, the generator didn't power the back sections of the shops; the storeroom was dark, and there was no sign of light

coming from under the door leading to the concrete passageways. Jodie fumbled in her pocket for her phone, but it was empty.

Where…? Of course, on the front desk—with everything else from my bag.

Jodie moved forward, feeling her way along the shelves, until she found the one she knew held the store's branded bags. The quiet squeal of a door being opened sent Jodie's heart into her throat as she felt around the box's base, searching for Allie's phone, and a gasp escaped her as her fingers fixed on the cool metal. She swiped it on, and the weak light spread through the room, illuminating the high-stacked boxes, the layaway bags, the piles of clothes…and the mannequin, standing just behind her.

She backed away from it, keeping her light focused on its face. Its eyes followed her from inside the shadowed hollows below its brow. Jodie reached her spare hand behind herself, feeling for the door that led to the hallways. Grasping the handle, she pulled it open.

The concrete passageway spread to her left and her right. The right path would take her toward the grocery store at one end of the center. The left path led to the loading docks, the center court, and the movie theater. She turned the door's lock before closing it, hoping it might delay the mannequins for at least a moment, then she ran. The motion made it impossible to hold the light steady, and it flashed across the stained concrete floor and dark chipped walls in erratic bursts.

Scraping, dragging, and creaking noises came from behind her. She tried shining the light over her shoulder, hoping that

would slow them down, but she nearly tripped in the darkness. Doors on either side of her led into different stores; most of them were locked, she knew, and the ones that weren't locked would lead her back to the quiet parts of the center.

The noises were growing closer, becoming louder, echoing off the concrete, and blending with the sound of her slapping feet. She didn't dare stop, but sucked breaths into her dry, sticky lungs as stress and exertion caused a stitch in her side. *Not far now. Just the next left—*

A white shape loomed out of the darkness, filling the hallway she'd been aiming for, and Jodie skidded backward, gasping. Her hands shook almost too badly to hold the light on the mannequin that had taken one of the back ways to block her path.

The loading dock! Get outside, into the parking lot. Run for the center court!

Jodie turned, using her momentum to swing herself down the opposite hallway, toward the loading dock, toward the place her nightmare had started. A flash of lightning ahead told her the doors were open—someone must be waiting for a delivery that night—and she raced for them, barely pausing to breathe. A new sound was building and pressing against her eardrums: torrential rain pounded the asphalt as the storm spent itself over the center.

As she leaped into the vast concrete room, another flash of lightning gave her a split-second view of the parking lot. She couldn't see a single car. The rain was coming at a sharp angle, heavy enough to obscure the trees grown by the ends of the parking rows. Litter, leaves, and even small branches that had

been stripped off the trees whipped across the asphalt, gripped by terrific winds.

Jodie lowered her head as she dashed under the loading dock doorway. Icy rain stung her face, blinding her, clinging to her hair, and slipping down her neck. It drenched her in no time at all, and she struggled to keep up her speed with the wet clothes flapping around her and a stitch digging into her side.

The center was shaped like a boomerang, with the parking lot nestled against the inside curve, and Jodie could see the lights at the opposite end—with the movie theater and food courts—shining through the rain. Trying to block out the sensation that she wasn't running alone, she focused on the light, blinking furiously as the rain dripped into her eyes and plastered her hair across her face.

She no longer tried to control the light from Allie's phone, but it flashed around her as she pumped her arms. For a split second, the light landed on a ghostly shape running abreast of her.

Jodie gasped and keened right, toward where a barrier of shrubs would divide her from the figure. She turned too sharply and skidded on a patch of oil left on the asphalt. Jodie lost her balance as her legs slipped from under her. Then a white shape appeared out of nowhere, striding through the rain, arms extended toward her. Unable to stop her momentum, she collided with the hard ceramic and tasted blood. The arms, colder than the rain, colder than ice, slipped around her in a dead man's embrace.

Just like I caught it on that first day.

She struggled to pull back and worm her way free, but the

grip was like a vice, crushing the air out of her lungs. Jodie raised her head as thunder pealed overhead; the deafening noise sent vibrations through her body. The mannequin's ghastly white face stared down at her, inscrutable in the darkness as rain pinged off its glossy ceramic skin. More shapes were materializing behind it and to either side as the mannequins moved in, surrounding them.

Jodie opened her mouth to scream, and the mannequin pressed a long, frozen finger to her lips as it smiled down at her.

———

Miho jogged through the shopping center, hands thrust into her jacket pockets as she tried to warm herself. She'd become drenched in the short run from her car to the center's doors. It was terrible weather, and the forecast didn't expect it to clear for another day or two.

Their store's doors were still closed, and Miho allowed her jog to slow to a brisk walk. She was late for the morning shift, but by the look of it, so was Jodie. As she fished her keys out of her bag, Miho vaguely wondered if the other woman had woken up as sore as she had.

The shutters slid up into their case with a scraping, grumbling noise. The inside of the store was intact that morning— thankfully—and Miho had settled into her space behind the counter before she realized Jodie had taken the clothes off the mannequins.

Why on earth?

Jodie clearly didn't like the dummies. After all that pressure she'd placed on Mr. Heinlein to buy them, she'd actually seemed quite paranoid since they'd arrived. *So why'd she go to the trouble of stripping their clothes off?*

Miho began picking the items off the floor and re-dressing the mannequins. If she was being completely honest, she wasn't a huge fan of them either. They were always watching her... which was, of course, impossible; they didn't even have eyes. Miho knew that it was meant to be a sign of good art if a painting's eyes followed someone around the room. She wondered if the same principle applied to statues.

She was slinging a sweater over one of the female mannequins when she sensed Jodie standing behind her. Miho swung around, shocked and half laughing as she said, "Jo, you startled me. I didn't hear you come in—"

The words died on her tongue as she faced the figure behind her. It wasn't Jodie, but another mannequin. The face looked remarkably like her friend's, though, almost as if it had been modeled off her. Miho leaned closer, frowning at it, wondering how she hadn't noticed the similarities before.

Then something happened that Miho had no answer or explanation for.

The mannequin blinked.

SUB BASEMENT

"It's your turn," Andrew said as he dropped a sheet of paper onto my desk.

I glanced over the list of names and cursed under my breath. There had to be at least twenty of them. "I could have sworn it was Carlie's turn next."

Andrew gave me a lopsided grin. "Nope, she did the archive run last week. It's tax time, man. Everyone wants their records dug up. You know that."

I glanced around and saw the half dozen employees within hearing distance had stopped their work to listen in on the conversation. Most of them had the decency to swivel back to their computers when I made eye contact, but Tyson, the office joker, took the opportunity to pull out his tie and hold it taut above his head like a noose. I hated Tyson.

"You know how it works," Andrew said. "Take a flashlight and

a jacket, and work fast. There're only twenty-two names here. It shouldn't take you more than half an hour. You'll be done before you know it."

I grudgingly took the list and headed for the elevator.

Everyone hated getting the archive run. It was a trip into the very bottom level of the high-rise to retrieve—or return—files of customers who no longer did business with us. Normally, the visits were infrequent—once every three or four weeks—but over the last month, we'd been inundated with customers wanting details of their canceled accounts so they could lodge tax returns.

I'd only done one archive run before, eight months previously, for two folders, and I had no interest in repeating the experience.

The archive's level wasn't listed on the building's floor plans, but most people called it the Sub Basement. It was permanently dark and icy cold and smelled like rotting paper and plants. Many rumors circulated about the neglected level. Most were probably hyperbolic, but enough had a ring of truth to them to make the Sub Basement a favorite gossip point in the office.

I got into an empty lift and selected the blank button at the bottom of the panel. The carriage held still for a second before beginning its descent. I wiped my sweating palms on my pants and loosened my tie.

"It's no big deal," I told myself. Dozens of people had made the run without seeing anything out of the ordinary. And even when… Well, Joan had suffered from a heart condition, anyway.

The display above the elevator's door listed the levels we were passing. I worked near the top of the building, on the eighteenth

floor. The numbers descended until they read 0—the first basement—then 00—the second basement. The display froze on 00 while the carriage continued to descend into the Sub Basement.

The elevator stopped with a jolt, and the doors slid open. Outside was a long corridor. I could only see as far as the elevator's light penetrated. Beyond that was ink black.

I stepped out and reached to the right. A row of flashlights and waterproof jackets hung from hooks on the concrete wall. I took one of each and turned my light on as the elevator's doors closed.

The Sub Basement's lights had failed four years ago, leaving it in permanent darkness. Management had hired electricians, but the lights couldn't be repaired without drilling into the concrete supports and compromising the stability of the building. Management had promised to put up temporary lights, but somehow, they never made it into the budget.

I shined my light across the walls of the corridor. The concrete was discolored from a steady seepage of water. Carts, the kind used in libraries, stood against the walls. Most were broken. Rust had stained many of them red. Twenty-two folders would be a large armful, but not enough to make me search for a working cart. I hurried past them.

The double door at the end of the hallway used a push handle to open. I pressed on it, but it stuck. I grimaced and rose onto my toes, putting my full weight on the handle, until it scraped down and opened the doors.

The stories about the Sub Basement were copious and of

dubious veracity. Paul from IT told anyone who would listen that it was never supposed to be built, but the construction crew made a mistake when reading the plans. I thought Paul was full of it.

Preeta had said she saw rats the size of small dogs when she was on an archive run. I'm a little more inclined to believe her—she tends to be honest.

The worst were the stories about the five employees who'd quit, each after going on an archive run. Supposedly, they'd asked for their unpaid salary to be mailed to them then walked straight out of the building, not even stopping long enough to clean out their desks or say goodbye.

I'd thought the stories were fiction—until I witnessed it myself. The most recent quitter was Riley, who had worked opposite me. He was a quiet guy, but we'd gotten along well. I'd always thought he was reliable. Steady. Then one afternoon, he went on an archive run and didn't come back. HR told us he had quit. They cleaned out his desk overnight. The rumor mill had a field day.

I moved my flashlight about the Sub Basement, squinting to pick out shapes in the dancing light. To the left were filing boxes stacked nearly to the ceiling. Immediately in front of me and to the right were shelves—nearly a hundred of them—with thousands upon thousands of files.

The air was incredibly cold. I held the flashlight with my teeth and tucked the paper between my knees before slipping into the waterproof jacket. It wouldn't provide much warmth, but at least it would protect me from the drips.

The room was about the size of a soccer field. Most of the files had been accumulated before the company went digital five years previously, and HR didn't have any motivation—or room—to move them to a higher, warmer level. I suspect HR would have found plenty of motivation if they were the ones responsible for archive runs.

The files were divided into three sections—one for each decade the company had been operating—and each decade was arranged alphabetically according to the customer's surname.

My list had the decades handwritten next to the names, and was arranged from most recent to oldest. First up were eight names from the last decade, which would be found in the boxes to the left of the door.

The universal advice was to get in and out of the Sub Basement quickly. The more time people spent there, the wilder their tales became.

Jerome said he believes there's a gas leak with hallucinogenic properties. He has warned every new employee not to light up in the Sub Basement in case it triggered an explosion.

I couldn't smell anything, but that didn't mean he wasn't right.

The first file—ANDERSON, Patricia—was easy to find, and I pulled it out of its box. Something rattled from farther in the room. I froze, listening hard.

Silence.

I exhaled through my teeth and started scanning the names again.

Gregory thought bats had infested the Sub Basement. He'd

supposedly found a nest of them in the corner of the room, but they were blind and deformed, and they'd screamed at him when he got too close.

I found the second and third names together and tugged them both out. I set my small pile on the ground and went to work looking for the fourth name.

Something brushed my ankle, and I jumped back, bumping into the shelves behind me and nearly knocking them over. The flashlight's beam was jittery as I angled it at the ground, but I felt a buzz of relief when I saw the strip of plastic wrap poking out from under the boxes. I must have grazed it.

I moved forward again to continue my search and felt something prickly stick into my neck. I swiped at it. The sensation clung to my hand as I pulled it away and angled my flashlight at it.

A glossy black insect hung on my fingers. It was large and flat, and its body was segmented like a wasp's. Its six legs had hooks that dug into my skin, and large mandibles protruded from its oblong face.

I let out a choked cry of disgust and tried to flick the insect off, but it dug its spiked legs in harder, piercing my skin. Desperate, I slapped the back of my hand against the bookcase, hoping to crush the creature. Its body convulsed on impact, and it dropped to the ground then scuttled under the shelf.

I drew in shallow, ragged breaths as I moved away and brought the flashlight up to examine my hand. The cuts were small, but they stung.

Something on my arm moved at the same time as I became aware of many small objects hanging on to my back. I froze then carefully turned the light toward my arm. One of the insects, larger than the first, clung to my elbow. Further up, another one had latched on to my shoulder.

The flashlight made a dull metallic noise as I dropped it on the concrete ground. I hardly dared breathe as I moved my hands to unhook the waterproof jacket's buttons.

Two of the insects shifted on my back. I squinted my eyes closed as my skin crawled and goose bumps rose on my arms. I unhooked the final button and, in a smooth motion, shrugged out of the jacket, skidded away from it, and scooped up the flashlight and paper at the same time.

I turned the light on the plastic jacket. Two of the insects burrowed into the cloth to hide. I let my breath out and shuddered then ran my hands over my hair, my neck, and my legs to check that I was clear.

They must have fallen on me when I bumped into the shelf. I'd never seen insects that big. *What were they? Wasps? Some sort of cockroach?*

"Work fast," I reminded myself. "Get the folders and leave."

I left the jacket on the ground and went back to my search, being careful not to touch shelves I didn't need to.

The fourth name was hard to find, but the fifth came easily. I took my stack of folders back to the doorway and left them on a dry bit of concrete. No point carrying them about with me.

The next folder I needed was on the other side of the

temporary cardboard filing cases. As I rounded the corner, I saw a kitchen and break room indented into the wall. Next to them was a door leading to the bathroom. Each floor, including the Sub Basement, had its own amenities.

Hanna loved to tell the story of how she'd needed to use the bathroom while on an archive run. The details seemed to get embellished with each retelling, but she did have the cuts on her legs to show for it.

I made quick work of the next three folders and put them on the stack next to the door. The fourth one was misfiled, and I had to crouch to search for it. Something cold and wet landed on the back of my neck, and I jerked back, frightened the insects had returned.

It was some sort of slime. I scraped it off the back of my neck to examine it. It was clear and thicker than water, but not quite jelly, like dense saliva, only icy cold.

I thought I heard rattling above me and pointed my flashlight toward the ceiling. Like the ground and walls, it was discolored, but I didn't see anything that could account for the drips. The slimy sensation on my hands made me feel nauseous. I didn't want to wipe it on my pants, and there was nowhere else I could clean myself—except the bathroom.

"Damn," I whispered. "Damn, damn, damn."

I nudged the door open and took a moment to shine my light over the insides. It was very similar to the bathrooms on the higher floors. Directly in front of me were three sinks, each with their own soap pump. At the back of the room was a hand towel

dispenser. To the right were four stalls with tall, dark-gray doors, all closed. The walls and floor were tile, while the ceiling was the same concrete as the rest of the floor.

Unlike the higher levels, the Sub Basement's bathroom was falling apart. Many of the tiles were cracked, and fungus and mold grew in the crevices. Dark stains ran down the sink bowls, toward the drains. The trash was overflowing with decaying paper towels, and the glass mirror above the sinks was clouded with age, showing a blurred imitation of the stalls behind it.

I placed my flashlight on the corner of one of the sinks. It reflected off the tiles, providing modest illumination for the room.

I went to the paper towels first, intending to blot off the ooze. The front of the dispenser was cracked open, as though something large had been rammed into it, and towels spilled out of the top. I pulled at one of them, but it fell apart between my fingers.

The air was too damp; moisture had gotten into the towels and rotted them during the five years the Sub Basement had been unoccupied. I grimaced and turned to the taps. I chose the sink with the least discoloration and turned the tap on. Grinding and shuddering rose from under the tiles at my feet, and I jumped back. The whole room sounded alive at that moment, filled with echoes of noise as long-unused pipes were forced to carry water.

Dark-red liquid spat out of the tap, splashing over the edge of the sink as it burst out of its pipes.

"It's just rust," I told myself, trying to slow my heart rate. "Nothing to be frightened of."

The red water flowed for nearly a minute before it became

clear. I waited until there was no trace of discoloration then dunked my slime-coated hand under the flow. The water must have been near freezing; my skin smarted wherever it touched, and I pulled my hand away as soon as it was clean.

I glanced into the mirror and jolted back. One of the stall doors stood wide open. I could have sworn they were all closed when I'd come into the bathroom, but it stood ajar, exposing a broken toilet inside.

The pipes below me increased their noise to a scream, and the water flowing from the tap reduced to a trickle then began to spew something thick and inky black into the sink.

I turned off the tap, but the liquid kept coming. It poured out in globs that contained something strangely brittle, like decayed plant matter, and painted the sink black. An oily, metallic smell rose from it, making me gag, and stuck in my nose even when I held my breath.

The gunk was too thick to drain quickly. The sink filled and began to overflow, and I stepped back to avoid the splatter. The pipes below my feet wailed and screeched, then abruptly, they fell silent. The thick black flow reduced to a drip.

I glanced around the room.

All four stall doors were open.

I grabbed my light and left the room—not quite running, but not loitering either.

Once I'd put a dozen paces between myself and the bathroom, I stopped and rubbed at my eyes with my spare hand. It was shaking.

Finish the job quickly. Ignore any distractions. Ten more minutes, and you'll be out of here.

I found the misfiled folder and put it on the stack by the door. I examined the list and found that I'd finished with the most recent section. The next batch of files would be in the tall wooden shelves.

My task became more difficult then. The boxes had been filed alphabetically, but the shelves only collected the first letters together, forcing me to flip through whole bundles to find the correct name. Frustration built in my stomach. I had fourteen names left—there was no way I would finish quickly.

The Sub Basement was freezing. My breath clouded in front of my face as I muttered names to myself. Occasionally, I thought I heard words being muttered back at me from across the room, but whenever I stopped to listen, it fell silent.

Jenna had said she'd heard people talking to her. The voices sounded like old men, and when she'd gone searching for the source, she'd found letters scratched into one of the walls. Other employees said they'd looked for the scratchings but hadn't been able to find them.

The stack of files by the door grew slowly. By the time I'd found the second-to-last name, I must have been in the Sub Basement for nearly an hour.

I was breathing hard from the repetitive crouching and stretching and shivering from the cold—but I only had one name left: PERRICK, Clarissa.

She was in a category of her own—the '60s to '70s decade.

Why she would want her records more than fifty years after she'd done business with us was beyond me.

I paced up and down the shelves as I looked for her section, but the records seemed to go back only as far as 1970. *Did Andrew make a mistake on the decade beside her name?*

Then I found the door hidden at the back of the room. It was tall and metal, with a push lever on the front, just like at the entrance to the Sub Basement. A faded plaque at the top read *Archives 1960–1970*.

"Hell," I whispered.

I dropped the four files onto the stack I'd collected at the entrance to the Sub Basement. I was tempted to return to the office without the last folder and claim I couldn't find it, but I knew management would be ruthless. Clarissa Perrick wanted her records, so she was going to get her records one way or another. They would either send me back down or send someone in my place—and that was a fast way to become unpopular in the office.

I returned to the door, rubbed my hands across my face, then pressed down on the lever. The door ground open, its hinges wailing, and brilliantly cold air blew through the gap.

I held the flashlight in front of myself as I crept through the doorway. My ears suddenly filled with the clang of my shoes on metal as the concrete flooring ended. Beyond the door was a staircase—not one of the solid, enclosed concrete ones, but a rusted metal fixture that had been screwed onto the wall. I pointed my flashlight over the railing, but the light wasn't strong

enough to bring the floor below into relief. All I could make out were some shelves and what looked like a lounge area.

"Damn it," I whispered. "A basement below the Sub Basement." No one from the office had said anything about another level.

I moved with intense caution, brushing one hand against the wall to my left and swinging the light across the steps in front of my feet. Ten steps down, the railing to my right disappeared. Where it ended was bent, as though someone had torn off a section. I moved closer to the wall.

Another five steps, and I nearly slipped. The metal slats had been dry up to that point, but some type of slime, unnervingly similar to what had dripped onto the back of my neck, coated the rest. I slowed down even more, placing each foot with painstaking care. A little farther on, the slime developed on the wall. It felt strangely warm under my fingers, and I recoiled in disgust. I became aware of the stench of organic decay. The farther down the stairs I went, the stronger it became, until it felt as if it were coating my tongue.

I reached the concrete floor and stopped to catch my breath. My fingers were shaking as I loosened my tie to allow for easier breathing. The room wasn't as large as the floor above had been, but it was deep. I angled my light up the stairs and could barely make out the top. I turned slowly, bringing shapes into focus with the narrow beam of my flashlight, and gazed into the room with sick fascination.

Shelves, much like in the room above, stood in two straight rows through the center of the room. Two of the closer ones

had fallen over like dominoes, the first propped up by a couch. Folders and pieces of paper had fallen out of it and were scattered across the floor.

I turned my flashlight over the mess. Many of the files had rotted in the dampness, but the ones toward the top were still mostly intact. Typewritten titles such as "Case 2461" and "Case 9330" were displayed on the front. I nudged one of the folders open with my shoe and instantly recoiled.

Inside was a black-and-white photograph of a disfigured man. He was missing both eyes, and where his nose should have been was a black hole. An open mouth showed badly deformed teeth. To either side of him, two doctors—passive, expressionless, and dressed in white lab coats—held the man still with a hand on each of his arms.

I shuddered as I turned away.

To the left of the shelves were couches. I skipped my light over them in morbid fascination. They were badly decayed, sagging and rotting—probably the cause of the stench.

Several had large stains on them. The discoloration was spread across the backrest and concentrated on the cushions below, almost as if…

No, I told myself. *No, not as if people had been left to rot in the seats. That's a dangerous way to be thinking. Find the folder, and get out.*

I moved between the shelves, looking for the familiar customer folder markings, but they were all numbers. "Case 0058," "Case 4902." No names.

"Damn it, where are you, Clarissa?"

I panned my light across the walls, looking for any bookcases or filing cabinets I might have missed. Paintings had been glued to the wall opposite me, creating a haphazard patchwork of color. They depicted strange faces and distorted shapes.

I was close to giving up when my light passed over a door at the back of the room. Bronze signs were posted above it.

Respite Rooms
Pharmacy
Conditioning Rooms
Brightwater Accountants—Archive

I chewed on the inside of my cheek. I'd thought the whole building belonged to Brightwater. *Maybe another business worked in the basement levels at one time.*

Perhaps the company's owner, Paul Brightwater, had rented the basement when he started his business then bought the entire building later on. That would explain why the file for Clarissa Perrick, one of Brightwater's first customers, was squirreled away in the nightmarish sub-sub-basement.

I glanced back at the numbered files and the rotting couches then pushed through the metal door. A long corridor with multiple doors stretched in front of me. I moved carefully, swinging my light to check the plaques above each doorway. The doors were old, many of the hinges were rusted, and the glass panes set in the front were blurry from accumulated dust and grease.

I peered through the window of the first door I passed, labeled *Respite Rooms*. Beyond it was another long hallway with many doors of its own. Medical trays were left abandoned along the walls. The window was too blurry to offer a clear view, but I thought I glimpsed movement near the back of the hallway. I paused, holding my flashlight still, but I couldn't see anything else.

My curiosity wasn't strong enough to make me linger, so I quickened my pace as I passed the other passageways. *Brightwater Accountants* was the last door to the left. I paused in the entryway and moved my flashlight over the room. It was a small office with a bare, defunct bulb hanging from the ceiling and age stains across the walls. A cheap desk sat to one side with two broken chairs opposite it. Behind the desk was a filing cabinet, which I hurried to and opened eagerly.

"Come on, Clarissa Perrick, where are you?" I muttered to myself. I checked under P and felt sick when I found only four files there, none of them belonging to Clarissa.

I'd come too far to turn back empty-handed. I checked under C, in case she had accidentally been filed under her first name. When I didn't find her there, I began to rifle through the other folders, desperate and frustrated.

She wasn't there. I slammed the drawer closed in a fit of anger and froze as the slamming noise echoed back at me from the hallway. I moved to the office door and shined my light down the length of the hallway. It was empty, but the door at the end was closed.

My breath whistled as I let it out through clenched teeth and

began jogging for the door. *To hell with Brightwater and their missing files. They'll have to do without.*

I pushed the door's handle to open it. It stuck in place. I pushed harder, then pulled, jiggled the handle, and pressed my entire weight on it.

It didn't budge. I'd been locked in.

My flashlight beam jittered over the walls as I turned and looked down the hallway. *Had the door locked itself, like they did in some hospitals? Was there a button to open it again?*

No, no button. I found only stained concrete walls, stained concrete floor, and blank metal doors with fogged glass.

I knelt beside the door and tried to slow my breathing while I thought. They'll come looking for me if I'm down here for too long. *Just like they'd searched for Joan…*

I cringed and pressed my sweating palms against my eyelids. I would never forget the moment they brought Joan out of the Sub Basement. Nearly everyone from my floor had stayed late as we waited for news. We'd congregated outside the lifts, talking in hushed voices as police and emergency workers swarmed through the building.

The lights above the only elevator that went to the Sub Basement lit up. We pushed forward, eager to see Joan, ask her what had gone wrong, and possibly hear a new tale of the macabre firsthand. But the elevator doors opened, and all that came out were four rescue workers and a sheet-covered body on a gurney.

She'd had heart problems, I reminded myself. *You're young and fit, and they'll find you.*

Eventually.

I stood up. There was another option. Health and Safety codes meant that every building above a certain size had to have two exits for each floor. There was another way out.

I started down the hallway. The room at the end, Brightwater's office, was a dead end. So was the pharmacy, which was missing its door. I glanced inside but didn't linger—every drawer and cupboard was open and empty.

The door to the conditioning rooms was locked. That left the respite rooms.

The handle creaked when I pressed on it, but it opened, granting me access to the long hallway of abandoned medical carts and closed doors.

I shined my light at the first door to my left. Through the blurred glass, I was able to make out a metal examination table. Leather straps were draped over its dulled surface, and the concrete floor was stained.

The following four doors all led to bedrooms. They had identical accommodations: plain, rusted metal bed frames held mattresses in varying stages of decay. A chair and a bedpan sat neatly against the walls. A single hand-painted sheet of paper hung above each of the beds—two had nature scenes, one was abstract splotches of color, and one depicted a face with no eyes.

The hallway turned a corner. As I walked, I became aware of a noise behind me. It sounded almost like shuffling, stuttering steps on the concrete floor. I froze. As though it were a switch being turned, the noise stopped.

An echo? I held my breath and scuffed my shoe across the ground. It made a dull thumping noise. No echo.

I started walking again. The noise was gone, but a horrible feeling of dread had taken its place. I walked faster and faster, and the flashlight's beam jittered erratically in front of me as I broke into a sprint. I didn't bother stopping to look into the rooms I passed—I just wanted to get out of there.

I rounded another corner, and the hallway ended in a double door, just like the entryway to the Sub Basement. Sweat trickled down the back of my neck even as the icy air coaxed plumes of condensation out of my breath. I was shivering almost too severely to keep the light steady as I pressed my face against the cold metal door and peered through the glass window.

It was too blurred for me to see anything. I flexed my shoulders, took a deep breath, and pushed the handle down. The door opened, and I could have laughed from relief. A landing stretched for a few feet ahead of me. Beyond that, stairs led upward.

Then I raised my flashlight and saw the rubble.

There had been a cave-in, probably a long time ago, from how settled it looked. Slabs of concrete, natural rock, bricks, and dirt mingled in a pile partway up the stairs, effectively blocking the exit.

I ran my hand over my mouth. *I might still be able to dig my way through. If the rubble isn't too deep, I could shift enough to get past it, get back to the Sub Basement, take the lift up to the eighteenth floor, and hand in my resignation, just like all of the other souls who quit after doing a Basement Run.*

The entire area was smothered in thick dust. I shrugged out of my jacket and tried to find somewhere clean to hang it. Eventually, I slung it over a metal support that stuck out from the broken wall.

I began climbing the rubble, moving slowly and testing each foothold to make sure it was solid. I hadn't gone more than a few steps when I noticed something strange—other footprints marred the dust. They were fainter than mine and belonged to smaller shoes. Someone had been there before me.

I crouched down to get a closer look at the print. I guessed it belonged to a woman's shoe, and, although it had left a clear imprint in the half-inch-thick layer of grime, fresh sheets of dust softened its appearance. It was old.

Maybe the owner of this print had been faced by the same obstacle as me but gotten through? I followed the tracks up the collapsed stairwell, turning my light backward and forward over the debris to follow the progress of the scuffed footprints and occasional smudge from where a hand had been used.

Near the top of the pile, the tracks stopped. I looked for a gap in the debris and held up my hand to feel for a breeze, but the way was clearly blocked. I sat down on a slab of concrete and evaluated my situation.

To my right, a strange shape leaned against the wall. I jerked backward in shock and turned my flashlight toward it.

Coiled up in the corner, leaning against the wall and holding a folder tightly to its chest, was a human body. At first, I thought it was a skeleton, but it still had skin, dried and stretched tight

across the bones after months of exposure to the icy air. Its eye sockets were empty, and its mouth was open, exposing a shriveled tongue and discolored teeth. Dirty blond hair lay in limp coils on its shoulders. I looked more closely at its clothes, and a horrible sick feeling surged through me as I recognized our office uniform.

The clue to the body's identity was the shoes: leather, with red buckles. Only one person in the office had worn shoes like that.

Joan.

I thought I was going to be sick. I ran my hands over my face as I tried to slow my racing heart. *This thing crouched in the corner can't be Joan. We all saw her carried out of the lift.*

That wasn't true, though. We'd seen *something* carried out on a stretcher, but the cloth had never been lifted. She'd had a closed-coffin funeral too.

I wiped my hands across my eyes, smudging away tears and leaving dust in its place. *If Joan came this far before giving up…*

Her bony hands were clamped over a plain manila folder. I had a terrible premonition of what it would contain, and I leaned forward just far enough to reach it. Without disturbing Joan's body, I pulled the folder's corner back to expose the name inside:

PERRICK, Clarissa

I slumped back, resting against the concrete block, a bitter taste permeating my mouth. Cold dust billowed around me, prickling my skin and irritating my eyes. I let out my breath in a long heave, watching it make the dust swirl.

Something on the other side of the door imitated my

exhalation. I scuttled back, my heart thumping, as something large and dark reached up to scratch at the foggy glass.

———

Andrew, arms crossed over his chest, listened to Thompson's speech as he leaned against Matt's desk. It had been cleared during the night.

"Yes, sadly, Matt handed in his resignation yesterday afternoon," Thompson said. He turned his head slowly to survey the gathered staff. "He was an excellent worker, and we wish him all the best in his future career. We understand it will leave a hole in this team, but we hope to hire a replacement within the week. Thank you."

The murmurs started immediately.

"I can't believe it," Madison said. "I thought he loved this job. I had no idea he was thinking about leaving."

"You know what this means, don't you?" Jacob said. "This is the sixth person who's left after a Basement Run. There's something not right down there. You know, during my last trip I—"

Andrew tuned out the chatter as a heavy hand landed on his shoulder. He turned to see Thompson beaming at him. "Andrew, right? I have a job for you. You see, when Matt was fetching the folders on Friday, he missed one—Clarissa Perrick. I can trust you to find it for us, can't I?"

"Sure thing."

THE WATCHER

It was a bad night to do the challenge. The thin crescent moon kept slipping behind the clouds, and a harsh wind tugged dying leaves off the trees and sent them skittering across the driveway. Jasmine got out of the van she'd been forced into and pulled her dressing gown tightly around her body. They'd parked in a large clearing that bordered a nature reserve, and banks of tall pine trees rose above them, making long shadows across the grass. They'd passed a home, its lights off and curtains drawn, farther up the driveway, but it was no longer in sight. Jasmine had seen a sign for a second in the van's headlights, but she hadn't been able to read it properly. *Trucket Pros and The Artical,* or something like that.

An animal cried in the woods, and another creature answered almost immediately. As her eyes adjusted to the dark, Jasmine began to make out details of her surroundings. The clearing was

about twenty feet wide and surrounded by trees on all sides. To the left was some sort of shed, teetering on the edge of a steep incline into a gully. The shed looked like a lighthouse sitting on the brink of a cliff, and the wildly swaying trees were the waves threatening to submerge it. To the right was an open workshop. Rusty saws and axes glittered in the thin moonlight.

Her masked companion got out of the van's driver's seat. "Down toward the shed," she instructed, and Jasmine reluctantly obeyed.

She was halfway there before she saw the three other hooded people standing in the shed's shadow. Like her companion, they wore thick black robes that trailed on the ground behind them. The hoods were drawn up over their hair, and blank white masks covered their faces.

"Welcome, friend," the middle figure said, and Jasmine recognized Erin's voice. Erin was the leader of the group and had probably planned the evening's entertainment.

"Hello," Jasmine said stupidly, hugging her body and shivering.

Erin stretched out her gloved hands, palms upward, and raised her masked face toward the sky. "We have brought you here tonight for a test of bravery. Pass, and you will be welcomed into our order. Fail, and you will leave disgraced."

The figure to Erin's left giggled nervously, but a glare from her companion quickly silenced her. The giggle gave away her identity, though. Only Hannah laughed like that.

They were piling on the dramatics, and Jasmine had to admit, it was working. The cloaks, the masks, and the remote location were making her skin crawl. She'd never been good at

handling fear. She hated horror movies and still occasionally had nightmares from a haunted house amusement ride her parents had taken her on as a child. *Of all the challenges they could have planned, they had to pick bravery, huh? Just my luck.*

Erin, who seemed to be getting a kick out of Jasmine's fear, raised her voice. "The rules are simple. When the bell tolls midnight, you will step into the Watching Room." She indicated the shed to Jasmine's left. "When the bell tolls one, you may come out. There is a window in the shed. As long as you are inside, you must be the Watcher and stare through the glass. If you look away from the window, you fail. If you turn the light on, you fail. If you leave the room before the bell's toll, you fail." She paused, letting the silence stretch out, then continued in a quieter voice. "But if you can watch for the full hour, you will have proven your courage, and your initiation will be complete. Do you understand?"

"Yes," Jasmine said, trying to smile. She wished they wouldn't make such a big deal of it. When Erin had told her she would need to pass an initiation to be a part of their book club, she'd assumed it would be an embarrassing prank or maybe a small act of vandalism. Erin had never given so much as a hint that she was interested in the cultish, horror-fueled test of bravery she'd established.

Jasmine looked at the three silent figures beside Erin. She'd gotten on well with them before, but it was so much harder to talk with them when they wore masks. "Did you all have to pass too?"

"Yep," Hannah said proudly before Erin could glare her into silence. "Even Erin did it."

"It was ages ago, though," the person to Erin's right added, and the accent told Jasmine it was Tasha. That meant the fourth figure, the one who'd driven her there, was Mel.

"We did it when we were kids," Hannah said. "This place has hardly changed, though."

"Some things never change," Erin said, making her voice low and ominous.

Jasmine could tell she'd been waiting for an opening for her story.

"Things like the Stalker."

Mel shivered under her cloak, and Hannah let out another nervous laugh.

Erin walked forward and began circling Jasmine with slow, ponderous steps, her feet scraping through the dead leaves. "The Stalker has lived in these woods for longer than anyone can remember. They say it's a horrible monster, half bat and half human, that drags its live prey deep into the forest to consume. It's often been seen from the window in the Watching Room as it stalks its victims."

Hannah's giggles became higher and more sporadic. She was really, truly frightened, Jasmine realized.

"Your job as the Watcher is to watch for the Stalker," Erin continued. "If you see it, don't look away. The Stalker won't attack as long as you keep your eyes on it, but as soon as you turn to run..." She drew her gloved finger across her throat in a slow

sweep then leaned forward to whisper into Jasmine's ear: "Don't look away."

What the hell sort of hazing is this? Jasmine rubbed at her arms as goose bumps rose over them. *I'm trying to join a book club, not a cult.*

She knew Erin was trying to scare her, and she was a little ashamed to admit it was working. The animal chattering from the gully was taking on a new dimension. The calls, the wails, and even the rustling of the leaves raised Jasmine's heart rate. *What would a Stalker sound like?*

The clamor of nature was suddenly interrupted by a deep, melodic boom. The town hall bell, the sound of which traveled across the woods, was announcing midnight.

"It's time," Erin said.

She, Hannah, and Tasha began walking up the driveway, leaving Mel to pull a large, ornate metal key out of her pocket and unlock the shed's door.

"I'll see you in an hour, I guess," Jasmine said, trying to inject some lightness into her voice. "Let's hope the Stalker doesn't show up, huh?"

The lock clicked, and Mel put the key back into her pocket. The town hall's bell was still ringing, blending with the noise from the gully.

"It's real, you know." She reached up to pull her mask over her hood. Her round face was flushed and sweaty, but her dark eyes were serious. "I know you think it's something Erin made up, but it's not. It's a local urban legend. There are stories about the

Stalker from when the town was being settled. You're new here, so you wouldn't have seen them, but the newspaper sometimes runs articles on it too."

"What?"

"Just thought you should know," Mel said, and Jasmine caught a glimpse of a wicked grin before the mask was lowered back into place. The town hall finished its twelfth chime, leaving the air saturated with its echoes, somehow heavier from the oppressive silence. Mel placed a hand on the wooden door and pressed it open. "In you go."

Jasmine could feel her fingers shaking, but she couldn't turn back. She'd been spending time with the four women for over a month, and when Erin had invited her to join their club, which they'd apparently started as children, she knew she would do anything it took to be included...even spending an hour as a Watcher.

She stepped over the threshold of the shed, and the door clicked shut behind her. Mel didn't lock it, though, and Jasmine was grateful.

The shed was completely empty and felt larger than it had looked from the outside. Wooden floors met wooden walls, which, in turn, disappeared into a wooden ceiling draped with spiderwebs. Erin had said there was a window, but that wasn't strictly true. Jasmine felt a swell of fear rise through her as she faced a wall made entirely out of glass.

There were no supports and no metal bars to segment the pane. It stretched seamlessly from the left wall to the right, and

from her slippers to five feet above her head. As she stepped up to the window, she felt as though she might be sucked through it and into the forest beyond.

The view would have been stunning at any other time, but that night, it was like something out of her nightmares. The incline dropped away from the edge of the shed, creating a slope of grass splattered with underbrush and scrappy weeds. The clearing rushed to blend with the claustrophobic woods beyond. It was a mess of shadows, where spears of moonlight and gashes of darkness mixed and fought for dominance, dancing and darting as the wind threw the trees' branches about with ecstatic abandon.

The sounds bled through the gaps in the shed wall. She could hear the calls of small mammals, the rasping chatter of bats, and a bleat from deep in the woods that rose in pitch before abruptly cutting off.

Jasmine struggled with herself, fighting to keep her feet planted where they were and to get her breathing under control as gnawing anxiety made her legs weak and her fingers shake.

Don't lose, she told herself. *Don't let their stories get into your head. This is fine. You're safe. Nothing can get in here.*

She felt vulnerable, though, exposed by that window, as though she could fall through it at any moment, to be dragged away by the Stalker.

There's no such thing as a Stalker! Even her internal voice sounded panicked. Jasmine closed her eyes for a moment then forced them open again. Erin and her friends were probably

making sure she didn't look away. They might have hidden a camera somewhere in the corner of the room, or they could have been in the woods at that moment, watching and laughing as she trembled, alone, in the shed.

Something moved between the trees, and Jasmine's heart skipped a beat. She focused on it, trying to make out the shape among the mess of shadows and plants. Some sort of animal sent up a chatter, a harsh *cht-cht-cht-cht*.

She tried to guess how long she'd been in the shed, but time felt unstable there, as if it passed differently in the outside world. She thought that at least half an hour had gone by, though. Her feet were starting to get tired. The wind picked up a notch, and the shed creaked, making a laborious sound that started to her right and traveled over the roof.

More movement appeared among the trees, though it might have just been a trick of the light. She scanned the scene, letting her eyes linger over the darkest parts, trying to identify shapes. A rock a little way down the gully looked as though it had eyes. Jasmine stared at it then smothered a shriek as it moved.

The rock wasn't a rock after all, but a creature hunched on the ground, watching her intently. It rose to a half crouch and began creeping up the gully.

All of her false confidence left her. She would have run if her legs hadn't been drained of their energy.

It can't be real, her mind insisted as she struggled to draw breath, watching the creature slink closer to her window. *It's got to be an animatronic or a special effect or…or a costume.*

She remembered the sign that had been nearly hidden by the trees at the head of the driveway, and the correct words came to her instantly: *Truskett's Prosthetics and Theatrical Makeup.*

Erin's surname was Truskett, but her parents lived near the town center. *This property must belong to an uncle or a grandfather, then. Someone who makes theater costumes and does makeup. Erin's resourceful. Of course she'd take full advantage of her relative's craft to make tonight an event I'll never forget. Why just talk about a Stalker when you can make one appear?*

This knowledge was like a rush of warm water. No wonder Erin had been so insistent that Jasmine not look away from the window. They didn't want her to miss a second of their elaborate fright fest. *Better luck next time, Erin.*

Jasmine tried to smile, but her face felt frozen. She was certain the thing in the gully was one of her friends dressed in an elaborate costume, but fear continued to crawl across her skin, itching at her back and making her feel sick. The monster in the gully was creeping closer, keeping its body low to the ground, its yellow eyes fixed on Jasmine's.

Don't look away.

It was entirely gray and wore no clothes. She couldn't imagine any of the friends stripping naked for a prank, so she guessed it was a monster bodysuit. *The yellow contacts would have been a pain to put in. They've really put a lot of effort into this.*

She would have been impressed with some quick makeup, maybe a wig and some tattered clothes—but the creature was above and beyond. It even moved animalistically, using all four

limbs to creep up the steep incline, its body twisting lithely. She could swear she saw the spine writhe under its skin.

"That's enough," she whispered. "Please, no more."

As if it could hear her, the creature turned, leaving its course, and circled the building. She watched it until it disappeared from view.

Her chest ached from the stress. Her heart was thundering, and her body was sticky with sweat under her dressing gown. She tried to swallow and found her throat was dry. *Please let that be it,* she begged. *I want this hour to be over already.*

A scream, shrill and inhuman, came from behind her. Jasmine jumped and shrieked herself, and it took all of her resolve to stay facing the glass wall. *You're the Watcher. Watch the window. Don't turn around, or you fail.*

The scream became raw, thick with terror, then it ended abruptly.

"Don't let them scare you. You're stronger than this." Jasmine reached up and rubbed the tears off her cheek. She'd never felt fear so intensely. "They're trying their best to make you leave, but you're going to win."

The silence stretched out. Jasmine kept her eyes on the woods below, following the rules to the letter. Her chest ached, and her limbs shook as she stood, watching the flickering shadows and swaying trees in the gully.

Then a deep, melodic boom came from the town. Her hour was up.

"I did it." She finally turned and stumbled toward the door,

her relief and exhilaration battling with her still-present fear. "I did it."

She opened the door, hoping for cheers and welcoming hugs, but the clearing was empty. Jasmine scanned the edges of the wood, looking for movement. *They must have gone to wait back at the house. Jeez, you'd think they'd be a little bit more considerate after what they put me through.*

She started walking and tripped over a dark shape at the foot of the shed. She screamed and landed in the dirt then pushed back quickly to see what she'd fallen over.

Erin lay on her front, her head twisted up to stare in horror at the crescent moon. Her face was painted white with dark patches drawn about her eyes. Plastic fangs peeked over her bottom lip, just above a dribble of blood.

A vampire. Erin's interpretation of half human and half bat. Jasmine's brain sluggishly put the pieces together as she sat on the ground, too shocked and frightened to move. *She must have been waiting for me to leave when the hour ended.*

Then she heard the noise, a *chk-chk-chk-chk*, from the opposite end of the clearing. Jasmine raised her eyes and saw it creep out from the trees. Its leathery gray skin slid over angular bones as it paced toward her, its body moving fluidly, its harsh yellow eyes fixed on hers.

Don't look away.

THE MALLORY
HAUNTING

THE MALLORYS' RESIDENCE DIDN'T LOOK LIKE A STEREOTYPICAL haunted house. The two-story brick building sat in the middle of suburbia, and the garden was full of freshly planted shrubs and green trees. A young, dark-haired woman opened the door when I knocked. "Can I help you?"

"Hi, I'm Cheryl White, ghost hunter. Paul Mallory called me about a spirit problem."

The woman's face lit up. "Oh, of course! I'm Anne, Paul's wife. Please come in."

In the sparsely decorated foyer, boxes were stacked into corners, waiting to be unpacked.

"When Paul booked the appointment, he mentioned you'd moved recently."

"That's right, we've only had this place for a few weeks. Excuse the mess; Paul hasn't finished unpacking, I'm afraid."

Anne led me into the kitchen and indicated that I could put my case of equipment on the table. Like the hallway, the kitchen was only partially unpacked. "Would you mind if I asked why you moved here?"

Anne let her breath out with a whistle. "Actually, the move was long overdue. We'd been staying with Paul's extended family. They had a large property up in the Blue Mountains and invited us to live with them after we got married—to save costs, you know? Then there was a death in the family, and Paul said he wanted to move out. We needed a fresh start, so we came out here."

I clicked open my case and pulled out my notebook. "How soon after you moved did the spirit disturbances start?"

Anne laughed. It was a rich, throaty noise. "You'd better talk to Paul about the ghosts. To be honest, I haven't had a problem with them. It's all focused on Paul. He's in the back garden, doing some work with Steven. Head on out there whenever you're ready. I've got a few chores to finish before the fun begins."

As Anne had promised, I found Paul in the backyard garden, planting a sapling with the help of another man. I cleared my throat as I approached, and they both startled.

"Damn," Paul said, wiping his hands and jogging up to greet me. "Sorry about that. You must be Cheryl, right? I wasn't expecting you until later."

I shook his hand and smiled. "I finished my morning job early."

That was a white lie. No one had hired me for a legitimate job in nearly a fortnight; funds were tight, and I was eager to start a

new case. If I was lucky, the Mallory house might have a genuine haunting, which would require multiple sessions of contact before we could make a decision about expelling or appeasing the spirit.

"Well," Paul said, "I'm glad you're here. I hope you don't mind, but I asked Steven to stay overnight, in case things get hairy. We used to be neighbors."

"Not a problem. Now, why don't you tell me what's been happening?"

Paul gave me detailed descriptions of the paranormal events he'd experienced as he led me through the building. "Sometimes, late at night, lights will turn on and off in the hallway—and for three nights in a row now, the door of the dresser in the corner has opened and slammed closed. It always happens late at night, regardless of whether I'm in bed or not."

I examined the dresser, opening both doors and bumping them gently to see if gravity or a breeze could be to blame. To my delight, the doors were heavy and stuck on their hinges. Slamming either of them would require force. If the event repeated itself that night, it would be substantial proof of a haunting.

"Curtains open and close themselves through the day," Paul continued. "The first time it happened, I thought someone had broken in—how else would the curtains be opened during the eight hours the house is empty? But nothing was stolen, and it happened again, day after day, until it became a regular occurrence."

"Have you heard any voices or unaccountable noises?" I asked.

"Yeah, if I wake up in the middle of the night, I'll sometimes hear noises in other parts of the house," Paul said, grimacing. "I'm pretty sure I heard singing last week. But I've searched the house countless times, and I can never find anything."

I jotted details in my notebook. "Well, that's plenty to start with. Let's get some equipment set up."

———

Paul and Steven stood behind me as I fiddled with the audio settings on my laptop. Anne sat in the bay window with a book, apparently content to watch from a distance.

I'd set up a temporary surveillance area in the spare bedroom—one of the few parts of the house where Paul hadn't experienced paranormal events—to monitor the cameras, audio recorders, and EMF devices I'd arranged throughout the house.

The equipment was my pride and joy. Not only did it look impressively complicated, but I'd also caught some amazing stuff on it.

Everything fed back to the laptop. Its split screen carried footage from four cameras I'd set up: one in the master bedroom, one in the kitchen, one in the living room, and one in the hallway. It also recorded audio from six microphones, and a bar along the bottom showed EMF readings from the hallway.

"We're ready." I plugged the final cable into the splitter. "The rest is up to your ghost."

Paul knelt next to me. "What should we look for?"

"Ghosts manifest in a range of styles. Some are white

mists—like a reverse shadow. Some look like glowing orbs. Others are transparent versions of their human forms, and if they're strong enough, they can even manifest to look exactly like they did when they were living."

―――――――――

The night dragged on. I stayed alert, watching the monitors, while Paul and Steven alternated between chatting and sitting in silence, and Anne dozed in the corner. Every few hours, I got up and inspected the house.

Sometimes, spirits will manifest for me but refuse to show themselves on cameras or to anyone else in the room. They can be fickle like that, so checking each room in person can pay off.

Our night of ghost hunting was a complete failure.

Dawn broke just before six, and I had nothing to show for my vigilance. The EMF meter had stayed dead, and I hadn't seen or heard a single thing that could be considered paranormal.

I was disappointed on so many levels. With the number of events Paul claimed had occurred in his house, I'd been convinced we would see something. It also meant I would have no repeat visits to the house—and very little chance of a referral. Who wants a ghost hunter who couldn't find the ghost?

Anne tapped me on the shoulder as I shut down the computer. "It's been a long night. I'm heading off to bed. Sorry we didn't see anything."

She slipped out of the room before I could reply, leaving me with Paul and Steven. They looked exhausted.

I hid my dissatisfaction and tried to offer some comforting parting words. "Just because we didn't see a spirit, doesn't mean there isn't one here. They can tell when they're being watched, and sometimes, they'll hide. There's some good news, though—the events you've described lead me to believe your spirit is harmless. Friendly, even."

"I guess that's something," Paul said as he helped me carry my equipment to the car. "But if I'm being honest, I'd be happier if it weren't happening at all."

"I'm sure." I felt both exhausted and disheartened but put on a cheerful smile for Paul's sake. "Sorry I couldn't be more help, but thank you for the opportunity to investigate your home. I'll mail you my invoice next week."

"No problem. Thanks for coming out."

"Say goodbye to Anne for me."

Paul froze at my words. "How do you know about Anne?"

I was confused. "What do you—"

"She's the reason I moved out of my old place." His voice was shaky with still-fresh grief. "Anne died last month."

CRAWLSPACE

THERE'S A TINY DOOR IN MY ROOM.

It's been covered with hideous blue-patterned wallpaper, but I can still see the outline of its frame and the little bump where the keyhole sits. It's only about two feet high and just as wide.

It's probably just a pokey storage hole.

I bet I could fit into it if I tried.

———

It was our first day in the new house. My parents were downstairs, fighting over how much to unpack. Dad was a borderline hoarder, but at least he was an efficient one. He believed that leaving most of our belongings in boxes would make it easier for next time we moved. We had at least a dozen cartons that were sealed nine years ago, when I was still too young to appreciate the insanity of his logic.

Mum also had hoarderish tendencies, but she preferred to have her clutter on display, decorating the house like her personal thrift shop. I was the polar opposite—anything that wasn't absolutely necessary for our comfort or survival could be thrown out. I didn't even have much furniture, just a bed, a wardrobe, a desk, and a chair. My small book collection sat atop my desk, but they were the only decorations I owned. Compared to downstairs— which Mum continued to fill with trinkets, vases, miniatures, and paintings—my room was spartan. I liked it that way.

The lack of furniture meant there was nothing to cover the door in the wall, though. It sat in the area between my bed and my desk. It was barely noticeable unless I was looking for it, but once I'd seen it, the door was hard to ignore.

It's probably empty, I repeatedly told myself as I made the bed and hung my clothes—five shirts and three pairs of pants—in the wardrobe. *It's not like there's some great big secret hidden in there.*

My unpacking took less than ten minutes. I could have gone downstairs when I finished, but I knew I would get roped into helping Dad squirrel away boxes marked "Don't Open," or Mum would ask me to help arrange dozens of her miniature horses and squirrels along the mantelpiece. I'd already done more than my share to help pack them, and the four-hour drive had exhausted me. *If they want clutter in their house, they'll have to deal with the consequences,* I decided and flopped onto the bed.

My window had a view of the large oak tree that grew beside the house, and I watched its fluttering leaves brush against the glass, mesmerized, until I drifted off.

I woke to the sound of tapping. The sunlight was hitting my face, so I rolled over to block it out and mumbled, "I'm coming. Hold on." When the noise didn't stop, I sat up and rubbed my palms into my eyes.

It wasn't Mum knocking at my door, as my half-asleep brain had assumed. I glanced toward the window, where the motion of the tree leaves had lulled me to sleep. The wind had died down, and the boughs were still.

I pushed my hair out of my face as I looked about the room. The tapping was quiet but, like a dripping tap, impossible to ignore.

"Hello?" I called.

Mum answered me from downstairs. "Dinner's almost ready! Come help me find the cutlery."

As the sound of her voice died away, silence rushed in to fill the space. The tapping had stopped, at least.

It was probably the tree, after all.

"Do you want to know what I found out today?" Dad asked.

Our real dinner table was crowded with half-unpacked cartons, so we sat our paper plates on a large packing box while we ate. Neither of my parents seemed to appreciate the irony.

"What?" I asked, scooping up pasta with a plastic spoon.

Dad swelled with excitement. "Apparently, this place used to

be an orphanage during the Depression. They had up to sixty children here at a time."

Mum paused, her fork halfway to her mouth. "How did you find that out?"

"Oh, well, I was setting up the office. The computer turned itself on—you know," Dad blustered.

I smothered a grin. I hadn't been the only one slacking off that afternoon.

"The real estate agent said it was built by a lord." Mum put down her fork and smoothed her cotton dress. I was sure she'd been born in the wrong decade. Necessity had forced her to work a part-time job most of her life, but she would have been much happier as a housewife. She even wore dresses and styled her hair as if she were living in the forties. Dad thought she was adorable.

"It was," Dad said, leaning forward. His enthusiasm was contagious, and both Mum and I mimicked his movement to hear him better. "When he died, he left it to a local church, and they converted it into an orphanage. It stayed that way until the eighties, when it was sold and renovated."

"Orphanage, huh?" I asked, glancing about the pokey kitchen. "It's not really built for it."

"Well, when you're desperate, you make do with what you've got," Dad said. "There were a lot of homeless children back then, more than any of the orphanages could keep up with, so they crammed the homes to capacity and had the children work—sewing clothes or running errands or whatnot—to help pay for food."

The house was big, much bigger than our last place had been,

but it still seemed far too small for sixty children. *Though, I guess, for a parentless child during the Great Depression, you'd call yourself lucky if you had a roof over your head and enough food to keep yourself from starving.*

Mum looked uncomfortable. She'd left her fork in her half-eaten meal and was rubbing at her arms. "I'm not sure I really like that."

"What's not to like?" Dad asked. He had shoveled so much pasta into his mouth that I could hardly understand him. "We get to be a part of the town's history!"

Mum seemed to be seeing the house in a new light. Her eyes darted over the stone walls and arched doorway, and her eyebrows had lowered into a frown. "I just hate to think about all those children… They must have been so lonely…"

Dad's whole body shook as he laughed. "Lonely? When there were sixty of them? I don't think so."

Mum pretended not to hear him. "That must be why the price was so low. It was even cheaper than that house half its size in Cutty Street, remember?"

"Their loss," Dad said, spearing more pasta onto his fork with a satisfied grin.

━━━━━

The tapping woke me in the middle of the night. I lay in bed and watched the opposite wall, where moonlight filtered through the tree outside my window and left dancing, splotchy shapes on the blue wallpaper.

The noise seemed to bore into my skull and knock directly

on my brain. I squeezed my eyes shut, willing it to be quiet so I could fall asleep again.

tk tk tk tk tk tk tk tk…

I groaned, rolled over, and pulled my pillow over my ears. It muffled the sound but didn't extinguish it.

tk tk tk tk tk…

If anything, the noise grew louder and more insistent, like a fly that was getting closer and closer to my head. I glared at the shadows cast on the wall, watching as they twitched and swirled, mimicking the infernal tree's movements. Maybe I could convince Dad to cut it down…

tk tk tk tk tk tk tk tk tk tk…

"Shut up!" I yelled, unable to tolerate the tapping anymore. I sat up in bed, feeling flushed, frustrated, and a little ashamed for yelling at a tree.

My room was quiet.

I held my breath, waiting for the noise to resume, but I heard nothing except beautiful, sweet silence. "Huh," I muttered and carefully lay back down. The shadows continued to sway over the wall opposite, but I didn't mind them as long as the noise had stopped. As I closed my eyes and let tiredness claim me, I wondered at how incredible it was that the tree had quietened at the exact moment I'd told it to.

━━━━━━━

Mum used a hot tray of muffins to bribe me into helping her unpack the next morning, and I spent the first half of the day

unwrapping, dusting off, and arranging her miniature collection. She fussed behind me, moving the animals and ball gown-wearing ceramic women into new arrangements, quirking her head to the side constantly to admire her work.

Finding out she lived in an old orphanage seemed to have shaken her; she was putting even more effort into turning this house into her domain than she had at our last place. She'd rescued her set of doilies and crocheted tablecloths from one of Dad's "Don't Open" boxes and flung them around the sitting room until it looked like a winter wonderland. Even more boggling, she'd brought out some of the Christmas decorations, including our fake wreath, holiday-themed trinkets, and bowls of plastic apples.

"Christmas in May?" I asked skeptically as I poked at one of the glittery apples.

Mum shrugged while she rearranged the miniatures on the fireplace mantel. "I think they look nice. Don't you want our house to be pretty?"

I didn't tell her, but I thought it was bordering on garish. I escaped back to my near-empty room, a pair of hedge clippers clutched in one hand.

Once I'd had a chance to think about it, I'd realized there was a simple way to stop the tapping noise without having to cut down the entire tree. I opened the window, pulled out the screen, and began snipping off all of the branches that touched or came near to the glass.

"I'm going to the shops," Mum called from downstairs. "Does anyone want anything?"

"Thanks, I'm fine," I called back at the same moment Dad hollered, "Beer!"

As I leaned farther out the window to prune branches that were nearly out of my reach, I saw Mum's car reverse out of the driveway and turn toward the town. Just past that, on the other side of the road, an elderly couple was standing on the sidewalk. They watched Mum's car pass them, then both looked back at our house. They'd inclined their heads toward each other and seemed to be talking animatedly.

About us?

Mum would probably get to meet them later when she went up and down the street to introduce herself. The elderly couple didn't look happy, I realized, and I paused my cutting to watch them. The woman had her arms crossed over her chest and was shaking her head, while the man scuffed his boot on the sidewalk. They exchanged another brief word then turned and disappeared into their house.

———

I found out what my mother's trip to the store had been for when I came down for dinner that night. At least two dozen fat candles had been spaced about the house, shoved wherever there was room between the miniatures. They were scented and lit, and their conflicting odors combined into a horrifically pungent smell.

"What's this?" Dad asked as he followed me through the doorway. His mustache bristled in disgust. "Smells like a perfume salesman died in our bleeding living room."

Mum sniffed as she dished up plates of fish. Our dinner table was clear of boxes, at least—but now four fat candles were clustered on a doily in its middle. "They're aromatherapeutic," she said. "They'll spread nice vibes through the house."

"This is a horrible fire hazard," I said as I watched a flame lick dangerously close to the wallpaper.

"Well, I'm sorry, but someone has to make this place feel like home," Mum said. She looked offended, so Dad and I dropped the subject.

"I'm going to visit some of our neighbors this evening," Mum said as she placed the plates of steamed fish and greens in front of us. "Does anyone want to come with me?"

Maybe I felt guilty for complaining about the putrid smell of her candles, or maybe it was curiosity about the odd couple I'd seen watching our house, but I found myself saying, "Sure. I'll come for one or two of them."

Mum looked delighted. "Well, I'm glad to see you're taking an interest in your new town, honey. Your father and I are hoping his work will let him stay here for at least a few years this time, so it would be good to make some friends."

"Hmm," I said noncommittally. Dad's work had a bad habit of jumping him across the country at short notice; this was the fifth house we'd stayed at in the last three years. That degree of unpredictability meant making friends was nearly impossible, so I'd just stopped trying. I wasn't holding out much hope that our most recent move would be very different.

I helped Mum wash up while Dad retreated to his office,

ostensibly to catch up on work, even though we could clearly hear him calling out answers to his favorite trivia game show. It was well past dark when Mum finally took up one of the small gift baskets she'd put together and led me out the front door.

"Which house will we start with?" she asked as we paused on the porch, looking at the twilight-shrouded rows of buildings that surrounded our house. "I'll let you pick, honey."

"That one." I pointed to the brick house on the other side of the road, where the elderly couple lived.

The woman answered the door before Mum had even finished knocking. I had the feeling she'd been watching us through one of the white-curtained windows. Her watery blue eyes skipped between my mother and me with a mixture of confusion and curiosity. "Hello?"

"Hello!" Mum gushed, showing her the gift basket. "We're new here. We moved into the house just across the street, and we wanted to say hi."

The woman, who introduced herself as Ellen Holt in between Mum's enthusiastic rambling, invited us inside. The house was smaller than ours, with peeling wallpaper, and it smelled like dust and dead mice. Ellen led us into the living room, where she introduced us to her husband, Albert, and asked if we would stay for a cup of tea.

"I'd love to." Mum placed the gift basket on the cluttered coffee table and settled into one of the lounge chairs. "Honey, why don't you help Mrs. Holt with the tea? Albert, I couldn't help but admire the beautiful vintage car in the driveway. Is that yours?"

I had to hand it to her—Mum was a genius at breaking the ice. Albert, a thin man with hair just as white as his wife's, seemed to light up at the mention of his Beetle and launched into a lengthy dialogue on it. Mum, who knew next to nothing about cars, smiled and nodded to encourage him.

Ellen led me into the kitchen. I leaned against the counter awkwardly while she filled the kettle, and she shot me a quick smile as her husband's monologue floated through the doorway. "Sorry, Albert loves to talk about his cars."

I chuckled, stared at my folded hands for a moment, then asked, "So, uh, how long have you lived here?"

"Oh, we bought the house when we got married, so…nearly fifty years, I suppose." Ellen pushed her glasses up her nose. "Where did you move from?"

"The city. But we hadn't been living there for long. Work keeps asking Dad to relocate, so…"

"Ah," Ellen said, picking a small jug out of the cupboard. Its inside was coated in dust, but she didn't seem to notice as she poured milk into it. "Do you think you'll be staying here long?"

"No idea." I watched Ellen place four teacups on a floral tray. A cat entered the room, fixed me with its amber eyes for a moment, then rubbed itself against my legs. "I'd like to settle down somewhere, but it's more likely that we'll need to pack up again in six months or so."

"That's not so bad," Ellen said, almost too quietly for me to hear.

"Sorry?"

The older woman paused and seemed to be on the verge of saying something more. Her cat gave a plaintive mewl as it left my legs and began rubbing its head over Ellen's shoes. "I...don't want to alarm you," she said at last, clearly picking her words cautiously, "because there's nothing really to be alarmed about. But..."

"Yes?"

"But you should be careful in that house."

She fished a can of cat food out from one of the cupboards and peeled its metal lid off. The cat redoubled its attentions.

I glanced from Ellen to the living room, where Mum was still pretending to be enthralled by Albert's history of the restorative work he'd done on the Beetle. "Why? Is there something wrong with it?"

"It's...a bit of a strange house." Ellen tipped the cat food into a bowl and bent to place it on the ground. When she straightened again, she fixed me with a searching stare. "I lived here when it was still an orphanage, see? Albert and I used to give sweets and oranges to the children, sometimes, when they passed our house. I heard some strange stories about things happening there."

I leaned forward. "Such as?"

"Well, a boy came up to me one morning while I was weeding the garden and said matter-of-factly, 'Henry isn't in the house anymore.' It sounded like he'd just realized it for himself. When I asked what he meant, he said, 'I haven't seen Henry for a month. He didn't get adopted, and he didn't die. I don't think the Sisters have noticed yet.' The lunch bell rang, and he ran off before I could ask any more questions."

The kettle finished boiling with a click, but neither of us paid it any attention.

"I waited for him to come and visit me again, but he never did. In fact, I didn't see him leave the house at all after that. I don't know if I should have told someone, but I was young back then and didn't want to look nosy. Albert thought the boy had probably found a nice family to take him in."

The cat had finished wolfing down its meal and gave my leg a final rub before leaving for the living room. Ellen kept speaking as she held an empty teapot and stared into the distance. It was as though she'd forgotten I was there, but I was too enthralled to interrupt her.

"Then they converted it back into a home—fresh paint and new doors and all of that—and the owners began renting it out. No one seemed to stay for long, though, a year or two at the most. And it was vacant for long stretches in between too. And then, about eight years ago, I woke up in the middle of the night to find police cars lining the street. A family's child had gone missing. I watched from the window, and all I could think was, *I should have told someone about the missing orphans, then maybe this one wouldn't have gone too.*"

She broke off suddenly, as though she realized she'd said too much, and turned back to me with a shaky smile. "I'm sorry. I didn't mean to yak your ear off. It's not something you should worry about, anyway…just an old biddy's imagination getting too excited…"

Ellen fumbled to fill the pot, pouring in hot water but

forgetting about the tea bag. I followed her mutely back to the living room and let my thoughts consume me as Mum made enough small talk to cover for both of us.

Henry isn't in the house anymore…

———

When we got home, I went straight to bed and lay on my back, watching the moonlight's patterns on the wall opposite.

Mum's anxiety about the house having once been an orphanage suddenly seemed much more rational. With sixty children crammed into a house during a time of hardship and suffering, it was beyond wishful thinking to imagine there hadn't been deaths.

I tried to picture what it must have been like while Ellen's story echoed in my head. *I haven't seen Henry for a month…*

If a child—a quiet, unobtrusive, and shy child—suddenly disappeared out of a hectic house with a constantly changing list of occupants, how long would it take before someone noticed?

Was Henry the only child to disappear? What if others had gone missing but were never remembered?

I tossed in my bed, trying to calm my mind enough to sleep. The air felt thick, and I was having trouble breathing properly. Downstairs, Mum's mantelpiece clock chimed one in the morning. I threw off my blankets.

I needed to know more about the house and the people who'd lived in it. My family only had one computer, and it was downstairs, in Dad's office, so I pulled my jacket on over my pajamas and crept out of my room.

The house felt eerily empty and quiet at night. I knew my parents were sleeping in one of the rooms down the hallway, but it was easy to imagine I was the last person on earth as I took the stairs two at a time and turned in to Dad's office.

It was a comfy, cluttered room, and he'd set it up almost identically to the way it had been in our old house. The TV sat in one corner with a couch opposite, and a desk and computer stood against the other wall. The main difference was the stack of boxes pressed into the space beside the lounge. Dad was probably still trying to find a place for them.

I turned on the computer and slid into the chair. As soon as the browser loaded, I typed our address into the search bar. The first few results were old real estate listings, but the third link belonged to a historical site. I opened it and started reading.

It must have been the same page Dad had found. It talked about how the house had been constructed in 1891 by a lord who'd owned a good part of the village. When he'd died, he'd gifted it to the local church, which had set up an orphanage under the care of nuns from a nearby convent. When the Great Depression hit, the nuns, who had a policy of helping anyone who came to them, took in far more children than the house had been equipped to hold. There were photos, and I scrolled through them slowly.

Some showed gaggles of scrawny children and teens playing in the yard. Another was of a young girl with thick brown curls, beaming so widely that it looked as if her face might split in half, holding hands with her two new adoptive parents. Another

showed how mattresses were stacked in piles during the day, so that the rooms would be usable, then unpacked at night to fill every available space. Even so, it looked as though three or four children had shared each bed, lined up like sardines in a can.

A blurry photo depicted a nun spooning soup out of a pot that was heated over an open fire outside. *So that's how they coped with the tiny kitchen.*

The final picture showed a different bedroom. The children weren't cramped four to a bed, but each had a mattress of their own. The room looked familiar, but not until I noticed a small shadowy bump in one wall—the secret door—did I realize it was my own room. I scrolled down to read the caption.

Children sick with scarlet fever in the infirmary. As many as one hundred children died at Hallowgate during its time as an orphanage.

"Infirmary?"

I recoiled from the computer as though it had burned me. Looking at the photo again, I saw that the children in the picture were clearly sick. A nun bent over one of the beds, ladling something—water, probably—into a boy's mouth.

I'd seen enough. I powered down the computer, turned off the lights, and slowly climbed the stairs.

It would be easy to move to a different room, I thought as I stood in my doorway and watched the shadows play over the place where dozens of children had struggled, and failed, to stay alive. *It's not like I have to stay here. I only took it because it's closest to the stairs.*

I wondered how angry Mum would be if I disturbed her by deconstructing my room and moving it in the middle of the night. *Probably very.*

C'mon, it's not a big deal. You've slept here before. You can change rooms tomorrow.

I sighed, stepped over the threshold, and closed the door behind myself.

tk tk tk tk tk tk

"Are you kidding me?" I gasped. I was sure I'd cut off all of the branches that were close enough to hit my window. I stormed toward the tree's silhouette, pulled open the glass, and looked out.

None of the boughs were even near touching the window. In fact, the air was still, and the tree's leaves weren't moving except for an occasional quiver.

What's the noise, then?

I closed my eyes and focused on pinpointing the infernal tapping. It wasn't coming from outside my room, after all, but from behind me. I turned slowly until I was facing the outline of the tiny square door hidden behind the wallpaper.

I felt as if I were in a trance as I walked toward the door. The rhythmic tapping seemed to be growing louder, closer. I knelt on the carpet so that my face was even with the door, and stretched out a hand to touch the surface.

My fingertips tingled where I felt the tapping lightly vibrate the wall. *Like a beating heart,* I thought as the intensity of the taps increased again. I drew my fingers back then brought my index knuckle forward to rap on the wall three times.

The noise stopped instantly. I held my breath, listening as hard as I could, then I heard three very distinct raps mimicking mine.

I scrambled away from the wall, my heart hammering as I tried to make sense of it.

"Hello?" I called, but my only reply was silence.

A single thought echoed in my head, drowning out logic as it consumed me: *I need to get the door open. Whatever's inside there has to be let out.*

I bolted from my room and raced down the stairs. My footsteps thundered on the wood as I abandoned all attempts to stay quiet. I found a small paring knife in the kitchen drawer and clutched it in my fist as I raced back up to my room.

By the time I knelt in front of my door again, I was panting, and a light sheen of sweat was sticking my pajamas to my skin. I put my head near the wall and called softly several times. There was still no answer, so I pressed the blade into where the wallpaper curved to cross over the edge of the door and began cutting.

The paper was thicker than I'd expected, and it took me several minutes to sever the wallpaper around the entire square. When I was done, I dropped the knife and dug my fingernails into the narrow gap I'd made. I pulled until my fingers ached, but the door stayed fixed in place.

Of course. There's a keyhole. It's probably locked.

I took up the knife again and carefully removed the paper from the bump on the inside of the frame. Behind it was a small bronze keyhole…and I thought I knew where I could find the key that fit it.

On the day my parents had signed the lease for the house, the real estate agent showed us a jar of keys. She'd said no one was really sure which door each key belonged to or which ones were no longer needed because the locks had been changed, but she left it with us in case we ever needed one of them.

As I went down the stairs for the third time that night, I tried to remember where the jar was. I checked in Dad's study first, then in the laundry, and I finally found the old jam jar perched in a cupboard above the fridge. Its collection jingled when I shook it, and I unscrewed it on my way back to my room. I knelt in front of the door, tipped the two dozen keys onto the floor, and spread them out.

They were all very old. Some were rusted, a couple were bent, and one looked partially melted. It only took a minute to find the key I needed, though. It was smaller than the others, and the bright bronze matched the keyhole. I picked it out of the pile and held it up to the light. It had a delicate, ornate carved design and was small enough that I could have covered it with one finger.

I pushed it into the keyhole. The lock was stiff after years of disuse, but I twisted it as hard as I dared. It unlocked with a gentle click.

The door swung open on its own when I removed the key, finally granting me access to the area beyond. My heart thundering, my palms sweaty, I bent forward to look inside. It was exactly what I'd expected, after all: an empty space that went on for several meters before ending in a solid wall.

I rolled back onto my heels and exhaled, uncertain if I felt

more relieved or disappointed. If there was no one and nothing behind the door, then the tapping must have been coming from somewhere else—maybe a pipe in the wall that wasn't secured properly or something in the rooms below that echoed into the tiny compartment my door guarded. Either way, I would change my room the next morning and not have to worry about it after that.

I'd half closed the door when something on the room's back wall caught my attention. It looked like white writing on the dark-gray stone. I squinted at it but couldn't make out what it said.

"Jeez," I muttered. I hesitated on the edge of the frame for a beat then crouched down and started wriggling my torso through the opening. *If I'm going to go to the trouble of opening the damn door, I may as well explore whatever mysteries it offers, no matter how mundane.*

It was a narrow crawlspace. I could reach my hands out to the side a little, but the ceiling was so low that I had to shuffle along on all fours with my stomach only just above the ground. At least it was a short passageway. I reached the end and lowered my chest farther so that I could raise my head and read the writing.

With my body blocking most of the light from the bedroom, I had to shuffle my mass about as much as I could to get illumination.

"Lots… Let's…"

The markings were crude, as though they'd been made by a child blinded by the dark, but once I figured out the main words,

I was able to piece together the rest. I read it carefully, making sure I had it right.

"Let's…play…hide…and…seek."

The door behind me slammed closed.

I was engulfed in perfect darkness. It was the blackness of nightmares, when you feel like you're drowning hundreds of miles under the ocean's surface, and no matter how hard you kick you can't see so much as a hint of light. I screamed and jerked, and my head hit the ceiling with a crack. Sharp pain flashed across my skull. I hunched down, pressing my forehead to the icy cold ground until the worst of the sting subsided.

My ears were ringing—whether from the slamming door or when I'd hit my head, I wasn't sure—and I felt dizzy. I reached a hand toward the wall to the left but couldn't feel it.

That gives me enough room to turn around, at least.

I shuffled in a little circle, trying to get myself facing the door without getting jammed in the narrow confines of the passageway, but not even my feet bumped the walls as I made my turn. I began crawling forward, occasionally touching the ceiling above my head to make sure I was leaving enough room. Then I stretched my hand forward to feel for the door.

One minute…two minutes…

Panic started to build in my chest as I moved farther and farther into the blackness without finding the exit. *It didn't take me this long to get inside, did it?* I kept reaching my hand forward, expecting to feel solid wood but grasping only air. My limbs started trembling from having to carry my body's weight at such

an awkward angle. My chest was grazing the floor, and every time I moved forward, my back bumped the ceiling.

It's getting lower, I realized with a stab of shock. *The ceiling is getting lower.*

Panic hit me, and I tried to scream, but even though my throat vibrated, I couldn't hear my own voice. I turned again, trying to find the walls, trying to find anything I could latch on to, but my fingers found no purchase, and every movement seemed to reduce the vertical space I had.

I rotated to face the opposite direction, desperate to find a wall. The stone felt ice cold under my burning, aching fingertips. The space had reduced so that I couldn't crawl anymore. I had to stretch my hands forward, press my palms to the floor, then use my arms and my toes to drag my body a few inches forward.

I tried to call for help again. Just drawing in the air to yell pressed my chest and my back against the floor and ceiling. Tears began to leak out of my eyes as I gasped. I was suffocating, my arms aching, my head pounding, my skin chilled from where it touched the unnatural stone enclosure.

I had no more wiggle room. My head was tilted, and even by exhaling as deeply as possible, I couldn't get enough space around my body to move. I was trapped in a vise that refused to let go.

tk tk tk tk tk tk tk

I turned my head toward the noise, and my eyes finally found something other than black. A shape was coming toward me out of the darkness—a child.

And yet…the figure was *not* a child.

Its eyes were the clearest; they had no pupil or iris, but they shined at me like huge white disks in the dark. Its face was narrow, gaunt, and unnaturally wrinkled, as though its skin had aged while the flesh and bones underneath remained those of a child. There was no color in its face—I could have been looking at a corpse.

My mouth tried to scream, but my lungs had no room to draw in air.

The child—the *thing*—dragged itself toward me. As its hand extended in my direction, I saw its nails had grown long. When the fingers hit the floor, they made the abhorrent tapping noise that had haunted my stay in the house.

tk tk tk tk tk

I couldn't move. I couldn't protect myself. I couldn't escape. All I could do was watch as the thing that belonged to the darkness scuttled closer.

Henry isn't in the house anymore…

Then I felt them touching me—creatures had approached me from behind, unseen and silent. With their bony, bloodless hands, they grasped my legs and arms, tugging at me, squeezing my flesh, and scratching at my skin. Henry's nails tapped on the ground twice more as he closed the distance between us, and his mouth spread into a toothless smile as he reached out two unnaturally long fingers to caress my face.

I drew in a deep, hungry gasp of air. It was such a shock to be able to breathe that, at first, I didn't realize where I was.

Shadows cast in moonlight by the tree outside my window danced over the wall, painting beautiful patterns on my wallpaper. I stared at them for a moment then moaned, flipped myself over, and stared at the door.

The keys lay scattered on the ground where I'd left them beside the jar and the knife. The door was open a little, its wallpaper edges jagged from where I'd cut it, exposing a sliver of the nightmare-black inside. The house was quiet, but I thought I could hear my father's faint snores from down the hallway.

I kept my eyes fixed on the doorway. It was almost possible to believe I'd fallen asleep on the floor and dreamed up the hellish tunnel with the slowly lowering ceiling and the decades-old forgotten children... But then, as I watched, unable to look away, the door closed slowly and carefully, until a faint click told me it was locked...and I heard him leave.

tk tk tk tk tk tk tk...

MANNERING HOUSE

MANNERING HOUSE LOOMED ABOVE US. THE FOUR-STORY BUILD-ing must have been decadent at one time, but half a century of neglect had left it dilapidated and crumbling. Someone had nailed weather-stained wood over the lower windows, and the porch seemed to sag into the moonlit, overgrown lawn. My eyes were drawn to the highest room, the attic, where a curtain fluttered in the open window.

I glanced at my three companions. Sanjit had his arm around Tara's shoulders, while Jason swung his flashlight in erratic arcs as he led us up the dirt path toward the house.

"We could go to a movie instead," Tara said, unable to keep the frightened squeak out of her voice. "I hear the theater is delightfully ghost-free."

"Re*lax*," Jason drawled, extending the last syllable as he jogged up the porch's steps. "This'll only take a minute."

The door's locks had been broken years ago—probably by looters or curious teenagers like us—and the carved wood slab drew open with a low groan. Sanjit hesitated on the threshold. "Someone probably owns this place."

Jason gave his friend's shoulder a light punch then stepped into the vast, shadowed entryway. "Shush, no one cares."

The bare rooms were dim and musty. I glanced to the right, into the living room, where knives of moonlight speared through gaps in the windows' boards.

"I hate this place," Tara whispered.

"Me too." I wrapped my arms around my torso as I reluctantly followed my companions deeper into the building.

"You guys know the story, right?" Jason asked, beckoning us toward the stairs. His delighted eyes landed on Sanjit, who sighed.

"You know I only moved here last year. Go on, then; tell me."

Jason beamed and began to jog up the narrow stairway, which creaked under his weight. "Well, this place used to belong to the Mannering family. They were a pretty big clan in the eighteen hundreds, but most of them died at the turn of the century." He raised his eyebrows. "Some people say they were cursed."

"Some people" was Jason, for the purpose of adding atmosphere. I rolled my eyes, but no one noticed in the dark.

"When the thirties rolled around, it was just Mr. Mannering, his three sons, and one daughter, Ruth. When the war hit, all four men were conscripted. Mr. Mannering came back. His sons didn't."

Dark patches on the stairwell's walls showed where family portraits had once hung. I shuddered as I passed them.

"The war made him crazy," Jason said, lowering his voice. We reached the landing and turned to follow the stairs to the third floor. I glanced down the hallway behind us. The doors were open, and the rooms' furniture decaying. "He locked Ruth up. Wouldn't let her go anywhere. Wanted to keep her *safe*, y'know? Only problem was, she'd fallen for the vicar's son, Mason, while her dad was away."

A spider spun down on its thread to hover in front of my face. I gasped, and Tara swung around. "What was that?"

"Just a spider," I muttered, skirting it.

Sanjit squeezed his girlfriend's hand. "Don't be frightened."

Jason coughed to bring the attention back to himself. "Remember how I said the dad was crazy? He really, *really* didn't want his daughter to leave. He forbade Mason from visiting, but the boy came during the dark of night, climbed the tree behind the house, and proposed to Ruth through her window. They made plans to elope the following night. But her dad found out, and he went ballistic."

We'd reached the top of the stairs, and faced a ladder that led to the final floor, the attic. Tara looked terrified, but she climbed the ladder when Jason waved her up. Sanjit and Jason followed, with me coming last.

Cobwebs hung from the angled roof like old lace. The window facing the driveway was to my left; its curtains fluttered in the wind. To the right was an open window overlooking an ancient elm tree. The room was bare except for a wooden chair.

"Dad takes an ax and drags Ruth up to this very room. When Mason climbs the tree that night, he can see them through the window. Dad bellows, 'You'll never have her!' Then *wham*, he chops his own child's head off."

Sanjit had turned a funny color. Tara nestled into his shoulder, shivering.

"The kid, Mason, breaks into the house. Mr. Mannering is standing over Ruth's body, laughing like the crazy man he is. Mason runs at him and pushes the both of them through the window, where they plunge to their deaths."

"Question." I raised my hand. "How do we know what happened if everyone died?"

Jason ignored me. "They say Ruth's ghost haunts this house. She appears on nights like tonight, ones with a full moon, to wait for her dead fiancé."

Tara squirmed. "I want to go home."

"Not yet. I haven't shown you my secret." Jason rubbed his hands together, grinning wildly. "Amy and I came up here last week for our date. Bit of privacy, you know?"

Sanjit snorted.

"And look what we found." Jason picked up the chair and turned it around for us to see. The seat had a deep gash, and the wood was stained nearly black. "I'll bet anything this is the chopping block dear old Dad used to behead his daughter."

"I want to go home," Tara repeated, sounding as if she were about to cry.

I leaned on the windowsill to get a better look at the elm tree,

and the wood creaked under my hands. Tara shrieked, and even Jason jumped then broke out into laugher.

"All right, all right. Let's get out of here."

I watched as the three friends climbed through the hatch that led to the floor below, then I sighed and turned back to the window. My throat tightened as my fingers clutched at my bloodstained dress, and I gazed at the branch Mason had clung to the last time I'd seen him alive.

STATION 331

Jen snapped her helmet into place, enjoying the quiet hiss and click that told her it was locked. A lot of outpost staff complained about having to wear the thick suits during routine patrols, but Jen liked them. They made her feel secure, as though nothing could get to her.

Carly locked her gloves into place. She wiggled her fingers experimentally then shot Jen a grin through the tinted glass of her helmet. "Damn, but I've been looking forward to getting out of this joint."

Jen had never asked exactly what Carly had done to get herself condemned to their tiny station on Perros's second moon, and Carly hadn't volunteered the information—but it must have been bad. People didn't end up on Station 331 by accident, and out of the three of them, Carly was the least suited to endure the isolation and monotony.

Jen checked her wrist controls to ensure everything was airtight. Carly was already at the door, hopping from foot to foot and swinging her arms. "C'mon, let's do this already."

A quiet voice buzzed through the helmet's speakers. "Jen, I'm ready for your all clear."

Jen turned toward the plexiglass window. Alessicka stood behind it, leaning over the control panel, her delicate face tensed in concentration. She was the only one of their three-woman team who kept her hair long, and it fell like a sheet down one side of her thin neck to brush over the panel.

"All clear," Jen said, shooting her two thumbs up as added reassurance.

Alessicka gave Jen a small smile then looked toward her companion. "Carly, how are you doing?"

"If I were any more ready, I'd explode." Carly swiveled in a semicircle to face the window. Her eyes were huge, and the need to be free was etched into every line of her face.

There was a pause.

"Carly, your monitor says your helmet isn't locked properly."

There was a tremor in Alessicka's voice. She hated arguing with Carly, but Jen knew her too well to think she would overlook any problem she found, no matter how minor. It was both a blessing and a curse; they were sometimes stuck in the air lock for an hour or more as she troubleshot problems…but at least Jen knew she wasn't going to be sent out in substandard conditions.

Jen's partner didn't share her view. Carly let out a string of swear words and kicked at the air lock doors. "We've been over

this before. A half dozen times. It's a problem in the feedback or whatever. I promise you, the helmet is locked."

Alessicka stared at the readings on the screen. Jen could see sweat beading on her face as she braced herself. "I'd like to run some diagnostics on…on…it." She trailed off at the murderous look on Carly's face.

"I swear, Lessi, you delay this patrol for another minute, and I'll murder you in your sleep tonight."

Alessicka's face blanched, and Jen decided it was time to intervene. "That's enough, Carly. Don't make jokes like that."

"Who said I was joking?"

Jen held up a hand to quiet her partner, then turned to the woman behind the console. "Lessi, I'm going to override you this time. We've checked out the helmet before, and you said it was probably a feedback glitch. Besides, it's been months since we've seen anything more exciting than sludge. I doubt Carly's going to need to test her helmet's seal today."

Alessicka gave a small nod and began pressing buttons on the console. "Prepare for gate unlock in twenty seconds."

"*Finally*," Carly groaned.

Jen stepped up to join her partner beside the door. They each took one of the stingers from the rack bolted to the wall and turned them on. Stingers were their main weapon against what lived outside the station. They looked like rifles with extended barrels, but the tip was shaped into a large metal needle. The idea was to push the needle into any unwanted creatures they found on their moon and pull the trigger. The stingers released a shot

of neurotoxins directly into the life-form's body, killing it within seconds.

That was one of their jobs on Station 331: keep the moon clean of hostile beings that came off comets or space debris. Some of the newer stations got more exciting infestations of aggressive creatures like parydonas and crawling Helens and had to call for backup from their ward planets, but even though Station 331 was on a remote moon near the edge of the system, the staff rarely had to deal with anything worse than poppers and sludge.

"External gate unlocking," Alessicka said through the helmet, and the metal doors in front of them hissed and parted.

"Yes," Carly moaned as she sprinted as quickly as her bulky suit would allow onto the surface of the moon. She took three steps then kicked the powdery ground, sending herself flying nearly ten feet into the air before gliding down to land in a billow of red dust. Jen followed at a slower pace, enjoying the sensation of weightlessness from the lower gravity outside the station.

The moon wasn't ugly, but it *was* dull. Its uneven surface was pocked after millennia of being beaten by asteroids and space rubble. Composed of four small living rooms, one air lock and one control room, the station had been built into a sheltered indent. Red rock surrounded it on three sides, so it got only four hours of natural sunlight each day.

Carly was sprinting ahead, stinger held in both hands, as she searched for a target to unleash her pent-up frustration on. She disappeared over the lip of a crater, and a moment later, Jen heard

a sharp pop through her headset, followed by a cackle of delight. Carly had found her first victim.

Jen went in the opposite direction and circled around the back of the base. Before long, she found a target of her own; a sludge was clinging to a rock formation just meters from the front door. The human-sized clump of coal-black slime undulated as its organs worked to convert the moon's minerals into nutrients.

Sludges weren't dangerous, but they could be a nuisance if they got out of control. They would clog doorways, damage equipment, and, given enough time, even eat through metal. Jen forced the tip of her stinger through the sludge's leathery skin, flicked the safety lock, and pulled the trigger. The gun kicked into her shoulder as it injected its poison, and she stepped back to watch as the sludge writhed and coiled in on itself.

Scientists said the sludges were no more intelligent than a plant, but Jen still hated seeing the creature thrash as its flesh bubbled and split. She stood with it until it was completely still, then she unclipped one of the hooks from her belt and snagged a corner of the sludge's frothing flesh.

She dragged it back to the waste disposal unit behind their station—low gravity had its benefits—and while she was feeding it through the slot, she heard another crack in her headset as Carly bagged her second target.

"Jen, Carly," Alessicka's voice said, "I'm getting a reading of a living shape by the weather vane. It looks like a sludge, but it's a big one."

"On it." Carly sounded breathless, but Jen couldn't tell if it was from excitement or overexertion.

Jen scouted around the perimeter of the station, making sure it was clean, before widening her loop. She could hear Carly humming as she made her way to the weather vane, which was located on an outcropping a kilometer away from the base. Twice, Carly stopped to use her stinger on creatures she found along the way, and once, she swore loudly, apparently having stubbed her toe on a rock. Jen started to tune her out as she focused on her job—injecting another sludge and a couple of thick, veiny plants that were struggling to survive on the barren moon—so she almost didn't hear Carly say her name.

"What's up?" Jen asked, clipping a sludge to her cable and beginning to pull it toward the waste disposal.

"This thing by the weather vane—it's not a sludge. It's… Hell, I have no idea what this is."

"Describe it," Alessicka said.

"It's…like…big. Maybe four times as large as I am. Black and lumpy, with red veins running all over its body."

"Red veins?" Alessicka asked. "Not yellow, like a crawling Helen?"

"No, definitely red. They're pulsing. And there are these… tendril things coming out at its base. Like roots. I think they're moving, but very slowly."

There was a pause, and Jen could hear Alessicka typing. "I haven't heard of a creature like that," she said, "and the system isn't bringing up any matches. Should I call Perros, Jen?"

Calling Perros, their ward planet, essentially meant asking for backup. Technically, that was the correct protocol for when they found an unidentifiable alien life-form, but hardly any station followed it.

"Aw, hell no," Carly said. "It looks harmless. It's actually managing to move less than a sludge. I'll just inject it real quick, and then we can get back to our damn jobs."

Alessicka's voice was tight with anxiety when she replied, "Don't proceed. You don't have clearance." She hesitated then added, "She...she doesn't have clearance. Does she, Jen?"

Jen sighed. Calling Perros was a huge inconvenience for everyone involved. Support wouldn't reach them for nearly twenty-eight hours, and if Carly was right and the life-form was vegetation or low risk, they wouldn't be happy about having their time wasted.

"Stay where you are, Carly. I'll come to you, and we can deal with it together."

"Sure you don't want me to get it now? It's an ugly son of a—"

"No." Jen unclipped the sludge from her belt. "Just stay put."

"Fine," Carly huffed, and Jen thought she heard a relieved sigh from Alessicka in the background.

Jen bounded across the moon's surface, her boots kicking up puffs of dust with each step. Perros rose over the horizon to her left, and she could see one of their sister moons, 384, to the right. There wasn't any proper *day* or *night* on 331, so the moon felt perpetually suspended in twilight; the atmosphere cast a red glow over the already-bronze landscape, dimming the sun's light and casting strange, leaping shadows.

Jen was still a few minutes from the weather vane when she heard Carly inhale sharply.

"What happened?" she asked at the same moment Alessicka said, "Carly?"

Carly laughed. "Oh, wow. I didn't expect that. I poked it, and it started moving."

"Moving?"

"Yeah, these tendril vine-like things are stretching out and waving all over the place. Are you sure we have to kill it? It's the most interesting thing we've had on this moon in months."

Jen kicked against the ground to leap over a rocky ridge. "Damn it, Carly. Stay away from it until I get there. We don't know how dangerous it is."

"Relax," Carly drawled. "It can't reach me. I don't even think it can see. It's—" She gasped sharply.

Jen heard scraping and rustling, then Carly shrieked.

"Carly?" Jen called. She increased her jog to a run, moving her legs as fast as the thick suit and low gravity would let her. "What happened?"

"Damn it," Carly said, over more scuffling. "It's got me, Jen. I dropped my stinger, and I can't get it off—" She grunted in pain then yelled something incoherent.

Fear spiked through Jen as she raced for the weather vane. She could hear Carly panting, interspersed with snapping noises. "I'm about two minutes away, Carly. Hang on."

Then Carly's screams filled Jen's helmet, drowning her in the rawness of the other woman's terror. Jen called to her, but Carly

either didn't hear or couldn't respond; she kept screaming and screaming. The shrieks' pitch rose—

Then there was silence.

"Carly?" Jen panted into the stillness. "Carly, can you hear me? Carly!"

"Her...her helmet's disconnected—" Alessicka's voice was thin with horror. "Audio's g-gone completely."

"Damn it!" Jen couldn't move fast enough, as if she were stuck in a nightmare where no matter how hard she ran she couldn't move any closer. Then she cleared a ridge and finally saw Carly's monster.

Clinging to the rocks at the base of a crater was a massive mess of black tendrils with pulsing red rivulets running down them. They were probing outward, feeling along the ground, seeking something to grip. Jen stopped well out of their reach and started sidestepping the creature, searching for the white suit that held her partner. She couldn't see it.

"Lessi, can you tell me anything? Do you have any reading on Carly?"

"No." She sounded as if she were hyperventilating, but her fingers were hitting the keyboard at an incredible speed. "It's... it's like her helmet has been separated from the suit. I can't get any stats at all."

"Okay." Jen's pulse pounded in her head as she weighed her options. "I'm going to try to sting it. If anything...*goes wrong*, don't come after me, but send a message to Perros immediately."

Alessicka made a strangled sort of noise. "Don't. Please, Jen. Please don't—"

The creature's limbs were tapping at the ground and seeking contact, but they seemed to be slowing their pace.

"I've got to try to find Carly. Under no circumstances are you to leave the base. That's a direct order, Lessi. Do you copy?"

"C-copy."

"Okay."

Jen began sliding down the incline that led to the life-form. Two of the tendrils stretched toward her, apparently sensing the motion. Jen hoped that if she could sting it and get enough neurotoxins in it to kill it, she might still be able to find Carly. She didn't want to think about the state the other woman would be in, though; the air on 331 was toxic. *If she lost her helmet...*

One of the arms shot out at an impossible speed and snagged Jen's ankle. She gasped and tried to jump back, but the creature was too fast. Before she could understand what was happening, she was in the air, held upside down, while another tendril wrapped around her chest.

She swung her stinger toward the nearest tendril. It missed its mark. A new arm came up and wrapped around Jen's helmet, blinding her. She heard cracking noises as the black pulsing limb strained to separate the helmet from its suit.

Is this what it did to Carly?

She could feel the creature becoming frustrated. She had only seconds before it tried a new method of killing her; she aimed blindly, felt the stinger's steel needle puncture something resistant, and pulled the trigger.

A horrific wailing noise rose around her, and Jen found herself

plummeting to the ground. She twisted around in midair in time to see she was headed for a crop of jagged rock, which would certainly puncture her suit, but at the last second, one of the thrashing arms batted her aside. She skidded over a dusty patch of ground and rolled to a stop.

The creature had gone wild. Its limbs waved in every direction, as though it were trying to fight an invisible attacker, and the bestial wailing noise filled her head. The arms seemed able to stretch to impossible lengths, and Jen realized she wasn't safe where she was. She began scrambling backward, up the incline of the crater, not daring to take her eyes off the waving, slapping arms until she was over the top of the lip and running for the base.

The terrible noise followed her. The poison had hurt the life-form, but it wasn't dead; a single injection probably wasn't enough for a beast that size, and there was no way Jen was going back to have another go at it—especially now that she knew for certain Carly couldn't have survived. The creature had tried to pop Jen's helmet off, just as it must have done to Carly. Jen's had only stayed on because it wasn't faulty.

Tears stung her eyes, and she blinked them back furiously. The guilt was crushing; she'd used her power as the team leader to override Alessicka when she'd tried to do her job, and now her partner was dead. *This is what you get for cutting corners. This is what happens when you don't take your job seriously.*

She squinted and ran faster. All she wanted, more than anything else, was to be inside the safety of the double-walled

metal station. She would never complain about how small it was again.

"Jen?" Alessicka breathed in her ear. She sounded terrified. "A-are you th-there?"

In her rush to get away from the monster, Jen had forgotten to tell her remaining partner that she was okay. Alessicka had heard the fight, but nothing afterward, and Jen had left her hanging in terrible suspense.

"I'm here," Jen said, fortifying her voice. "I'm fine, and I'm coming back now. Carly...isn't."

"Okay," was the only thing Alessicka managed to say. She sobbed quietly and discreetly the entire time Jen was jogging back to base. She was young, and Jen didn't think she'd ever lost a team member before.

Relief spread across Jen's chest when the hulking metal structure came into view. She approached the air lock doors and asked Alessicka to open them. The girl must have been waiting with her hand poised over the button; they drew apart immediately, and Jen entered the air lock.

They looked at each other through the thick plexiglass screen that separated the air lock from the control room. Alessicka's face was pale and covered in tear tracks, but she kept her voice from breaking as she stepped Jen through the protocol they'd followed so often that it was like second nature. This time was different, though. This time, Jen stood alone as she waited for the chamber to be filled with breathable air, stepped out of her suit and stored her equipment.

"Central doors unlocking," Alessicka said at last, as the metal doors separating them parted. Jen stepped into the control room, and Alessicka threw herself onto Jen. Trembling, she hugged her fiercely, and Jen patted her hair until she pulled back. The girl's red eyes searched Jen's face, and for a moment, Jen was frightened Alessicka would blame her—tell her it was all her fault for ignoring the warning about Carly's helmet—but instead, she said, "What do I need to do?"

Ignoring the guilt and the pain had been easier when she had a purpose, so Jen latched on to Alessicka's opening and led her to the command board. "We need to get a message to Perros. Explain about the life-form we found. Explain about...Carly. Ask for assistance."

They would also need to request a replacement team member, but they could do that after the creature was dealt with and Carly's death was confirmed.

Jen watched over Alessicka's shoulder as she typed the message. Because of the location of their outpost, communication with Perros was difficult. Their ward planet would receive the message, but it wasn't likely they would send a reply. Any discussions would have to wait until the backup arrived.

"Sent." Alessicka swiveled in her chair to look up at her leader. "What else should I do?"

She needed work to keep her mind off Carly just as badly as Jen did. Unfortunately, work was one thing they were low on: the patrols usually took most of the day, so they'd finished all of their regular chores that morning.

Jen opened her mouth to suggest they go over inventory again, but a sharp noise interrupted her. They both jumped and looked through the plexiglass window into the air lock. Something large and dark was pressed against the outside door.

It's the monster from the weather vane. It's followed me back to base, Jen thought with a spike of panic, but as the shape moved and she realized what it really was, she somehow felt even more horrified.

"Carly!" Alessicka shrieked.

Their missing team member stood outside the base. She wasn't wearing a helmet, and her crop of curly black hair was stuck to her forehead with sweat. Her dark eyes bored into them intently, desperately, as she banged a fist on the door.

Alessicka slammed her hand on the button that opened the air lock, and Carly stumbled inside. Jen stared at her, shocked that she had survived the unbreathable air long enough to get back to base, let alone lived through having her helmet ripped off. Alessicka was talking rapidly over the speaker as she changed the settings on her control panel.

"Hang on, Carly. I'm depressurizing the air lock—filtering in oxygen—stabilizing the seal. Just a moment, and we'll have you back in the base."

Jen couldn't take her eyes off Carly as the woman leaned against one of the walls, panting and shivering. It seemed incredible that she could have made it back. *More than incredible, actually. Impossible.*

"Carly?" Jen asked. "Are you hurt?"

Carly was unzipping what remained of her thick suit. Jen saw tears in it; one arm had been shredded completely, and Jen thought she saw a splash of red on the inside as Carly shimmied out of it. "A few bruises," she said, flashing them a shaky smile, "but I'm alive and in one piece, so I guess I can't complain."

"Thank goodness," Alessicka said. She was adjusting the levels in the air lock to filter out the planet's toxic air before she opened the doors to their base. "We thought—"

"Yeah, I thought that for a moment too," Carly said. "I heard you come for me, Jen, but it had me pinned, and I couldn't help. I'm glad you got away okay."

"Me too," Jen said automatically, raking the woman over with her eyes. She looked fine, completely fine, and that terrified her.

"It's dead, by the way." Carly took one of the towels from the storage closet and rubbed at her sweaty face. "The monster. Life-form. Thing. Once you stung it, it let me go, and I was able to get my own stinger and finish it off."

"I see."

Alessicka looked ready to cry again, but a wide smile spread over her face. "Okay, Carly, central doors unlocking."

"Wait." Jen grabbed Alessicka's wrist to stop her from opening the metal doors that separated them from Carly.

The girl blinked up at her in confusion. "Did I do something wrong?"

"No. Uh, Carly, I'm sorry about this, but you need to stay in the air lock. Quarantine."

Carly's jaw dropped. She walked toward the plexiglass window. "Is this a joke? Because it's really sucky timing. I want a shower, damn it."

"I'm sorry, Carly, but you were exposed to that thing. We don't know what it was or if it infected you with anything. You need to stay in there until the team from Perros arrives."

Carly swore at her. "This is ridiculous! Let me back in, Jen!"

"Surely—surely she's fine," Alessicka said, offering a weak smile.

Jen let go of her wrist. "We can't take that chance. It's only twenty-eight hours, Carly, then we can decontaminate and release you."

Carly stared pure hatred at her leader, and Jen felt her resolve slipping. *Maybe I am being overcautious. We were told the air was poisonous, but not* how *poisonous. Maybe someone could survive in it for short amounts of time. Maybe it isn't so unbelievable that she's still alive.*

But then Jen looked at the torn, helmetless suit crumpled on the floor, and she knew, with complete certainty, that she wanted to keep the doors closed.

"Alessicka," Jen said, "could you bring Carly some food and water?"

The young woman still looked shocked that they were keeping their partner inside the air lock, but she nodded and got up. Carly slouched away from the window to sit against the back wall, scowling. As Alessicka's footsteps faded down the hallway, Jen said, "Carly, you know why I have to do this, right?"

"I'm your friend," she spat. "We've been stuck on this forsaken lump of rock for three years. Don't you trust me?"

Not at this moment, I don't.

The day passed slowly. Alessicka and Jen stayed at the control panel. Carly refused to touch the bottles of water and peach-flavored slurry packets they'd cautiously tossed through the door, but sat in her corner and sulked. After trying to make small talk for a few minutes, Alessicka gave up and joined them in silence.

When the clock ticked over to the third quarter of the day, Jen turned to Alessicka. "You'd better get some rest."

She looked ghastly. Her doe-like eyes were bloodshot from crying, and her face was pale, but she still smiled. "I'm fine, Jen."

Jen sighed. "No, you really need sleep. I'll stay here with Carly. Go on."

Alessicka obediently got up and waved goodbye to Carly, who flashed a grin back at her. Jen waited until she heard the bedroom door close before speaking.

"You haven't touched your food."

"Not hungry."

"So you're going to starve yourself until we let you out?"

Her only reply was a very slow blink.

"Carly," Jen said, choosing her phrasing carefully. "I don't believe you escaped from that creature."

The other woman didn't say anything.

"I felt how strong it was. It would have torn me in half if I'd given it another minute."

"I'm sure it would have."

Something about how she said that—almost with a hint of arrogance—made Jen pause. Carly was watching her through half-closed lids, a smirk hovering around her mouth.

"You don't have so much as a scratch on you."

"I was lucky, wasn't I?"

"The air isn't breathable."

"Are you sure about that? I swallowed it. It was fine."

"So you think the scientists lied to us when they said it was toxic?"

"Yes." Another slow, languid blink followed.

Jen pursed her lips. She had always gotten along reasonably well with Carly, but at that moment, she would have been glad to never see the other woman again. "I'm going to get some sleep too."

"Do you know why I was condemned to this hellscape?" Carly asked, and Jen froze halfway out of her chair. Carly's smile widened, but it wasn't a pleasant expression. "I know you've seen my work history. I'm beyond overqualified for a place like this. You probably think I did something really bad to end up here, don't you?"

Now it was Jen's turn to play the silence game.

"You'd be right." Carly was speaking so quietly that Jen had difficulty hearing her. "Before this, I was in charge of a mineral processing plant. Big place, dozens of people under me. There was this one conveyor belt that was designed to crush rocks into

gravel, and I took a walkway above it every morning on the way to my office."

She glanced to the side, and her eyes went hazy as she relived the memory. "One man there—I don't remember his name; Jon or James or something—tried to talk to me every morning about this idea he had. A way to streamline the plant. He'd follow me from the front door until I locked myself in my office. Tried to corral me every lunchtime too. His plans were flawed and wouldn't have worked in a million years, but no matter how often I told him that, he'd keep on, like a fly you can't catch, chasing me every morning. And eventually, I couldn't stand it any longer."

Jen swore under her breath, and Carly smiled, her dark eyes flicking back to watch her companion's face with relish. "You can guess what happened, can't you? He was still alive when he hit the conveyor belt, but the crushers took care of that pretty quickly. He painted the floor red." She laughed and licked her lips. "I told them he slipped. No one saw me push him, so they couldn't accuse me, but they guessed. And they punished me in the most effective way they could: they sent me here."

"Enough," Jen said. She was shaking.

Carly had never spoken like that before. She was sometimes brash, rude, or reckless, but Jen had never seen such maliciousness come from her.

"Just thought you'd like to know," Carly said sweetly, before closing her eyes and pretending to sleep.

Jen turned on her heel and marched toward the bedroom. Her

head was throbbing from stress and frustration. *I need a time-out. A chance to center myself, away from Carly.*

The bedroom was dark and cool. She paused in the doorway, listening to Alessicka's breathing from the bed at the back of the room, using the sound to reassure herself. She didn't bother changing—she didn't expect to sleep more than a few hours—so she crawled into her bed fully clothed.

Jen didn't fall asleep for a long time. Images of the black pulsing creature kept drifting across her closed eyelids. She saw Carly, too bold for her own good, snatched into the air. Then the tendrils latched on to and tore off her faulty helmet. Jen heard her scream. She was running toward her, but the faster she tried to move, the less progress she seemed to make. A tendril forced itself into Carly's mouth; she struggled against it then bit it, and ink-like blood burst from it to coat her face.

A loud bang pulled Jen out of the nightmare, and she sat up in bed, drawing in thick, ragged breaths. Sweat coated her body as though she'd just finished running a marathon, and her blanket had fallen to the floor. As she sat still, trying to rein in her thundering heart, she realized something was wrong: she couldn't hear Alessicka's breathing anymore.

A second bang and a drawn-out scraping noise came from the main part of the building. Jen launched herself to her feet. Alessicka's bed was empty, the sheets pushed neatly back into place. Jen ran for the hallway.

"Please no," she muttered as she ran. "Please don't be in there. Don't be in there. Please."

The noise had quieted; the rooms were so still that she could have been the only living person in Station 331 as she rounded the corner and opened the door to the control room.

The air lock door was open, and Alessicka was inside, slumped on the ground with her back to Jen, while Carly knelt in front of her. Jen froze as Carly looked up, a wide, unnatural smile stretched across her face. Their gazes met for a second before Carly's eyes flicked to the open door.

They moved at the same time. Carly dashed toward freedom, and Jen lunged for the control panel. Jen was a second faster; her hand hit the flashing red button, and the air lock doors slid closed just in time for Carly to hit them.

"Damn it, Jen!" she yelled.

Jen pulled back from the panel, feeling terror and nausea rush through her. Alessicka sat crumpled on the ground, looking like a doll that had been propped up into an imitation of a sitting pose.

"What did you do to her?" Jen called. Her mind raced, fighting to think of a way to get the girl out, desperately hoping she wasn't too late.

"She's *fiiiiine*, Jen," Carly said. She'd reverted to a complacent drawl as she paced back into view. "Aren't you, Lessi?"

As if on cue, Alessicka's body jerked. Slowly, like a puppet being pulled by strings, she began to twitch herself upright. It looked so unnatural that Jen wanted to scream.

"Lessi?" Jen asked as the girl rotated to face the window.

Alessicka's face was slack, and her eyes were blank as she stared at a space somewhere behind Jen's shoulder. Then she blinked,

and her whole body shuddered. Her hands twitched up, her neck straightened, her back aligned itself, and a look of awareness returned to her face.

"Jen!" She clasped her hands in front of her chest, blinking quickly and giving the worried look she wore whenever she thought she was in trouble. "I'm sorry, Jen. I opened the door to give her some food, and we sat down to talk. I must have fallen asleep, and—did you lock the doors?"

"Yes," Jen's lips moved to say, but no noise escaped her.

Alessicka looked normal again. Completely normal. Yet Jen couldn't erase the memory of her body, crumpled on the ground, as if the life had been sucked out of her…

"You can let me out now," Alessicka said, hurrying to the plexiglass window and giving Jen a sweet, apologetic smile as she pressed her hand to it. "I'm really sorry. I know I should have asked you before going in, but she said she was hungry, and… I'm so sorry. Please let me out."

"No." Jen wanted to cry as she said the words. "You're in quarantine now too."

Something flashed over Alessicka's face—anger or maybe resentment—and was covered over so quickly that Jen doubted she'd seen anything. "Oh, Jen," the girl said, her voice a tremulous whisper, "please don't be mad at me. I was just trying to do the right thing."

Jen turned away from the console so Alessicka wouldn't see how badly her words had cut.

On the day Alessicka had arrived on Station 331 to complete

their three-woman team, Jen had realized the girl was too gentle and too young for a job that would entail years of isolation. As Alessicka examined the console station she would be in charge of, Jen had watched the woman's hands flutter above the buttons with the anxious motions of someone who'd never been outside a simulation room before. She'd made up her mind to watch over her newest ward carefully. She'd told herself she could shelter her, protect her, and guide her until her contract was up. Then she could usher her into an easier, more enjoyable job on Perros. She'd failed. Whatever had happened to Carly had taken over Alessicka, and Jen hadn't been able to stop it.

"Jen?" Alessicka called, and she sounded so much like herself that it was agony for Jen to leave the doors closed. "I'm sorry, Jen. I didn't mean to upset you."

Jen grimaced then turned back to the window. Alessicka stared back, her smile apologetic, her doe eyes begging for forgiveness. Carly was near the back of the room, standing beside the shelves holding the equipment. She kept her eyes averted, seemingly trying to blend into the background, almost as though she hoped Jen would forget she was there.

Jen couldn't let Alessicka out... But she didn't want to leave her alone either. She sat in front of the console, ignoring the girl's curious gaze, and turned off the intercom. If she couldn't hear her, she wouldn't be so tempted.

As soon as she saw Jen wasn't going to open the doors, Alessicka turned away and joined Carly near the back of the room. They sat together, Carly's arm around her friend's shoulders, in the

same pose Jen had once sat with Alessicka when she'd been crying from homesickness. Jen ignored them.

The console recorded and stored audio for up to forty-eight hours. Normally, it was Alessicka's job to retrieve it if they needed to check any of their patrol data, but Jen knew enough about the machine to fumble her way through it. She rewound it to a point just a few minutes before the door had been opened, and pressed play.

"Hi, Lessi," Carly's tinny voice said. "Couldn't sleep?"

"No."

"Neither could I."

A few minutes of silence was punctuated by rustling noises. Jen imagined Alessicka sitting in front of the desk and Carly moving toward the window.

"Lessi, I can trust you, can't I?"

"Yeah, of course you can."

She heard Carly sigh. "There's something wrong with Jen."

"Wha...in what way?"

"The creature didn't attack me, Lessi. It snagged my ankle and tripped me over, but it wasn't dangerous. It was Jen who pulled my helmet off."

Alessicka was silent.

"I didn't want to say anything in front of her, in case it panicked her and she tried to hurt you too...but I think she wanted me to die out there. She pulled the faulty helmet off and left me to suffocate. I guess she thought the plant would be a very convenient explanation."

There was a thin sound; Jen thought it must be Alessicka trying not to cry.

"I'm so sorry, Lessi." Carly's voice was low and anxious. "I don't know what to do. She's locked me in here to divide us. Quarantine is just an excuse. Why would I need quarantining, anyway? I'm not hurt, and I'm not sick."

Alessicka mumbled something Jen couldn't make out.

"No. The creature was harmless. It was Jen all along. She doesn't want me working here. She wanted to get rid of me. I can prove it to you; she left a bruise on my neck—come in, and I'll show you."

Alessicka mumbled again. It was a wonder Carly had been able to understand her.

"No, it's okay. Just come in, and I'll show you. Then we can figure out what to do. We'll find a way to help Jen, I promise, but we'll need to work together. We'll need to be able to trust each other. You do trust me, don't you, Lessi?"

The squeak of a chair being vacated was followed by the slick whoosh of doors being opened, silence for a moment, then the loud bang that had broken through Jen's sleep. She heard a whimper, followed by another bang and a dragging sound. Then footsteps—her footsteps—raced into the console room.

Jen turned off the recording. She'd been so engrossed in it that she hadn't noticed Alessicka and Carly had moved. They stood in front of the window, equally calm faces holding tranquil eyes that stared down at her. Carly raised her hand and rapped on the plexiglass. Knowing what she wanted, Jen turned on the intercom with trembling fingers.

"You don't remember, do you, Jen?" Carly asked.

"What?" Her mouth was dry. Their stares were almost hypnotic.

"You don't remember attacking me."

"Because I didn't! The plant—"

"The plant was harmless. It tangled around my legs, and while I was trying to pull myself free, you grabbed me from behind. I screamed, and you pulled my helmet off, disconnecting the audio so I couldn't get any word back to Lessi."

"No!" Jen shouted, launching herself out of the chair to face them. "That's a lie!"

"You've been acting strange for weeks," Alessicka murmured. "I confronted you about it yesterday. Don't you remember? You've been mumbling in your sleep and refusing to talk to us."

"That's…not true," Jen stammered.

Alessicka's gaze held her, mesmerizing her.

"It is true," Carly continued. "We've been so worried about you, Jen. It's this place. This station. It's too small and too remote for someone as strong as you. You've been gradually losing your mind for months."

"No…"

"Yes," Alessicka said. "And you finally snapped yesterday. You knew how wrong it was, how terrible what you were doing was, so your mind built a fantasy. A fantasy about a monster that tried to kill Carly…but it was you all along."

Jen pressed a hand to her cheek and found it was wet. Her body was shivering. They were lying to her, she knew, trying to chip away at her resolve and make her doubt herself.

"Do you remember what you did to be sent to this station?" Carly asked. Her lids were half-closed, and her voice was a low, comforting murmur. "Do you remember?"

"I—I talked back to a superior—"

"No, Jen, you tried to strangle your superior. You always protested your innocence. Your mind washed it over. You couldn't stand to think of yourself as a killer."

"No—no—"

"What will the relief unit from Perros think when they arrive and find you've locked both of your team members in a room with no food or water?"

"But I haven't..." Jen stammered. "We gave you food."

Carly waved her hand at the room. "No you didn't. It's just your mind telling you that you did."

Jen stared at the ground, the shelves, and the boxes, trying to find the packets of food and bottles of water she'd passed through the door. *We did give Carly food, didn't we?*

"You see?" Carly said, her voice a sweet song in Jen's ears, her eyes drawing the other woman back to drown in them. "You can't trust your mind. But you *can* trust us. We want to help you, Jen. Let us out before the relief team arrives, and we can protect you, look after you...make sure no one hurts you."

"Let us help," Alessicka whispered. She was standing so close to the glass that her breath fogged it. "We want to help you."

"It's okay, Jen. Just open the doors."

"Open them, Jen."

"It's okay."

"You can trust us."

Jen found her hand hovering over the red button that would unseal the air lock. Her body was shaking, and her head was foggy. Tears dripped off her chin as she stared at her teammates, the two people she'd relied on, cared for, and watched over for nearly three years. They smiled at her so warmly and so kindly that she knew denying them would be insanity.

Her hand pressed the button. The doors drew open with a gentle whoosh, and it felt good to give in, to stop resisting, and to stop fighting her friends. That's what they were—friends. They walked through the doorway, came to her with open arms, and embraced her. The women held her still as she cried, stroked her hair, and told her she'd done the right thing.

Then Jen looked at Alessicka and saw a hairline fracture running down from her scalp, between her eyes, down her nose, and over her lips, chin, and neck before disappearing behind her shirt's collar. Jen frowned at it, confused and mesmerized. It began to part, splitting open, peeling the girl's smiling face back to show the pulsing, black mass inside her. Jen tried to pull away, but they held her firmly. She looked at Carly and saw she'd mimicked her partner; her skin was coiling back in on itself as the black tendrils reached out of their shell, tasting the air, and stretching toward Jen's face…

———

Jen stood in front of her station, suited up to protect against the toxic air, as she watched the ship from Perros land. It kicked up

huge clouds of red soil as it touched down, and even though she was wearing a helmet, she raised her arm reflexively to shield her face.

The ship's doors opened, and three suited figures jumped out. Jen waved them over and led them into the air lock.

As soon as breathable oxygen had replaced the toxic air, they unlocked their suits. "Thanks so much for coming," Jen said as soon as her helmet was off.

"That's our job," the team's leader, a tall and wiry man, said. "What's the problem?"

Jen watched as they unsuited. Their team was composed of two men and a woman; they all looked tough and capable— exactly what she needed. "Long story," she said as they hung up their suits, "but it's been pretty crazy down here. Come in, and I'll explain everything."

The doors slid open, and they entered the main part of the station. Jen turned to smile at the assistance team as Alessicka and Carly, as quiet as shadows, appeared behind them. Jen didn't need to give any signal; they all knew what needed to be done.

"Have you ever heard of body snatchers?" she asked, beaming at the three newest additions to their small colony as her sisters shed their human skins.

HITCHHIKER

THE SETTING SUN WAS UNPLEASANTLY HOT ON HELEN'S BACK. Her car, a decades-old model with more replacement parts than originals, had tapped out halfway through the drive to Surry. The town, where Helen's new apartment was waiting, was still two hours away.

She was on a long, derelict road flanked by tangles of sickly shrubs and dry weeds. She hadn't seen another car since leaving her own vehicle more than an hour before, and there was still no sign of the next town. The dirt road crested a few kilometers ahead, and Helen prayed she would top the gentle hill and find a sprawling town on the other side, preferably one with a pay phone and a car repair station that catered to customers who were borderline broke.

The insects hidden in the reeds that poked through swampy land sent up a shrill chatter. A long way away, a bird of prey

screeched. Helen shifted her bottle of water to her left hand and rubbed her sweaty right palm on her jeans. She'd kept her burden as light as possible; the bottle of water was vital for the long walk into town, and she'd tucked her wallet and car keys into her pocket. Everything else, including her dead cell phone and the eight large cardboard boxes full of possessions waiting to be unpacked into her new house, were still in the car.

At least I had the forethought to change into walking shoes, Helen thought as she scuffed her sneakers through the long brown grass that crept onto the dirt road.

A low hum made Helen turn. A truck was coming up behind her, sending clouds of gray dust up in its wake. For a moment, Helen entertained the idea of hitchhiking. It would save her a huge amount of time, no small amount of frustration, and probably a few blisters, but she dismissed the idea almost as soon as it came into her head. She'd heard more than enough stories about hitchhikers going missing and their remains turning up months, or even years, later. There'd even been a spate of disappearances around the area she was moving away from. Young women walking home from the train station and waiting for a bus late at night had vanished. The police were urgently seeking any information the public could provide, but the clues were so sparse that they were almost nonexistent.

Helen focused on watching her feet, hoping the owner of the truck wouldn't try to stop for her. As it drew closer, its engine's noise became clearer; the deep grating rattle seemed both

unhealthy and unnatural. *Keep your head down. If you show no interest in him, chances are he'll just pass you by.*

The wheels crunched on loose rocks as the vehicle drew up beside her and, to Helen's frustration, slowed to a crawl.

"Found a problem, miss?" a man asked.

Cancer. That's exactly how Uncle Jerry sounded when he had throat cancer.

She made herself look at the vehicle. It was old, almost as old as her own ill-fated car. Except, where she'd taken care to keep hers clean and well maintained, the stranger hadn't. Trash littered the front carriage: crumpled cigarette packages, empty brown bottles, plastic bags, wadded receipts that were so discolored Helen thought they must have been sitting there for years, and a used Band-Aid that had been casually discarded on top of the dashboard.

The man behind the wheel matched his car perfectly. Helen guessed him to be around fifty, but he looked much older. Greasy, steel-gray hair hung too long over his wrinkled forehead, and three days' worth of stubble covered his sunken cheeks. He looked sick—the sort of sick of cancer that's progressed too far to be treated. His skin seemed thin, like crepe paper, and his fingernails were long and stained yellow from nicotine.

As he turned to face her properly, Helen felt a pang of shock; his left eye was an intense sky blue, although age and illness had sent red veins and a yellow tinge over the whites. His right eye, however, was opaque. A bump and a slightly darker circle where his iris had once been pointed at an odd angle compared to the

other eye, as though it were blindly staring at a space far past Helen's left shoulder.

"I'm fine," Helen said bluntly, averting her eyes. Instead of stopping, she increased her speed as she moved off the dirt road and began marching through the underbrush.

"You sure about that?" the man slurred. "Pretty woman like you shouldn't be walking this road alone."

Helen didn't answer. Her heart was thundering, and her stomach was cold and tight. *Leave me alone. Can't you see I don't want to talk? Just keep driving.*

She was drawing ahead of him, so the man tapped his accelerator to push his truck forward, sending black smoke from the exhaust. Motion just above the dashboard attracted Helen's attention—a trinket hung on the rearview mirror danced around. At first, she thought it was a strange furry fruit, but then it rotated on its cord and Helen caught sight of a nose, two eyelids sutured closed, and a mouth distorted into a bizarre grimace.

What the hell? He has a shrunken head. A shrunken head in his car. Is it real? She spared a second glance at the tanned, stitched-up skin then looked away again as nausea rose into her throat. *It looks real.*

"This isn't a good road." The man licked his dry lips. His good eye was skimming Helen's body, while the blind eye stared intently at the sky.

"I'm fine," Helen repeated, and her voice sounded very strange and weak in her own ears. She was all but running, but the man in his truck kept abreast of her easily. He was grinning at her, and

Helen saw that although he still had the majority of his teeth, many of them were rotting.

A thousand scenarios ran through Helen's mind. *Keep off the road so he can't run you over. Use your keys as a weapon. He's old; you could probably beat him in a fist fight if it came to that.*

Then the man said the one thing Helen had been dreading. "Lots of people go missing on this road, you know."

Heart in throat, bottle of water sloshing in her sweaty hand, Helen started running. The truck's engine revved as it lurched forward to match her pace. The man was saying something to her, but she couldn't hear him over the engine.

Don't turn around. Don't slow down. Don't look at him—

———

Something hard was digging into Helen's stomach. She rolled backward, trying to escape it, and dry, prickly weeds scratched at her face. She opened her eyes to see the sky filled with dirty twilight.

With a groan, Helen sat up. Her back, arms, and legs ached, almost as though she'd been run over. She pressed her palm to her swimming head, waiting for it to clear.

What happened? Did he—

Suddenly panicked, Helen did a quick mental inventory. Her jeans were still buttoned, and while her back ached and her limbs felt bruised, nothing hurt where it wasn't supposed to. She let her breath out and pushed her loose hair out of her face. *What happened, then?*

She was sitting on the edge of the dirt road, in almost the same spot she'd been before she blacked out. The gnarled tree to her left looked familiar.

The twilight didn't seem to have deepened much either. Shapes melted together and played tricks on her eyes. Insects were chattering in the weeds beside her, and a bird of prey cried out in the distance. The truck and its repulsive occupant were nowhere to be seen.

Get into town. Find somewhere with a lot of people. You can worry about everyone else once you're somewhere safe.

Helen's legs felt unsteady as she pushed herself to her feet. She stretched, felt the bruises along her arm flare, then started walking. When her sneaker hit something solid, she looked down, surprised to see the bottle of water lying barely a foot from where she'd been left. She picked it up then remembered about her wallet and keys. Both were still in her pocket.

If he didn't assault me or rob me, what exactly did he do?

Helen unscrewed the bottle of water and took a deep drink. Then she started walking again, suddenly wanting to reach the town more than she'd wanted anything in her life. *Maybe I'll splurge on a hotel room and wait until morning before continuing the drive.*

Then she heard the rumble of another approaching car. The reaction was immediate; her heart rate rose, and a sheen of sweat covered her body as her adrenaline prepared her to respond to the threat.

Relax. It's just a car. Not every human on this planet is dangerous. Keep your head down, and it'll pass you by.

She couldn't stop her reaction to the noise, though. Fear clotted in her chest and left a metallic taste in her mouth as she increased her pace to a jog. The roar of the engine felt familiar; it had a rattle and unnatural cadence similar to the man's truck. Almost...*exactly* the same.

Helen glanced over her shoulder, and the fear, previously just a whisper in her ear, commandeered her body. The truck, its dashboard littered with long-empty cigarette cases and beer bottles, was gaining on her quickly. Its shrunken head bobbed and danced on the string as its owner's sallow, diseased face watched Helen.

The bottle of water fell from Helen's hand. She was running, dragging in terrified breaths. Squeezing her eyes shut against the image, she prayed she was going crazy and that it was all in her mind.

He's come back for me. Come back to finish the job. He'll skin me, probably, turn my face into a new shrunken head so I can bob along beside his other trinket for the rest of eternity—

"Found a problem, miss?" the man crowed at her as the truck's engine roared.

This time, the rock was digging into her back. Helen gasped, feeling disoriented as she rolled onto her hands and knees. The dizziness had returned, and the bruises on her limbs made her shudder. She lurched into a sitting pose and waited for the ache in her head to clear.

He came back for me. Why? What for? Did he run me over with his truck? It would explain why everything hurts…

But it didn't explain why she was still alive. If she'd really been hit by the truck going at that speed, she would have broken bones and serious internal damage at the very least.

Helen rubbed her hair out of her eyes and looked around. She was still on the same stretch of road, with the same twisted black tree sticking out of the reeds to her left. The insects were humming; above her, a bird of prey gave a loud cry.

This feels so familiar. Like déjà vu.

Helen scanned the ground and saw the bottle of water lying there, waiting for her. She picked it up and swirled it around, confused by what she saw. It was half-full. *Didn't I drink most of it earlier?*

She looked at the sky. It was still twilight, hovering in that indefinite time that never lasted more than a handful of minutes.

Don't go there, Helen told herself as she unscrewed the bottle of water and took a drink. *Don't you dare start thinking about time travel.*

But what if? the other, more adventurous half of her mind asked.

Don't start asking what-ifs. The last thing we want is to see that damn truck again.

She glanced to the right, where the empty road behind her stretched into the distance. She let her breath out in a sigh and massaged her left shoulder, where the bruised muscles were tight. *Something very strange has happened, but you can worry about that*

after you reach the town. What's important is that you're alive, you've still got all of your limbs attached, and that truck is nowhere to be seen.

She'd barely gotten to her feet when she heard the rumble of an engine behind her. Dread, icy cold and uncomfortably familiar, filled her chest as she turned around.

The truck was topping the ridge down the road. It was still too far away to see clearly, but she was sure it was the same dirty vehicle. Helen licked her lips, which suddenly seemed very dry.

Should I run? Hide?

Running hadn't helped her before. After two encounters with the truck, she was reluctant to turn her back on it again.

The vehicle was gradually gaining on her, kicking up black dust behind it as it roared down the road. Helen stood her ground, shivering and sweating as stress built in a tight ball inside her. She felt as though she might be sick.

Don't run. Don't let him out of your sight.

Helen carefully pulled her key ring out of her back pocket and gripped it in her fist so that the keys stuck out between her fingers like tiny, blunt blades. The truck had come close enough for her to see its occupant; the grizzled man's face split into a rotten-toothed smile as he met her gaze. The shrunken head bobbed like a Christmas bauble below the mirror.

He slowed down as he drew closer and eventually came to a halt right beside her. Helen was close enough to smell the truck, which stank of beer, cigarette smoke, and urine.

"Found a problem, miss?" the man asked for the third time that day.

"I don't know," Helen said, choosing her words carefully. Her hand holding her keys was hidden behind her back, and her muscles were tense as she prepared to lunge and attack at a second's notice if the man made a move toward her.

"Pretty woman like you shouldn't be walking this road alone." He tilted his head back to scratch at his stubble with yellowed nails. His good eye roved over her as though assessing her for the first time, while his blind eye watched the slowly rotating shrunken head.

Helen hesitated. She wasn't sure if she should tell him about her broken car, but she guessed he must have passed it and would have put two and two together already.

"This isn't a good road," the man continued when Helen didn't speak. "Lots of people go missing round here."

"Why?" Helen asked, surprised by her own boldness. Her nerves had been charged with electricity; she shifted from foot to foot, intensely uncomfortable but determined not to show her fear.

The man regarded her for a moment, head cocked to one side, dry lips pursed. Then he said, "You've not long left Carlton's border. If you continue up the road a little way, you'll be in Mellowkee. But here, this little patch of road, is Harob land. You heard of Harob before, miss?"

"No." Helen couldn't guess where he was going. The twilight was gradually fading into true night, and the insects behind her had quieted.

"Not many people have." The man scratched at his grizzled

chin again. "'Cept, of course, for the souls who live there. I suppose most folks want to forget it exists. Strange things happen in Harob. Things that might give you and me some trouble sleeping at night. If you find yourself in Harob country, you're best if you move on as quick as you can."

Helen shook her head slowly, indicating that she didn't understand what he was implying. The man reached forward, digging through the litter on the passenger seat, and Helen reflexively took a half step back. He was only searching for a cigarette box, though, and when he'd found one that wasn't empty, he pulled out one of the rolls and clamped it between his cracked lips.

"A more immediate concern for you, at least, is the sinkholes." He cupped one hand around the cigarette as he lit it, then took a long drag and blew the smoke out of the open windows. It occurred to Helen that the shrunken head might not have been that brown when the man had bought it. "Lots of sinkholes around here. They're hard to see in the day, and even harder at night. You'll want to be careful."

"Okay." Helen shifted uneasily and glanced at the road to her left, where she could still see the lip of the ridge, silhouetted in the fading light. "How far's the next town?"

"Augh, it'd have to be—what? Twenty minutes' drive." Another puff of smoke, then he raised his eyebrows at her. "Want a lift?"

"No. But thank you for offering."

Again his single working eye roved over her, assessing her dirty sneakers, jeans, light cardigan, and near-empty bottle of

water. "You sure about that? It'll be a bit of a hike for a little lady like you."

"I'm sure." Helen put as much force into her voice as she could and managed to flash him a tight smile. "Completely sure."

"Suit yourself." He moved the cigarette to the other side of his mouth and turned back to the steering wheel. "Watch out for those sinkholes, now. They're hard to see."

"I will."

The sound of the truck's revving engine grated at Helen's nerves, and the vehicle picked up speed as it followed the road toward the ridge. Helen watched it until it had disappeared, then she let her breath out and sagged.

She wasn't dead, kidnapped, skinned, or any of the other terrible possibilities she'd been preparing for. If the man had been telling the truth, the town would still be a few hours' walk away, but that was bearable. Helen drained her bottle then screwed its cap back on and began following the road.

The sounds had changed. With the end of daylight and the emergence of a smattering of weak stars, new insects had started a shrill song. An owl called from behind her, and one of its companions to her right answered. Helen had to slow her pace and focus on where she was walking to make sure she didn't step on a loose stone and twist her ankle.

There was a strange, dark patch in the ground ahead of her, mingling with the weeds and pressing against the side of the road. It looked like a shadow, but there was nothing to cast it. Helen had to crouch down in front of it before she recognized

what it was: a hole. Plants and vines grew so heavily around its edge that it was almost perfectly camouflaged in the bad light. It was at least two meters wide and three meters long. Helen leaned over its edge to see how far down it went, but she couldn't see for more than a few feet.

Watch out for those sinkholes, now.

The water bottle was empty and would have been just useless luggage for the rest of her walk. Helen dropped it into the hole and listened to the hollow tap as it hit the sides again…and again…and again, before fading from her hearing.

"Damn," Helen muttered, sitting back on her haunches. The old man had been right; sinkholes like this were a hazard for anyone walking the roads in poor light—or anyone who wasn't paying attention to the road, for that matter.

Helen glanced behind herself, to the spot where the truck had pulled alongside her. She'd been running in this direction, keeping off the road so that the truck couldn't easily hit her. It was a miracle she hadn't fallen into the sinkhole.

Suddenly uneasy, Helen stood up. She had barely a second to realize the ground was shifting under her feet, collapsing as the ledge she hadn't realized she was standing on crumbled, and then—

The rock was poking into her shoulder. Helen groaned. Her whole body ached as though she'd been hit by a truck…or fallen down a very steep incline.

She sat up slowly, waiting for the dizziness to pass. The light was fading as twilight converted day into night. To her left was the grizzled tree poking out of the marshes. Helen put her hand out to where she already knew her bottle would be and picked it up, feeling the water slosh inside it.

This can't be happening.

She sat where she was for a long time, waiting for the aches to ease as she listened to the hiss of insects and the bird of prey's single call. When she saw the truck top the ridge farther down the road, she carefully got to her feet, brushing her hands over her jeans to clean off the worst of the dust.

The truck pulled up beside her, and its haggard occupant focused his one good eye on her. "Found a problem, miss?"

Helen hesitated only for a second before answering. "Yes, actually. Can I get a ride into town?"

He gazed at her for a moment, taking her measure, before saying, "Sure thing. Hop in."

She opened the door and waited for him to scoop the litter off the passenger seat. The shrunken head rotated slowly until its stitched-closed eyes were facing Helen, then it continued to turn to survey the road. Helen climbed into the truck and pulled on her seat belt.

"Where're you heading to?"

"Town," Helen said simply, watching as the twilight gradually eased the landscape into darkness, her half-full water bottle clasped in her lap with both hands. "As quickly as you can, please."

A

DARCY COATES